THE FINAL BATTLE

THE BEGINNING OF THE END

PURNELL MYLES

FINAL CHAPTER
PUBLISHING

Published by Final Chapter Publishing Dardanelle, Arkansas

ISBNs:

Paperback: 979-8-9992011-0-2

EPUB: 979-8-9992011-2-6

Hardcover: 979-8-9992011-1-9

Cover design by 100 Covers

PROLOGUE

OUR STORY STARTED thirty-five years ago on a small road in Yell County, Arkansas. A car's headlights blurred in the fog down a narrow two-lane mountain road. The man was behind the wheel, driving very slowly because of the thick fog. The woman was turned with her knees in the seat, taking care of the baby in the back. They were arguing about something, and for a second, the man looked away. There was a thump as if they hit something, and the woman quickly sat back down.

"What was that?" she asked, trying to look out the back window.

"I don't know, dear," the man answered as he put the car in park and took his foot off the brake.

He then reached over her and opened the glove box, pulling out a pistol.

"What are you going to do?" she asked as he checked the rounds in the revolver.

"It may be an injured animal. I can't leave it out there to suffer." He then squeezed her hand tightly and smiled.

He opened the car door and stepped outside, walking toward the back of the car. The woman watched as he looked around and then walked to the front of the car. Her eyes grew as big as silver dollars, and she screamed at the top of her voice. She turned and jumped into the back seat where her baby was sitting.

Her husband, at that time, came flying through the front window of the car. Half of his body was inside, and half was on the outside of the windshield. The woman then grabbed the baby, opened the back car door, and jumped out. She screamed for help as she looked and saw the figure standing there. She took off running into the woods, carrying her baby in her arms.

"Please, somebody help me, please! Lord God, please help me!" she screamed as she ran.

She could hear it getting closer by the heavy footsteps behind her. She then heard more steps to her right, and as she looked, something hit her left calf. The woman fell to the ground and saw a knife that went through and stuck in her bone. She saw a shadow in front of her and looked to her right. There, she saw a giant cypress tree and crawled over to it using her right hand. The baby was in her left hand; she laid it by the giant tree and turned and sat on the ground. She pulled the knife from her calf, then turned to her baby and placed her right hand on it. She could see the figures getting closer to her from three different directions. She lifted her head toward heaven and started praying to God and cried.

"Lord God, I know I haven't been the Christian that I should have been, and please forgive me for that. Please, God, take my life, but please don't take my baby's, I beg of you."

The figures were right upon her now, and she rose to her feet with knife in hand. The figures could be seen clearly now, and she lunged toward the one right in front of her. The three figures grabbed her, and it lasted about three to five seconds as she lay on the ground. She could feel the warmth on her skin from the blood covering her body. Her body on the inside was getting cold as her blood poured from her small body. Unable to move her body but only her eyes could she move. She saw the three creatures standing over her with their bloody hands and mouths. They were looking toward the tree where she had placed her baby. Please, God, no, she begged.

She then cut her eyes toward the tree and saw another figure holding her baby at the giant cypress.

"Give us the child," she heard one of the creatures say with a deep, growling voice.

She then heard another speak out from the north, so she cut her eyes to the left. She could see the figure clearly and looked to heaven, crying aloud. "Thank you, my Father." She looked back at the tree, and the figure holding the baby drew a sword from their left hip with the right hand. She then looked to her left and saw the larger figure draw a six-foot sword from its back.

"If you want the child, then take it," the smaller figure said to them with sword in hand.

She saw the larger figure charge one of the creatures, cutting off its head with one mighty blow. The other raised his axe as she also saw it cut down very swiftly and brutally. The last creature she saw ran toward the smaller figure holding her child, and it sliced its head off.

The smaller figure walked toward her and knelt down, holding her baby.

"Your baby is safe now," it told her.

Not being able to feel her body, she felt the figure as it touched her hand. It was placed on her baby's cheek as she then moved her head, starting to breathe really hard. The other figure knelt on the other side of her with a calming, gentle smile. She started gasping for breath now, not being able to catch her breath as the large figure bent over her.

"Shh," it said as her breathing calmed, and it placed its left hand on her forehead. "Know that you are loved, and your child is loved. Now, go in peace," it whispered as she took her last breath.

THE NEXT MORNING, a game warden was traveling down the road on a routine patrol. It was still foggy heading up the mountain on the two-lane road, so he was traveling at a slow speed. He noticed a vehicle about twenty-five feet away and pulled up behind it. He also noticed that there seemed to be no one around, so he called in the tag number on the new Ford LTD.

He then got out of his pickup, holding his flashlight in his left hand with his right placed on his sidearm. He started to walk around the car and noticed something at the front. He walked to the front and saw a man halfway through the front windshield, with half of his face missing. He pulled his sidearm from its holster and looked around with the flashlight. He then called it in using his handheld radio and started shining the light inside the car. He shined it in the back seat and saw a baby that was not moving in a car seat. He then walked around to the passenger side back seat where the baby was and opened the door. It was very cold in the car, but when he touched the child, it was warm. He saw no injuries or blood anywhere around the baby, so he called it in with his handheld. He stayed by its side, not wanting to move it just in case there was something wrong he didn't see. Before long, search and rescue units, the sheriff, city police and fire units, ambulances, and more arrived.

The body of the lady was found with her spine ripped from her back, lying dead with a smile on her face. There were no traces of anyone or anything else being there, not even wild animals. When the autopsy was done, it read that between her spine being ripped from her body and her dying was about fifteen minutes. It also read that it was completely impossible that she could live that long. The pediatric doctor said that the baby was in perfect health, not even having a sniffle. It had been below freezing that night, yet the baby seemed to be as if it was by a warm fire all night.

Three months later, the case was closed and filed under mystery murders, case closed. Over the years, detectives from almost every law enforcement agency tried to reopen the case to no avail. The case file was eventually put in a closed case no-reopen file and was used only for learning now.

CHAPTER 1

PRESENT DAY, Northern Pacific Ocean, Two and a Half Days Out of Pearl Harbor, Hawaii

The United States warship, the USS Tiger Shark, had been on a mission in the Gulf of Aden off the coast of Somalia. It had a six-month mission but had to cut it short by one month due to mechanical issues. It was experiencing engine troubles along with electrical issues throughout the ship. It was based out of Norfolk, Virginia, at Norfolk Naval Base and was classified as one of eight SADs.

SAD stands for "stand-alone destroyer" and sails alone about 99 percent of the time. These ships and their crew are known as SOS (special operation ships) and work with the same crew at all times. The crew usually gets from 30 to 90 days off and 120 to 221 days at sea. The reason these ships only have one crew is that they have to know and trust one another. These sailors and their ships go anywhere at any time under any circumstances to do whatever needs to be done. These few ships carry smaller crews so they can be fitted with more armaments. One sailor on an SAD has to do the work of two, sometimes three, sailors due to the size of the crew. These destroyers carry not 90 but 150 guided missiles and are larger than the others. Instead of being 510 feet long, the SAD destroyers are 605 feet long.

On the bridge of the Tiger Shark, it was just before dawn, and a sailor yelled out, "Captain on deck!"

Commander Mathew Bolders stepped onto the bridge and walked over to pour a cup of coffee. "I take it everything went well last night since I slept all night without interruption?"

"Aye, sir," the duty officer replied, "just a few minor electrical problems. We were good, sir."

"Fantastic! Good to hear that. We may just make Pearl without any more major malfunctions," Bolders said.

The captain then sat in his captain's chair and looked over the nightly report as he drank his coffee. He closed the log and placed it back in the pouch in his chair. He then got up and walked back to the coffee urn to get himself another cup of coffee. Bolders looked out the front window as the sun was just starting to come up, and the first crew was coming on deck.

"If anyone needs me," he told the officer on deck, "I'll be around the ship. Just give a shout."

"Aye, sir," the duty officer replied.

Bolders exited the bridge as he heard a sailor yell, "Captain's off the bridge!"

Lieutenant Commander William Taylor was headed to the bridge himself after just finishing breakfast, passing right by the Combat Information Center (CIC). As he was passing by the CIC, one of the sailors called out. He stopped and walked inside the room, and the sailor led him over to a station with two sailors. One of them mainly controlled the radar, which combed the area for potential threats and other activity. The other, sitting beside him, was the radio officer who listened to traffic both in the air and on the ocean. They explained the situation to him, and he picked up the ship's phone and called the bridge. He asked to speak with the captain and was informed that he had left the bridge about thirty minutes ago. He told them to call the captain and have him report to CIC at once and bring the security level to two.

Bolders was walking on the main deck outside around the ship when he heard the level two security being announced over the intercom. He then heard his name being mentioned, telling him to report to CIC. He immediately turned and ran back, entering the ship's passageway and heading to CIC. Once he walked through the door, he saw his XO, Commander Taylor, standing by a radar.

"Mat, over here," Taylor said, raising his left hand and motioning Bolders over to him.

The captain walked over to where he was and asked, "What do we have here, Will?" calling Taylor by his first name.

Taylor looked at the sailor by the radar and put his right hand on the sailor's left shoulder. "Give the captain a sit-rep."

The sailor, looking up from his seat at Bolders, started to fill the captain in on the situation. "Well, sir, I have been following this Coast Guard cutter headed back to Hawaii at top speed, it seems."

"What is so strange about that, sailor?" Bolders asked him.

The sailor, pointing to his screen, started to explain. "That wouldn't be so weird by itself, sir, but a little over an hour later, I noticed this." The sailor had the radar where he could only see the cutter and nothing beyond it. "Now, this is how I had my screen set, sir, and we kept getting foreign chatter, so I widened the screen. I couldn't make out whose ships they were until Lieutenant Manners here heard them talking."

Bolders looked at the female radio and radar officer as she was still listening to the foreign chatter. The sailor sitting beside her tapped her on the right shoulder with his left hand. She tried to widen her screen and was shaking her head in frustration.

"Lieutenant, is there something that you would like to share with the rest of us?" Bolders asked her.

She turned her head to the right and partially turned her chair in the same direction to look at Bolders more easily. "Sir, as Ralph," she said, indicating the sailor, "explained, he had been tracking a Coast Guard cutter for close to an hour. He told me that on one of the upper channels he heard a foreign language and asked me to listen in on it. I tuned to the channel and heard Iranian ships talking back and forth to each other."

Bolders spoke up and asked Lieutenant Manners, "Are you sure it was Iranian? You're absolutely sure?"

"I am sure, sir," Manners answered the captain. "It was Iranian. I speak it very well. The thing about it, sir," Manners continued, "is that they are chasing that cutter."

Ralph added, "They are catching it, sir."

Bolders and Taylor exchanged a look of concern, and Bolders asked Manners, "What are they chasing them for?"

"They have something on the ship that they don't want anyone else to see, sir; that's all I know. There is one more thing, sir," Manners told the captain as he was turning to Taylor to say something. Bolders looked back at her, and so did Taylor as she said, "There is another ship out there that's giving the orders."

"So how many is that total, three or four ships?" Taylor asked Manners.

"It's definitely four, sir," Manners answered.

"How do you know that if they're all speaking Iranian?" Bolders asked her.

"That's the thing, sir; not all are speaking Iranian. One of the ships is speaking Russian, sir," Manners told them.

"Russian!" he said in a somewhat high-pitched voice, looking at her a little shocked. "You also speak Russian, Lieutenant Manners?" Bolders asked, looking at her.

She answered, "Yes, sir."

The captain looked at Taylor. "Get me Norfolk on the line and get Pearl also." Bolders looked at Manners. "I'm going back to the bridge. Make sure the XO is informed of any changes." Bolders left the room and went straight to the bridge.

Taylor stayed behind in CIC. As the captain entered the bridge and was announced, a sailor holding a ship's phone said that Norfolk was on the line. Bolders walked over to the sailor and took the phone with his left hand, putting it up to his ear.

"Commander Bolders," he answered.

"Bolders, Captain Pettus here. I have been informed about the situation, and your ship is in no shape to engage. Let me make this perfectly clear, Commander Bolders, you are under no circumstances cleared to engage," Captain Pettus ordered.

Bolders stood there, not saying anything; Pettus repeated his order again in a stern voice. "Do you understand that, Commander?"

"Yes, sir. Order is understood, sir," Bolders acknowledged the base commander's orders and then slammed the phone down.

Taylor, at that time, walked onto the bridge just in time to see the captain slam the phone onto the receiver.

"Mat," Taylor called Bolders by his first name, "that must have been Pettus. Is everything okay?" he added.

Bolders looked at Taylor, not hiding it from anyone on the bridge. "That ass wants us to do nothing. They're slowing down even more from what CIC is saying, and at that rate, they will destroy that cutter."

Taylor told him, "They're not going to fire on them, or they would have already done so."

"Captain," he heard someone say as he turned his head to look behind him.

It was a sailor holding the ship's phone up.

"It's Admiral Riley, sir, from Pearl Harbor."

Bolders walked over to the sailor and took the phone with his right hand and thanked the sailor as he put it up to his ear.

"Commander Bolders," he answered.

"Commander, this is Admiral Riley. Have you spoken to anyone else about this yet, son?" he asked.

"Spoke with my CO at Norfolk, sir, to engage," he answered the admiral.

"What was his answer?" Admiral Riley asked the captain.

"I was not to engage because of the condition of my ship, sir."

"How do you feel about it, Commander? Do you think you, your crew, and ship can do it, son?"

The crew on the bridge, which now included Lieutenant Tanya Manners, could only hear what Bolders was saying and not the admiral.

"I think if I got an order that overrides my base commander, my crew and I would show them what American warship power is, sir."

"Well, Commander Bolders, the order stands overridden; show them what the United States military is all about, son."

"In the meantime, I am directing the carrier Benson to send you air support, which is about forty minutes out, sir," the captain said in acknowledgment to the admiral and handed the phone back to the sailor.

He then turned to Taylor and saw Lieutenant Manners also standing on the bridge.

Bolders walked over to where the two were standing. Looking at Tanya, he said, "I need you here with me." He then looked at Taylor. "Will," calling him by his pet name, "get me a track on everything unfriendly around us."

Taylor turned immediately and ran to the phone behind him, calling CIC.

Bolders looked at Tanya. "If they don't understand me, then I want you to explain word for word, understand?" he said to her.

He walked over to the radio with Manners following him, and he picked up the mic and waited for her to do the same. Bolders then put the radio close to his mouth, pressed the receiver button, and began to speak.

"This is the captain of the United States naval warship Tiger Shark calling Iranian warships."

There was no answer, so he looked at Manners, and she translated to the Iranian ship. They waited for a minute.

"We understand what you're saying, American. Please do not interfere, and we will leave when we get what is ours."

"What is yours on that ship?" Captain Bolders asked the Iranian officer.

Once again, there was silence for about thirty seconds.

"I think it is above your pay grade, Captain, if you don't already know," he said in Iranian.

Manners translated to him what the captain of the enemy destroyer had told him.

Bolders raised the mic once more and started to talk on it. "Iranian warship, please change course."

When there was no answer, Manners translated to the enemy ship, and still, there was no answer.

"Iranian warship, this is the United States destroyer. Divert from your course now, or we will stop you."

CHAPTER 2

"AMERICAN WARSHIP, this is the last time I will say to you. Do not interfere. Now, go away. I'm tired of you. I will not have this translated, so I hope you understand. If you try and board or fire on that ship or this one, I will light you up so bright it will make a Christmas tree jealous."

There was no response as they waited, and then they heard something come over the radio.

"Tiger Shark, this is the Coast Guard cutter High Seas. We have got lights back under generator power. We should be to you within the next five hours."

"High Seas—" Bolders began to reply.

All at once, he heard, "We're being boarded. Repeat, our ship is under attack, Tiger Shark."

"I need to go to CIC quickly, sir," Manners told the captain.

He nodded his head, telling her to go.

One of the sailors who answered the ship's phone yelled out, "Captain, incoming birds [missiles], sir!"

Bolders grabbed his binoculars, looking at several balls of fire coming from a southerly direction.

"Those things are not headed in our direction," Bolders said as he looked at them from many miles away.

They were so large that the crew from Tiger Shark could see them from fifty miles away.

Bolders, looking at one of the sailors to his right as he brought the binoculars down from his face, said, "Get me High Seas."

Taylor called up to the captain from CIC, "Did you see that?" he asked in an excited voice.

"We're fifty miles away and saw it clearly from here," Bolders told him. "Did you see where they came from?" he added.

"It came in the direction of Devil's Island, Mat," Taylor told the captain. "Devil's Island doesn't have any defensive capabilities like that, only a couple of missions for the locals and a National Guard unit."

Bolders then thought for a couple of seconds and called Taylor back on the radio. "Get hold of the army unit on the island."

All at once, everyone on the bridge heard emergency alarms and the voice, "Incoming, incoming." Then they saw the two Phalanx systems on the ship go off, destroying three missiles. Bolders grabbed the ship's phone, calling CIC again; a sailor answered it, and Bolders told him to have Manners translate to the Iranians.

"She's not here, sir," the sailor told Bolders.

His reaction was, "Of course she's there."

"Sir, hold please for the XO," and the sailor told Taylor what Bolders had said about Lieutenant Manners.

"She's not here, Mat," Taylor told Bolders. "She left about ten minutes ago headed that way. She didn't make it here, Mat," Taylor added.

Before either man could say anything, they heard incoming again.

At that time, Lieutenant Manners entered the room, and Taylor looked at her, noticing her right pant leg torn.

He said to her, "Get over here and talk to these assholes and tell them we didn't fire those missiles at their ships."

Bolders heard Manners come over the radio from the bridge and listened as she spoke in Iranian to them. Once again, the alarm went off for incoming, and Bolders once again called CIC.

"Fire three missiles at that damn ship and sink it before it does us," the captain ordered Taylor.

Bolders and everyone on the bridge could see and hear three AShM (anti-ship missiles) fired from the ship headed toward the Iranian ship. There was another alarm, and three more missiles were fired from the enemy destroyer. The Phalanx once again took care of two of them, and the third struck the rear of the ship. All three missiles fired from the Tiger Shark hit the Iranian warship and destroyed it. There were a few injuries, nothing major, and the ship had a small hole in the deck at the rear.

When Bolders heard this, he took a deep breath and released it with a sigh, then sat in his chair. Bolders looked to his right at a sailor and told him to get Taylor and Manners to report to the bridge right away. Bolders sat in his chair for a few minutes waiting for his XO and the lieutenant to show up. Even though the outside of his body wasn't shaking, the inside was trembling like crazy. When it all started to happen, he really didn't have time to be scared; it was all about the ship and crew. Now, it was, for the most part, over, and he just wanted to ball up on the floor and lay there.

Then he heard Taylor's voice behind him, "Captain, the lieutenant and I are here, sir."

"Will, get the helo ready and a security team ready to go over to the cutter."

"Sir, about the lieutenant—" Taylor began.

Bolders cut him off. "She's a big girl, XO. Go and get everything ready, XO," he told Taylor, "and I want you to oversee the mission," Bolders added as he got up from his chair.

Bolders watched as the XO went off the bridge, and he looked at Lieutenant Manners, telling her to follow him.

He walked out the bridge door onto the catwalk, and Manners followed him, closing the door behind her. Bolders walked over to the port side edge of the catwalk where no one could read his lips or see his facial expressions. He then took his left hand and patted the top guardrail of the catwalk and told the lieutenant to come stand there. She followed his order and walked over, standing beside him on the catwalk.

"I know you are young, but you are an officer, and a lot is expected of an officer at all times. In emergencies, people depend on their officers, especially in situations like we just went through. Do you understand that, Lieutenant?" Bolders told her in a calm but authoritative voice.

"Yes, sir, I understand that, sir," Manners answered, then asked, "Is there something that I did wrong, sir?"

"You left the bridge and told me you were going to CIC, and when the shit hit the fan, you weren't there."

She started to say something, and the captain cut her off by saying, "I'm not done yet, so just listen. I want to know that I can count on all my officers in any situation, no matter what it is."

"I know you are just temporary onboard for this trip, but for now, you are one of my officers. Having said that, I expect you to act and perform as an officer should."

Bolders went on to say, "I hope we are clear on that, Lieutenant." Then he turned his head to the left. He looked at her. "We are clear on that, aren't we, Lieutenant?" he asked Manners.

She answered, "Aye, sir."

"I want to hear from you as to why you weren't where you told me you were going to be when you said you would be there," Bolders asked her.

"When I left the bridge, sir, the ship started making drastic maneuvers, and I fell, hurting my ankle and my knee, sir," Manners told him. "I got up as quick as I could and went straight on to CIC and reported to the XO."

"I stand corrected," Bolders told her as he couldn't help himself from looking in her gray eyes, just like a lot of others on the ship.

"You stand corrected about what, sir?" she asked him.

He just looked at her, and she smiled. "Is there something wrong, Captain?"

He caught himself and answered her, "Yes, I apologize for not asking you what happened first before jumping to conclusions."

She looked at him for a moment and thanked him, then they both turned, watching the helo lift off, headed to the cutter High Seas.

"Well, Lieutenant Manners," Bolders said as he straightened up from leaning on the rail, "shall we go back in?"

They walked back inside onto the bridge and could hear the ship-to-helicopter traffic talking back and forth. Taylor came back onto the bridge, and he looked at Manners, raising his eyebrows and widening his eyes for just a second. She knew it was a gesture asking her silently if she was okay, and with her hands to her side, she gave him a hidden thumbs-up. Bolders did not see it because he was looking out the front window and not at them.

Listening to the radio traffic, they heard, "Five Zero Six [helicopter] fifteen miles out, Tango Sierra [Tiger Shark]," the pilot radioed to the destroyer.

A couple of minutes later, they heard, "Five Zero Six two miles out, Tango Sierra, no movement on deck or on the bridge as far as can see."

About one minute later, the helicopter came back over the radio. "Five Zero Six going into hover position. Tango Sierra security team rappelling onto the cutter now, remaining in hover," the pilot told CIC.

The pilot then radioed once again. "All cargo off, coming out of hover, moving out to one hundred yards to cover team."

The CIC crew on the Tiger Shark acknowledged and approved what the pilot said.

"Sir, I'm going to head back to CIC," Lieutenant Manners told the captain as she was getting ready to walk away.

"Stand easy, Lieutenant," Bolders told her. "You're here with me until this is over, just in case you're needed."

"Sir, yes, sir," she acknowledged to him that she understood and stayed by his side.

At that time, everyone on the bridge heard, "Team lead to home base, we found survivors."

"How many do you have, lead?" CIC asked the security officer.

"Five plus the captain, home base."

Then CIC came back. "What is their condition, lead?"

"The captain is in bad shape along with three others, and they're conscious but in bad shape. Stand by on the other two, home base, waiting for the doc's [medic's] word."

The Tiger Shark finally got up beside the High Seas and secured transport lines from ship to ship. They started transporting the wounded sailors from the cutter to the Tiger Shark, and Bolders went to the main deck. When the few surviving crew members from the Coast Guard cutter were retrieved, Bolders started to head to sick bay. A sailor caught him before he could go back inside the ship.

"Sir, you're needed in CIC right away, sir."

Bolders followed the sailor to CIC with Taylor and Manners following behind. He walked into the room with the other two, and they walked over to Ralph, who was sitting in Manners' empty seat beside him.

"What do we have, Mr. Ralph?" Bolders asked him as he patted the young sailor on his left shoulder.

20

"I have team lead on the radio, sir. He says that he needs to talk to you, sir."

Bolders picked up the headset from Manners' desk where she worked and didn't put it on but held it up to his left ear.

"Lead one, this is the captain. What do you have?" Bolders asked the security lead.

"You need to get over here, sir, and bring that lady to translate with you, sir," the security officer told him.

"On the way, lead," Bolders replied.

The security officer responded, "Will have someone meet you on the main deck, sir."

Bolders turned around, looking at Manners and Taylor. "XO, you have the ship. Lieutenant, you come with me," Bolders added.

All three left CIC at the same time. Taylor went to the bridge, and Bolders and Manners went outside to the main deck. They walked over to where the transport lines were connected, and Manners and he were sent over to the cutter. Bolders went over first and then waited for Manners, and the security officer and the captain helped her on deck.

"If you both will follow me, sir, I'll take you to one [speaking of the team lead]," the security officer said.

They followed him down a passageway to the very last room on the left where the team lead was waiting outside.

"Sir, ma'am," he greeted them. "You're not going to believe this, sir." He turned and walked into the room, followed by Bolders and Manners.

Bolders looked and saw a room full of people, mostly women and old men. There were two children and one baby, which the mother was holding and crying.

Bolders looked at the team lead and asked, "Who are they?"

"We have no idea, sir," he answered. "That's why I asked you to bring her, sir. We have been trying, sir, and they don't speak a word of English, or they just don't want us to know they do."

Bolders then turned his head left and looked at Manners. "See if they speak one of your languages, Lieutenant."

She spoke to them in a few different languages, and then one old man spoke up. They started talking back and forth, and before long, two more men started to speak with her.

Bolders looked at her in shock. "Just how many languages do you speak, Lieutenant?"

"I speak several, sir." The captain and the team looked at her in amazement. "This man," pointing to him, "speaks Eastern Aramaic, and this man," pointing to another, "speaks Western Aramaic, sir." Then she looked at another man, pointing to him. "This man speaks Old Aramaic or Middle Aramaic."

The security team lead asked Manners, "What is the difference? They all understand each other, right?"

"The Eastern and Western do understand for the most part, but they don't understand the old language."

They all looked at her, and she could tell they needed an explanation.

"Old Aramaic, or Middle Aramaic as some call it, is the first language. It is called the language Jesus spoke. It was spoken about nine hundred years before the Messiah, and very few speak it."

They all looked at her in total amazement.

Bolders said, "What are you doing on my ship, Lieutenant?"

She looked at him with wide eyes.

He explained, "You could be doing anything you wanted with your knowledge. The lady with the baby, what is wrong with her?" Bolders asked. "She has been crying the whole time."

CHAPTER 3

"THE DOC [medic] checked out the baby, and it's dead, sir," the team lead explained. "We haven't been able to get her to let it go," he said. "It is one of the saddest things I've ever seen."

Manners walked over to the lady, and they all listened as she spoke an even different language this time. The lieutenant was sitting on the floor where she could look at the lady face-to-face.

When Manners finished talking, the young woman had stopped crying and smiled at the lieutenant. Manners placed her right hand on the lady's left cheek and told her something in a soft voice. The young lady then gave the lieutenant her baby, and Manners held it against her left breast tightly. Everyone watched the lieutenant as she placed her lips on the top of the baby's head. She started whispering something, then singing to the baby in a whisper, with her tears dropping on the baby's head.

Manners was rocking back and forth and started kissing the top of the baby's head. Everyone watched in unbelief as the baby's head jerked up, and it started to cry for its mother.

"I swear," the medic said, looking at Bolders and the security lead, "that baby had no heartbeat, and there was no life in it."

Lieutenant Manners got up and kissed the mother of the child on her forehead and said something in her language. The lieutenant then walked over to where the captain and medic were standing and looked at the medic. She slightly tilted her head to the right and, with a small grin, told the medic, "You were wrong this time." She then looked back at the child.

Bolders and the security team leader stepped outside the room, and something caught the captain's eye. Down the passageway, out of his peripheral vision, he saw a shadow pass the other passageway.

"Nelson, did you see that?" he asked the team lead as he looked in the direction the captain was pointing.

"No, sir, I didn't see anything, but I'll have a couple of the guys check it out," he told Bolders.

"No," the captain told him, "I probably just need a little more coffee this morning." He smiled.

"Okay, let's get everyone off this ship, starting with you and the lieutenant, sir," Nelson told Bolders.

"The Tiger Shark just informed me that a storm is moving in, and it looks pretty rough. Let's get everyone else on board first," Bolders told him as everyone started walking out of the room.

The captain and lieutenant followed behind everyone, with a security team member behind them. About halfway through the ship-to-ship transfer, the weather started getting bad, and the skies started getting really dark. Bolders, looking at the sky, had Nelson radio the ship, telling them the mission needed to pick up speed. One of the older men was on the line and being pulled across when the slack went out of the line. The older man went down into the water as the two ships started to come really close together because of the waves.

Taylor was on board the Tiger Shark and was doing a great job in controlling the ship from the bridge. He knew, as well as Bolders, that it was going to get really hard now with only one ship under power and the other dead in the water. The older Aramaic man completely submerged under the water as everyone looked on help-lessly, waiting for the line to tighten back up. It tightened back up as Taylor and the helmsman kept the destroyer off the Coast Guard cutter, and the man appeared back above water. The waves started getting higher, about eight to ten feet high, causing the two ships to move around a lot. Bolders had to make a decision quickly before it was too late whether to release the lines or not. The captain looked at Nelson, taking a deep breath, and told him to have his team release the lines. Nelson did so and then told Taylor, who came out on the catwalk, watching Bolders and the rest of the crew on the cutter. Taylor saluted them, and they looked on, seeing him all at once run back inside the bridge.

Nelson heard a voice come over the radio. "This is helo Three-Eight-Eight and Three-Zero-Two, sixty miles out."

Nelson jumped into the air, shouted out loud, and was pointing in the opposite direction into the air. Bolders and everyone else looked and saw two helicopters flying toward them.

Nelson, still excited, yelled out, "Hell, yes, two CH-53 Super Stallions, baby!"

Everyone started cheering.

"Three-Eight-Eight to cutter."

Nelson answered, "Go ahead, you big beautiful bird. We're going to send a line down with a couple of my crew and get you all off that ship before the weather gets too bad."

Everyone was transported from the cutter back to the Tiger Shark by the carrier Carl Vinson's Super Stallions. The crew on the bridge of the Tiger Shark watched as the two helicopters dropped off the last of its passengers. One of the lookouts on the bridge, as he watched the two helicopters leaving, headed back to their carrier. He noticed something in the distance that looked like someone standing on the bridge.

He got the binoculars and looked. "What the hell!" he said in an excited voice.

The duty officer walked over to him. "What's up?"

The lookout pointed and handed him the binoculars. "Oh shit!" the duty officer said loudly, and everyone on the bridge turned and looked at him.

He started over to the radio to contact the helos, and before he could, he heard, "Stallion Three-Eight-Eight, did we leave someone?"

The duty officer told one of the sailors on deck, "Go, get the captain now!" shouting the order. "Stand by, Three-Eight-Eight. We are checking now."

Then the helo replied, "Weather is getting rough, Tiger Shark."

The duty officer could see the huge helicopters being tossed around by the strong wind that was getting even stronger.

The helo pilot looked again and looked at his second seat. "Do you see them? I lost them."

"Negative. They're gone and confirmed that with the two crew members in the back of the aircraft."

Bolders came on deck along with Nelson just as the pilot finished talking on the radio.

"What's going on?" the captain asked the duty officer.

He explained to the captain that someone had been spotted.

Bolders took the radio. "Three-Eight-Eight, this is Commander Bolders, captain of the Tiger Shark. Do you still have eyes on?" Bolders asked him.

"Negative, your one [captain], we have no joy [not seen], repeat no joy."

The helo descended closer to the water where the crew could

take a good look on the bridge of the cutter. The winds were really picking up now and had blown both helicopters all over the place. Water was beginning to splash on and inside the helo, and the crew chief told the pilot they needed to rise.

Bolders took the mic from the duty officer. "Vinson, helo, we got everyone that we could find on board. Get out of there."

The pilot responded, "Affirmative, your one. I guess your man and me and my crew all drank from that same water bottle, seeing ghosts, I guess. This is Three-Eight-Eight and company. We are RTB. Good luck, Tiger Shark," the pilot added.

Bolders turned around and looked at Taylor. "Lieutenant Manners and I are going below deck. You have the bridge."

The two of them went below straight to sick bay to check on what was left of the cutter crew. As Bolders and Manners walked into sick bay, two of the sailors raised up in bed, looking at Manners.

"It's you," one of the sailors said to Manners. "You are her."

Bolders and Manners were puzzled.

"What are you talking about?" Bolders asked the two sailors. "Just who do you think she is?"

"She's the lady that saved us from whatever that was that killed everyone on board."

At that time, the captain walked through the doorway into sick bay and stopped in his tracks. He just looked at Lieutenant Manners, and Bolders turned and looked at him.

"Who are you people?" the captain asked Bolders.

"What are you talking about?" Captain Bolders replied.

"She came on our ship and killed everyone that was attacking us and then brought my men to where I was."

One of the sailors spoke up, "She picked me up with one hand and carried me like a purse."

Then the other one spoke, "Yeah, I saw it, and that was while fighting whatever that was with the other hand."

The captain spoke up again, "And she threw one of those things twenty or thirty feet down the passageway with one hand." He went on, "Then she grabbed another one and bounced him off the walls like a rag doll."

Manners looked at Bolders, then at the captain of the cutter. "Sir, whatever you think you saw, it wasn't me."

"You would pass for that thing's twin, Lieutenant," he told her, still a little in shock.

"I've got a question for you," Captain Bolders asked him as he turned and faced him. "If whatever this woman or thing was saved you, why be afraid of it? I would think you would be grateful," Bolders said.

"Commander, we are all grateful, but the strength it had. Trust me, Commander, you wouldn't want to meet something like that."

The doctor stepped forward. "You suffered a drastic blow to the head, and we don't know what kind of damage it has done," he told the cutter captain.

"Look, Doc, I'm not crazy or imagining things," the cutter captain told the doctor. "Besides," he added, "we all saw the same thing."

They finally gave the cutter crew a shot that relaxed them for the night, and everyone left except two security officers.

One day had passed, and out of the five cutter personnel that were rescued, three were up and able to move around parts of the ship. Another day passed, and the storm had passed, and the ship was two hours out of Pearl Harbor. Bolders was in the galley with Nelson, Manners, and the captain of the Coast Guard cutter.

A sailor came into the galley. "Captain, helo from Pearl inbound, five minutes out, sir."

28

Bolders turned, looking away from the sailor and at Manners. "Lieutenant, let's go see who is coming to visit."

Bolders and the lieutenant walked onto the bridge, and he saw Taylor upon entering the bridge. Taylor turned to him, laughing a little. "Looks like we have become famous, Captain."

"Really?" Bolders replied, walking up to the front window and looking out, seeing Pearl Harbor in the distance.

CHAPTER 4

TAYLOR POINTED to the east and, while pointing, looked at Bolders. "There's our lunch guest, Captain," he said, pointing at a helicopter.

Bolders looked at the helicopter, then back at Taylor. "Do we know who it is yet, XO?"

"Yes, sir, it is Admiral Riley himself," Taylor told him. "We didn't get any warning until they were inbound."

Bolders looked out at the helos that were inbound and then back at Taylor. "Sounds like a hush, hush deal, doesn't it?"

"That is what I was thinking too," Taylor replied. "Wonder what he is trying to hide?"

Bolders lifted his eyebrows for a moment, looked at Taylor, then at Manners. "I guess we're about to find out."

Bolders watched as one helo broke away from the other one and started circling to the back of the ship.

"Well, let's go meet our guest." Bolders started walking, and Taylor followed behind him.

Bolders stopped just before exiting the bridge and turned around, looking at Manners. "Lieutenant, tag along. You're in this too."

The three went to the landing pad and watched three people get off the helo and start walking toward them. "Admiral, sir," Bolders said as the admiral walked up to them. "Secret mission, sir?" he said jokingly.

"Actually, it is, Commander," Riley told Bolders. He then added, "Is there somewhere we can talk in private?"

"Yes, sir, follow me," Bolders told him as he led the way back into the ship to his quarters.

The admiral kept looking at Manners strangely all the way to the captain's quarters. Bolders noticed the admiral looking at Manners all the way from the main deck to his quarters. After they arrived, he had a small table that would be comfortable for two people, but it could seat four. He had a small love seat which would seat two and a counter with three stationary swivel stools. He also had a chair where he usually sat when he relaxed in his room with a book or reading over paperwork.

Bolders opened the door to his cabin and walked inside, holding the door as everyone walked in. After all of them had entered the room, Bolders closed the door and looked at them standing in the middle of his room.

"Please take a seat," Bolders told everyone as they began to look around and started to pick their seats.

The two officers that Admiral Riley brought on board with him both sat on the love seat, holding their briefcases in their laps. Bolders did not sit yet and waited on everyone else to take their seats. Admiral Riley, Taylor, and Manners took a seat at the small table, moving the seats around for more room.

After they all took their seats, Bolders asked, "What would everyone like to drink?"

Taylor asked for a Coca-Cola while Manners asked for a bottle of water, and he looked at the admiral.

"What about you and your party, Admiral?" Bolders asked as he looked at all three naval personnel.

Riley looked at him. "I would like something just a little stronger if you have it, Commander." The other two men asked for water.

Bolders handed everyone their drinks, and then he walked over to a small cabinet that was made on top of a small bar.

He opened the door, which had lattice work over the glass, making it look very decorative. He reached inside and pulled out some Irish cream liquor, some Jack Daniel's, and a new bottle of El Dorado cream rum and set them on the bar.

The admiral looked at them. "I'll have some Irish cream and coffee."

Bolders put the rest of them back in the cabinet.

He took two coffee mugs down and looked at the admiral. "I hope a mug is okay, sir; don't have normal coffee cups."

"That will be just fine, Commander," the admiral told him. He then added, "Pour about half rum and half coffee."

Bolders did it, then handed it to the admiral, then walked back to the bar and put the top back on the bottle, starting to put it up.

"You're not going to have one?" the admiral asked him.

"I'm just going to have coffee, sir," Bolders told the admiral.

Riley looked at him and, pointing at the bottle, said, "I think you need to have a strong one also, Commander."

"I don't drink that much," Bolders told the admiral as he turned and started to return the bottle back to its case.

The admiral got up from his seat and walked over to the small bar where Bolders was standing and pointed at the bottle, holding out his hand.

"May I?" the admiral asked. Bolders gave Riley the bottle of Irish rum and watched as he took the top off it.

He then watched the admiral as he started pouring a generous amount into his cup that was sitting on the bar.

"Ah, no, Admiral, I really don't drink that much," Bolders told the admiral again as he watched him pour it into his cup.

Riley finished pouring the rum into his cup, then handed it to Bolders. "Top it off with coffee there, Commander."

"Wow," Bolders commented, "that is a lot of liquor," as he looked in the cup, then topped it off with coffee, looking at the admiral.

"I'm going to set the bottle on the table," the admiral said as he went back and sat down at the table. "You're going to really need that when you hear what we have to tell you." He then pointed to the bottle. "Everyone else may want one too." The admiral took a sip of his coffee that he had well-diluted with the Irish rum.

He turned his body in the seat, holding his coffee mug in his right hand and his right elbow on the table.

"Commander," the admiral said as he looked at Bolders, "your base commander Captain Pettus evidently doesn't like you much."

"Why do you say that?" Bolders asked as Manners and Taylor also looked at the admiral, waiting for an answer.

"Well, he is coming all the way from Norfolk to get you with the blessing of our current president, Jeffery Banes. Then once he gets you back to Virginia, he plans to file charges against you for disobeying a direct order and attempting to start World War Three."

"What?" Bolders burst out, saying in an angry voice.

Taylor spoke up, "How can he say that? He wasn't there."

One of the gentlemen that Admiral Riley brought on board with him spoke up.

"Commander, he claims to have someone who is willing to testify that you were—and I quote—directly the cause of what happened."

Manners looked at him. "That is impossible because a witness

34

would have to be"—and then she paused—"they would have to be onboard," she said as she looked around the room, then paused. "And not one of you better point to me," she added.

Bolders spoke up, "I don't think anybody thinks you did it, Lieutenant," he paused, then finished, "I know you didn't."

The other guest of the admiral spoke up, asking, "Is there anyone else onboard that is new or untrustworthy?"

Taylor and Bolders looked at each other, trying to figure out how many new people there were on board.

The lieutenant looked at them. "Really, I'm new onboard, and I know how many you have and you don't," she said.

"Oh, and can you tell us who the new people on the ship are, Lieutenant?" Taylor asked in a smart tone.

"Actually, sir, yes, I can," Lieutenant Manners told him. She started saying, "There is the new engineer in the engine room."

Taylor looked at her. "Yeah, maybe," he said, then looked at Bolders, "it could be."

Manners then said, "No, it's not him. I'm pretty sure of that," she said, looking at Taylor then everyone else.

The admiral, looking at her, asked, "Why are you so sure that he isn't the one?"

"He is going through puberty or something, and between chasing women and the engine room, he doesn't have time."

"Okay," Bolders said, "who else do we have besides you that's new onboard that we can look at?"

Manners then looked at the admiral and Bolders. "The security team member that came on board when I did."

Taylor looked at her and poured her a drink of rum in her coffee mug. "So he could be the one?"

"No," she answered defiantly, "he's out of Pearl and has put in for a transfer to Master Chief Nelson's security team."

"Okay, how many more?" the admiral asked her.

"There is only one that has just come on this cruise."

Taylor looked at him. "The second shift helmsman."

Manners looked at him and smiled, leaning back in her seat. The second shift helmsman and Manners leaned forward and toasted Taylor, then leaned back again.

Bolders, looking at them, said, "We have to be sure about this before accusing someone."

"Okay, what about this?" Taylor said, "Let's just go and confront him and tell him we know about everything."

Manners, sitting across the small table from him, started to shake her head, not believing what she just heard him say.

Taylor looked at her. "What? I really think it would work," he told her. He paused then added, "You have a better idea?"

Bolders looked at her also then said, "I think that would work."

CHAPTER 5

TAYLOR, looking at him, said, "Thank you, Captain."

"May I speak freely?" Manners asked the three officers.

The admiral, looking at her, said, "Please, I would like to hear what you've got to say."

"Thank you, sir," she said to the admiral. "I guess it's because I'm a woman that I notice things more than you men."

"Just what kind of thing did you notice that we didn't, Lieutenant?" Bolders asked her, leaning forward in his chair.

"Every time, before something happens, he has to go to the bathroom," Manners said, "so he has a very weak bladder or he has a satellite phone hidden somewhere."

Admiral Riley looked at her. "If he has a satellite phone, then someone knew something was going to happen."

"Exactly," Manners said, "and if, and I say if, I am right, whoever he is contacting has known everything for the past five months."

"Okay, do you have any idea how we can definitely find out that he is the one?" Nelson asked.

"I'm glad you asked, Master Chief," she said, smiling at him and slightly raising her eyebrows, "because I sure do."

She didn't say anything and just looked at no one else except for Bolders in almost a seductive way.

"You going to make me ask just what you had in mind before you tell us, Lieutenant?" Bolders said with a small smile.

The other four men, seeing this, looked at Bolders then back at her. "Okay, Lieutenant, let's hear it," the admiral said.

"First, we need to get to the bridge and put everything into motion."

As she explained everything, all five officers arrived on the bridge, and Manners looked out and could see Pearl Harbor about an hour away in the distance.

"There it is, Captain," Manners said, looking at Bolders.

Then Taylor spoke up, "Everyone, clear the bridge." Taylor then looked at the helmsman and pointed at him. "Don't you move," he ordered.

The Lieutenant Commander then walked up behind the helmsman, saying, "Were you going to leave your post, sailor?"

The helmsman, just for a second, turned and looked at Taylor. "No, sir, I wasn't, sir."

"Looked like to me you were about to leave with everyone else. Douglas, isn't it?" Taylor asked.

"Okay," the admiral said, "we need to get you off this ship and onto the base before we reach port. Then they can't touch you, at least for a few days. By then, we may be able to get the paperwork to keep you and the crew at Pearl for a while."

Everyone was close enough to the helmsman that he could hear every word they said, and he wouldn't misunderstand anything.

"Lieutenant Commander," the admiral said to Taylor, "get to CIC and get the helicopters back out here before we get to Pearl."

Taylor left the bridge and went to CIC. He wasn't gone but about five minutes when the helmsman started to get fidgety.

"You okay there, sailor?" Bolders asked him.

"I really need to go to the head, sir," he replied to Bolders.

"You go to the toilet a lot, son; you okay?" Bolders asked the young ensign, sounding concerned.

"I am okay, sir. I just drank too much tea and water before coming on duty, sir," he told Bolders.

"Sounds like you have weak kidneys, ensign," the captain told him. He then added, "Go ahead, just hurry back."

Admiral Riley stopped Bolders as he was about to take over driving the ship. "It's been a while, Captain." He then stepped up to the wheel. "If you don't mind?" Riley asked Bolders.

They all watched as the young ensign exited the bridge and waited for about a minute. Bolders then looked at Manners, not saying anything, telling her to follow him. He leaned his head to the right and moved his eyes in the same direction. Manners, understanding what the captain was telling her, knew it was time to follow him.

Manners went down the stairway and to where the passageway connected with another and put her back against the wall. She then peeped her head around the corner just as the ensign was going into the restroom. Once the door closed behind him, she gave it a few more seconds and then walked around the corner.

She then saw Nelson at the other corner and another security team member further down the passageway. The captain and Nelson had discussed earlier before departing for the bridge what they were planning, so they made sure the passageway was clear.

"Lieutenant, walk up to the door."

With a thumbs-up from Nelson, she cracked the door and heard Douglas talking to someone. She turned a recorder on and held it just inside the doorway where she could get everything. She heard the toilet flush and eased her arm out of the door and gently closed it. Nelson motioned for his team member to disappear and then motioned for Manners to hurry to him. She ran down the passageway to Nelson, and they went down the adjoining passageway to an outside door. Nelson, watching his watch, gave Douglas (the helmsman) a couple of minutes to get back to the bridge.

Back on the bridge, the admiral was at the helm really enjoying himself, and Douglas, the helmsman, walked back onto the bridge.

With Douglas being gone for twenty minutes, Bolders said with a smile, "Must have had to do more than turn the sprinklers [pee] on."

"Yes, sir," the helmsman said. "Sorry, sir, it took so long, Captain," he told Bolders.

"You gotta go, you gotta go, son. Don't apologize for that," Bolders told him, smiling.

The admiral then looked at Douglas, saying, "Helmsman, I stand relieved." He then backed away from the wheel.

Douglas stepped up to it.

At that time, Bolders heard Nelson's voice come over the ship's radio. "All team members, report for pre-dock inspection station 1." Then again, he heard the Master Chief's voice. "Captain, please report to station 1 for pre-dock inspection."

Bolders looked at Riley. "Admiral, would you like to accompany me to the inspection, sir?"

"I would like that, Commander," Admiral Riley replied to Bolders as he started following him toward the exit.

He looked at Taylor as they passed him. "XO, please join us," Bolders told him.

Then all three men exited the bridge. Instead of going to the inspection point, they went straight to Bolders's quarters, where Nelson and Lieutenant Manners were also waiting for them. Bolders opened the door to his quarters, and they all walked inside. Nelson left a team member from his security team outside the door to make sure no one interrupted them. Just as they all sat down, there was a knock on the door.

Bolders said aloud, "Enter."

Knowing that the security member outside his door had approved it, he wasn't worried.

It was Ralph from CIC. "Sir, you said to keep you informed in person, sir."

Bolders answered, "That's correct, ensign. What do you have?" he asked.

"The helo is ten minutes out, sir, and we are thirty-three minutes from the shipyard, sir," Ralph told him, then left.

Admiral Riley looked at Nelson, then Manners. "Have you listened to the recording yet?"

Nelson got up and placed it on the table as he answered the admiral, "No, sir, we were waiting on everyone to hear it at the same time."

Everyone got up and walked to the table and stood around it waiting to listen, including Admiral Riley's two guests.

"Well, let's hear it," Bolders told Nelson.

The Master Chief, with his right pointing finger, pushed the play button. They all listened as they heard the helmsman start to speak to someone from the bathroom.

"Captain Pettus, sir, this is Ensign Douglas, sir. I have some information for you and can't talk long. There is a helo coming in to get the captain, and they are going to hide him out 'til they can get paperwork to keep him at Pearl." Then there was a pause, and Douglas spoke again, "That is what they said, sir." Then there was a longer pause, and then the helmsman spoke again, "Yes, sir, I heard the admiral himself say that, Captain Pettus." After another short pause, Douglas spoke again, answering what seemed to be a question, "Yes, sir, the XO Taylor and a lieutenant that the captain can't keep his eyes off of is also in on it."

Nelson looked at Bolders, saying, "You old sly dog," making Manners blush and everyone else laugh.

Then they heard Douglas tell Pettus, "Your plan is working to perfection, sir."

Nelson then took his finger and hit the stop button on the recorder; looking at the admiral and captain, he said, "That's all we got."

Riley looked at the two gentlemen that came with him. "Do you think that's enough to make it backfire on them?"

"If we can find the phone, we could make this work," replied one of the ones who came in with the admiral.

Riley then looked at everyone and said, "I am sorry, everyone. Let me introduce these fine gentlemen." Riley pointed to the one closest to him first, putting his right hand on the sailor's left shoulder. "This fine gentleman is Lieutenant Timothy Slate, lead attorney for the admiral's office." He then stepped back one step and walked behind Slate, placing his left hand on the other's shoulder. "And this fine gentleman is Lieutenant Melvin Benton, the assistant attorney to the lead for the admiral's office. The reason I didn't have them dress as they should was because I wanted to keep this under wraps for now." Then the admiral turned to Manners, looking at her again in a loving and tender way. Lieutenant Riley said, "I owe you an explanation here in front of everyone before this is over and an apology also."

"Sir, you owe me nothing," Manners said. "You have done nothing to apologize for, sir," she added.

He then looked at her again in that same way. "I know you've noticed the way I've looked at you, Lieutenant, and that is inappropriate."

Nelson jokingly said, smiling, "Admiral, if half the wives of the sailors on this ship have seen the way they've looked at the lieutenant, they would all be divorced."

CHAPTER 6

EVERYONE LAUGHED FOR A SECOND, then watched as the admiral pulled out his wallet with tears forming in his eyes.

Bolders placed his right hand on the admiral's back, looking at him. "Are you alright, sir?" he asked.

Riley opened his wallet and unzipped a compartment on the inside of it and pulled something out with his right hand. Tears now started dripping down his cheeks as he wiped them away with his left wrist and opened a small ziplock bag.

"I met a woman—the most beautiful woman that I have ever seen in my entire life until I got on this ship." His shoulders bounced once, and he skipped a breath as he bowed his head, and a few more tears rolled down his cheek. "My wife knows about her, and my wife knows how much I loved her. This woman was the love of my life. She is the one that brought me back to God," he said, with a few more tears coming out.

Nelson reached inside his jacket pocket, got a clean handkerchief, and reached in front of Bolders, handing it to the admiral. His eyes were also starting to water up as the admiral took it and kept explaining to everyone.

"She was the love of my life, and her life ended. I was heart-broken over a year until I met the next love." He pulled out two laminated wallet-sized pictures out of the ziplock bag and handed them to Bolders, who was at his left.

Bolders looked at the pictures, then looked up and handed them to Nelson to his left. They did this until they got to Manners, and she looked at them and looked up at the admiral.

As she looked up at him, he told her to look at the back of the pictures and read what was written. She turned it over, and Nelson asked her what it said, and she read it out loud.

"To Nicholas Riley, the man I love, Tanya Manners."

The admiral sat down, and more tears flowed now. Manners walked around to him, holding him by his shoulder, wanting him to stand, and he did so. She put her arms around his neck and, for about a minute, held him really tight as he started to cry aloud. She then released him as he did her, and she looked up at him as he stood straight.

"I'm glad you got to see her through me, Admiral." A couple of tears dropped to the floor from her cheek. "I'm glad I was the one that brought those loving feelings back to your heart," she said as she held his hands. "Those are more the tears of a happy love than those of sadness, and it makes me happy to be part of that."

The admiral couldn't say anything, and neither could anyone else at the table; Manners smiled at him.

"Let me say one more thing, Admiral, and this is for everyone, not just you, and it is the truth. If we listen to God, things don't always go the way we want them to, but they turn out better than we wanted. We don't understand why God does some things he does, and we will never know some of those things. We have to trust, and one day, we will have all the answers to questions our hearts and mouths have ever asked."

At that time, there was a knock on the door, and Bolders told them to enter. It was one of the security team members. He opened the door and looked around the room at everyone in there with tears in their eyes.

Nelson spoke up, "Have you never seen a room full of men then looking at Manners and one woman crying?" he asked.

"No, Master Chief, never, not even at a funeral." He then thought for a second. "No one died, did they?" he asked with a serious look on his face.

"No," Nelson said. "Did you come in here to talk about our tears or to tell us something else?"

"Yes, Master Chief, the helo is inbound, Chief, five minutes out," he told Nelson. Then he stood there as if there was something else that he needed to say.

Bolders asked, "Is there something else, Ensign?"

"Actually, there is, sir," he replied to Bolders. "The master chief said if we found anything suspicious, we needed to bring it to him."

Admiral Riley stood up and asked him, "And did you find something, sailor?"

"Yes, sir, Admiral. Hidden in the ceiling tile was a satellite phone, sir, and there are only supposed to be two on the ship." Manners looked at him. "And where is it, Ensign?" she asked the sailor as he held out his left hand with a bag. She took it and turned to everyone else in the room, walking over to them. "Let's get the helo, and then we can have our guys do a call analysis on it to see when and where it called." The sailor held up his right hand with a couple of papers in it. "We took the time to have that done also, Captain." He walked over and handed it to Bolders. As Bolders opened it, the sailor explained the numbers he was seeing. "That main number that you're seeing, sir, is to Malcolm Pettus's private phone number and was called every day. The second number you see on there was made to a number that is nonexistent anywhere in the world." When he said that, the sailor touched his ear where his receiver was and said, "Roger that. Sir, the helo is landing now, sir."

He looked at the sailor. "Thank you, we will figure the rest out."

Douglas could see the helicopter and saw that someone was getting on it and breathed a big sigh of relief. At that time, Bolders, the admiral, Manners, and Nelson with his security team walked onto the bridge. When they were announced, the helmsman jumped slightly, turning around to look at them. His eyes got very big as he saw Bolders standing there in front of him.

"Sir," he said nervously, "I thought you got on the chopper."

Bolders tilted his head slightly and shrugged his shoulders. "I changed my mind and decided to face your boss." He then noticed the other helmsman standing behind everyone.

"What are you doing here?" Douglas asked him. Nelson stepped forward and motioned for two of his security team members to step forward also.

"Mr. Douglas, you are hereby placed in custody of the ship's security team until you can be turned over to the proper authorities at Pearl."

"What did I do?" the helmsman asked in a very nervous and scared voice.

Nelson walked up to him and as he looked around Nelson, he asked again, almost crying now, "What did I do wrong?" None of the officers said anything and just looked at him as one of the team members had him step away from the wheel. The two team members turned him around, putting his hands behind his back and placing handcuffs on him. They turned him back around to where he was facing Nelson and the officers behind him. Nelson looked at him.

"Ensign Douglas Wang, you are hereby placed in custody until you can be turned over to shore authorities at port. You are charged with having and hiding an unauthorized transmission device and using it to spy on officers of the ship." The two security team members started to walk away with him, and he looked at Bolders as he passed by.

"Captain, please let me explain. I'll tell you whatever you want to know," Douglas told him.

Manners looked at Bolders. "We might want to keep him onboard for a while to see what he knows."

Bolders turned, looking at Nelson. "Master Chief, make sure to keep him in the brig, and don't notify anyone of this yet." Nelson acknowledged the captain's orders and went to catch up with his team members as they escorted the helmsman to the brig. The admiral looked at Bolders and held out his left hand toward him.

"Let me be the one to make this call."

Bolders handed him the phone, and all four officers walked out on the deck above the main. "Let's dial this number. Why don't we—"

CHAPTER 7

ADMIRAL RILEY PUSHED the number and redialed it. "Ensign Wang," a voice answered very sternly on the other end, "what is it now? We're waiting on the helo."

"Well, Captain, you might be waiting for quite a while."

The voice on the other end asked, "Who the hell is this?"

"Well, this would be Nicholas Riley - as in, Admiral Nicholas Riley."

There was no answer from the other end. "Captain, are you there?" the admiral asked Pettus.

"Yes, sir, I am here, Admiral. What is this all about, sir?" Pettus asked.

"Captain Pettus, I need to be asking you the same question, specifically considering what I have just found out."

"Where are you, Admiral?" Pettus asked him.

"Here with Commander Bolders and your spy, Captain. It was on speaker, so they all heard."

"If we could meet up, sir," Pettus asked the admiral, "I can explain everything to you in person, sir."

"Meet us back at the shipyard dock, and we can talk further there," Admiral Riley told him, then hung up.

"That was smooth, sir," Taylor said to the admiral as Riley chuckled.

"Well, we will see how smooth it was."

They watched as the ship came through the Pearl Harbor entrance, and Bolders turned to the admiral.

"We might ought to try and find out what we can before we meet Captain Pettus at the dock, sir." They all went back to the brig where Nelson and one other team member were waiting with the prisoner. They stood up, and the admiral told them to stand easy. He then asked, "How is the prisoner?"

"He's been begging and crying a lot, sir," Nelson replied as he opened the door leading to the four cells. All the cells were on the left side of the short passageway, and Douglas was in the last one. Riley, Bolders, and Taylor walked into the cell where Douglas was and set up chairs they had carried in.

"I need to know everything you know, son, if you ever want to stand a chance of getting out of this," Riley told him, leaning forward slightly.

"Yes, sir, I will. Just please don't kick me out of the Navy, sir, please," the young sailor begged, tears welling up in his eyes. The admiral and Bolders stayed in the cell with the young ensign for twenty minutes and then emerged, escorted by Nelson. Taylor and Manners rose from their seats, exchanged looks, and saw the admiral shaking his head.

Bolders said, "Nothing, he gave us nothing." "Let me have a try at him just for five minutes, and I guarantee you, he'll talk," Taylor said with a very upset voice, stepping closer to the admiral.

"Thank you, my friend," Bolders told him, patting him on his left shoulder. "It won't do any good," he added.

"Either he doesn't know why he was doing it or he knows he's

52

very protected, one of the two," the admiral said, a frown crossing his face.

"Could I have a chance at it?" Manners asked, looking from Bolders to Riley. "What can it hurt? Please, just five minutes." She waited for a few seconds, and no one said anything. "Three minutes, give me three minutes, and if he doesn't talk, I'll stop." They all exchanged glances, and then Bolders turned to Nelson.

"What do you say, Master Chief?" he asked Nelson.

A team member walked over to where they were standing. "Master Chief, we will be docking in five minutes."

"Look, I've been on missions where a woman talking to someone young like him and showing some compassion got people to talk," Manners added, her eyes pleading. Bolders looked at the admiral, and neither one spoke, but they seemed to understand each other.

Bolders looked at the lieutenant. "You have five minutes, Lieutenant Manners, and if nothing happens, that's it. We will be out of time." Nelson led her back to the cell, unlocked it, and then sat in a chair right outside the cell. Manners walked in, turned around, and looked at Nelson.

"Is there any way we could be alone, Master Chief?"

"I can't do that, ma'am," the Master Chief replied firmly.

Then she looked up at the camera and said, "I'll be okay, please."

Bolders opened the door that led to the cells and said to the Master Chief, "It's okay, Nelson, come wait with us."

Nelson got up and walked out. Douglas sat on his bunk while Manners moved her metal chair closer, crossing her legs.

Seeing this, Nelson started to rise from his seat. "What is she doing?" he said. "She was told four feet at all times."

Bolders reached out, touching his arm. "Just give her a few minutes to work it the way she needs to."

Taylor chimed in, "Yeah, Master Chief, come on, we can see and hear everything."

Nelson sat back down with the others as a team member entered. "Master Chief, we are about to tie off."

"She doesn't have five minutes, Admiral," Nelson replied, "so she better get something quick."

Manners smiled at Douglas. "Where did the name Wang come from?" she asked.

"My mom is half Chinese, and my dad left before I was born, so I got her last name."

Nelson looked at Bolders as they watched the camera together. "She really needs to hurry, Captain."

"Why wouldn't you tell the captain and admiral what you were doing and why, Douglas?"

"There's really nothing much to tell, ma'am. I told them everything, but that's not going to help me."

"No, it's not, but I can't believe you would just do something like this knowing it was wrong without questioning it. It doesn't seem like your mom raised you like that," Manners said. "What would she say about this?"

"It would break her heart; she was so proud when I graduated boot camp, bragging to all her friends."

"Douglas, listen to me, I promise you no one on this ship or anyone else will ever know about this."

"Really?" he said, looking at her.

"No one," she replied. "No one, Douglas. You just have to tell me why."

"Will you help me tell my mom and girlfriend why I'm no longer in the Navy, Lieutenant?" he asked.

She leaned forward in her chair, smiling at him. "There won't be any need for that."

He looked at her, confused.

"I'll make sure you return to work without any jail time."

He smiled at her. "Okay, I'll tell you what I know. It's not much, but it's what I was told."

Lieutenant Manners leaned in more, taking his shaking hand. "It's okay," she said.

"I was told that the captain was a suspected terrorist, and they had gotten word that he may try to start World War III," Douglas continued. "I was given the sat phone and was supposed to call in at least once a day. I really thought I was doing a good thing for my country, Lieutenant. I really did, ma'am."

"Douglas, I really need to know who told you this, and what else they told you, okay?" she said, squeezing his hand. "You will be going away for a long time, and you don't want that," Manners continued, still holding his hand to keep him from shaking. "Douglas, look at me."

He raised his head and looked at her for a couple of seconds.

"Do you have a girlfriend or a fiancée back home, Douglas?" she asked.

"Yes, ma'am," he answered. "I've got a girlfriend but hope she'll soon be my fiancée."

"Well, I promise you, if you talk to these people, you will be around to ask your girlfriend to marry you."

"Ma'am, there is a man. I was told to call him Mr. Drake, and, Lieutenant, he is a very scary person."

"Douglas, look at me," she said, still holding his hands but raising them slightly.

"If I tell you, ma'am," Douglas said, starting to look at Manners, "I am afraid of what might happen to me and my family, ma'am," he continued, shaking a bit more now.

The lieutenant softened her voice a little and asked, "Did someone threaten your family, Douglas?"

"Not in so many words, ma'am. It was just the way he said it," he replied.

"What happened? Tell me," Manners asked. "I promise you, if I can't help, I will not bother you anymore."

The four men watched on, listening to see if and who had threatened him or his family.

"The captain sent a message that he wanted to see me in his office right away, and the shore patrol escorted me," Douglas told her. "When I got to his office, Captain Pettus started explaining about Captain Bolders being a terrorist. I was promised a promotion to petty officer if I did what I was told." He continued, "Ma'am, I barely made it through Naval A School. I wasn't given much of a choice."

"I thought the captain asked you to do this, which means you had a choice, correct?" the lieutenant asked.

"I was under that impression, ma'am, until the captain had to leave the room for a few minutes," Douglas replied.

"What happened or what was said that changed everything when the captain left the room?" Manners asked.

"That's when Mr. Drake walked over to my chair, grabbed me around the throat, and lifted me off the floor. My throat hurt for a week, ma'am. I could barely swallow. It hurt so bad."

Nelson looked at the other three officers, laughing. "This guy has quite the imagination, doesn't he?" he said.

Douglas continued telling Manners about the man who picked him up with one hand. "He told me I had a very nice family and a very pretty girlfriend, and it was a shame about my father. No one knows about my father's condition. We're trying to keep it in the family. Then he said it would be bad for me not to be around for my mother when it's finally time for my father to go."

Manners looked at him as his eyes started to fill with tears. He bowed his head, looking at the floor.

"I take it you and your father are very close?" Manners asked.

"I'm close to both of my parents," Douglas replied. "I was a late child, ma'am. My mom and dad had me in their late forties. When they came to my graduation, everyone thought they were my grandparents, but that didn't bother them. Anyway, back to Mr. Drake—he threw me back down in the chair just before the captain returned. He told me if I loved the things in my life, I would do whatever I was asked to do. Then he said if I told anyone, no man could stop him from getting to me."

"Well, I'm not a man. I am a woman, and I promise you I can protect you with no problem, Ensign," Manners said.

Douglas looked at her with doubt in his eyes. "Lieutenant," he said with a forced smile, "if you could protect me, I'd tell you everything."

Manners turned and looked over her left shoulder at the camera on the corner wall of the cell.

"What is she doing?" Bolders said, looking into the camera.

Nelson added, "What is she saying? She can't protect him."

At that moment, only Douglas was visible, and where Manners should have been on the camera was blacked out. The four men tried to fix the screen but couldn't find anything wrong.

They heard Manners talking to the ensign. "Look at me, Douglas. I promise I can protect you," she said.

The four men watching the camera saw Douglas's eyes widen, and a large smile spread across his face.

"What is he smiling at?" Nelson said aloud, looking at the monitor.

They saw him lean forward, and the camera came back on, showing him grabbing her.

All four men ran to the entrance door to the cells, but it was jammed and wouldn't open. When they finally got it open, they rushed to the cell and found Manners and Douglas laughing and talking. "Are you okay?" Bolders was the first to reach the cell and shouted out to her, waiting for Nelson to open the door.

"I'm fine," she replied, looking at them. "Douglas is going to tell us what we need to know."

"Really?" Taylor said. "That's great."

Admiral Riley stepped forward. "Let's go meet with Captain Pettus." Turning to Douglas, he added, "I want to trust you, but I'll have to keep you here until we get your testimony."

The four men and Lieutenant Manners walked out onto the main deck and saw Pettus and three men waiting. Three of Nelson's team members were also there, with one at the top of the gangway.

Admiral Riley looked at Bolders. "Well, let's go meet this guy and find out who the other person with him is."

Manners chuckled at his words, and they walked down the plank to the bottom of the ramp.

Captain Pettus and his party saluted, while a man not in uniform stood about ten feet away. Pettus looked at Bolders and his crew without saying a word.

"Is there a problem, Captain?" Riley asked.

Pettus looked at him. "Waiting for them to show me the respect I deserve."

Admiral Riley nodded to Bolders. "Salute him."

Bolders, Manners, and the rest saluted Captain Pettus. Riley then turned to Pettus. "Now that they've shown you respect, can we get on with why you're here?"

Pettus was visibly offended. "I'm here for that," he said, pointing at the Tiger Shark, "and him," pointing at Bolders.

"The ship needs work, and it's unsafe to sail. As for the commander, his feet are on my dock, so no to both," Riley replied.

Pettus looked at Bolders and then at his two sailors. "Take the commander into custody."

The two sailors started toward Bolders, but Nelson made a hand gesture, and his team members blocked their path.

The Norfolk security officer looked at Nelson. "Master Chief, they need to move."

"I have my orders too, so stand down," Nelson replied.

The sailor turned to Pettus. "Captain, should we proceed?"

"Stand down," Pettus said, looking at the admiral. "This is your base, and you outrank me. We'll see you in court."

They watched as Pettus and his sailors walked away toward the tall man at the end of the dock.

Riley nodded to Nelson. "Thank you, Master Chief."

"Just following orders, sir," Nelson replied.

Out of the corner of his eye, Riley saw two attorneys approaching. He turned to face them, and everyone else followed suit, waiting for them to reach the group. Bolders could tell from their expressions that it wasn't good.

He tried to joke, but it fell flat. "Oh, it's that good, huh?" he said, attempting a grin.

Slate looked at the admiral and then at Bolders. "Honestly, Commander, we can't submit this account from the Ensign."

Manners, standing beside Bolders, squinted at Slate. "Why not? What's wrong with it?"

Benton replied, "Lieutenant, it sounds like something straight out of a thriller novel."

"What can we do, or what other options do we have?" Taylor asked, looking at Benton.

"We have the sat phone and its recent call info," Slate paused, then added, "and we have Ensign Douglas Wang. Isn't that enough to keep the commander out of a court-martial?" Manners asked the two attorneys.

Slate looked at everyone, then at Bolders. "Sir, we have the weekend. Let us work on it and see what we can come up with."

"Well," Taylor said, looking at Bolders, "what are you doing tonight?"

The commander shook his head.

"Nancy and the kids are here, so why don't you come out with us?" Taylor suggested. "The family would love to see you."

"No, Will, thank you," Bolders replied, tapping his left hand on Taylor's upper arm.

Everyone started to leave. The admiral asked Bolders again if he wanted to come.

"I'm sure, Admiral. I'm going to stay on the ship tonight and maybe catch up on some reading or just relax."

"Very well," the admiral said. "I'll check in on you in the morning then, Commander." He walked away.

Bolders turned to Manners. "Are you staying on base tonight, or on the ship?"

"After I take you to a nice steakhouse I know, I'm going home to see if it's still there," Manners replied.

"Home?" Bolders asked, confused. "You mean temporary billeting, don't you?"

"No, sir. This is my base, and I have a home here."

Bolders looked even more puzzled. "Your base? Didn't we get you from California?"

"You did," she said, smiling at his confusion. "I was on loan to San Diego Naval Station."

He smiled and shook his head. "Okay, well, thanks for the invitation, but I'm going to my quarters to relax like I told the admiral."

Manners just stood there, looking at him. He laughed. "Seriously, I'm staying on the ship tonight."

She remained still, arms crossed. He walked about ten steps, looked back, and saw her still standing there. He stopped and turned around.

"I'm serious," he told her.

She stood there, smiling. "I don't like rejection," she said, arms crossed.

He looked at her and felt his heart skip a beat. She was the most beautiful woman he had ever seen. Her slim figure and long dark brown hair looked black in certain lights. Her beautiful gray eyes took his breath away. On the ship, he always tried to avoid direct eye contact with her for that reason. His two best friends, Nelson and Taylor, sometimes laughed at him for it; even the admiral could see it.

"Okay," he said, turning and starting toward the plank to board the ship. He turned once more to look back.

She was still just standing there, and he laughed a little, saying aloud for her to hear, "You can come onboard and wait for me; I have to take a shower first."

She walked up to him, and they walked up the plank together, not saying much.

"You know, Captain, you can just get your clothes to save time and shower at my home. I have two of them," Manners said.

Bolders turned to her, smiling, still avoiding direct eye contact. "What? Two homes?" he asked.

"No, silly, two showers." She laughed, and so did he as they entered the ship.

They arrived at the captain's quarters. He opened the door and held it open for her, then walked in after she did.

"Have a seat, and I'll get some clothes together," he said, opening a small bag and setting it on his bunk.

He looked at her and asked, "Are you wearing your uniform or plain clothes?"

"I'm wearing my civvies," she said, smiling. "I wear my jeans whenever I get the chance."

She watched as he went into his closet and got a pair of blue jeans and a flannel shirt. He then walked to a small dresser and took out a pair of socks and underwear, holding the latter to his side so she wouldn't see them.

Manners began to laugh. He looked at her, smiling. "What's so funny?" he asked.

With a small smirk, she said, "Boxers, huh? Very impressive; don't see that too often anymore."

His cheeks turned red, and her grin widened into a smile. "You embarrass easily, don't you?" Manners asked as he went to his bathroom to get a few extra things.

He came out with both hands full, and she laughed again. She stood up and walked over to him as he laid everything on the bed to pack it neatly.

Manners picked up a bar of his soap and a washcloth. "I've got soap, and I've got these too," she said.

He looked at her chin to avoid her eyes. "Sorry, I'm just not used to packing to go to someone else's home."

She threw the washcloth and soap to the foot of the bed, then zipped up his bag. She picked it up, handed it to him, and said, "Okay, let's go. I am hungry."

Bolders opened the door and let Manners walk out first, then followed and locked his door. The two walked off the ship, and the base security called for transport. They were taken to the front gate, and she noticed Bolders looking up and down the main road.

"What are you doing?" she asked.

"Looking for a taxi," he replied.

"Captain," she said, "we don't need a taxi to get to where we're going."

He turned to his left, looking at her. "You live pretty close to the base?" he asked.

She laughed and said, "Oh my God, no. To the main base parking lot. That's where my car is."

62

Bolders looked at her for a moment. "You leave your car here when you go on your cruise?" he asked, surprised.

"Yes, I do," she said. "It's a twenty-minute ride by car and twice as long to my house by bus."

The bus pulled up then, and they got on, walking toward the back as it was so full.

One of the lieutenants sitting in the back recognized Manners. "Tanya, you finally back?"

"Just got back this morning," she replied.

"What about an early dinner, then?" the lieutenant asked.

She turned her head toward him but looked up at Bolders, who was standing beside her seat first. "I've got a late lunch date," she said.

The lieutenant looked at Bolders and then at Manners. "Oh well, enjoy," he said, pulling the stop wire.

CHAPTER 8

BOLDERS TURNED sideways to let the sailor and two more pass, and Manners put her arm around his waist, pulling him in.

The bus started again, and they heard the driver over the intercom, "Next stop, main parking lot."

A sailor sitting in front of her turned to look at Manners. "Lieutenant, how was your cruise?" the young ensign asked.

"It will surely be one to remember; that's for sure," she replied.

"It's good to have you back, ma'am," the ensign said. "I loved when you told him you had a date." She then whispered to Manners, "You did really good, Lieutenant Manners."

Bolders, smiling, bent over and whispered, "He's right here and can hear you."

The intercom crackled again. "Main parking lot," and the bus began to stop.

Bolders let the ensign and Manners go first. They walked down the aisle and exited the bus. Manners and the young ensign walked just ahead of Bolders, talking and laughing softly.

The ensign looked back at Bolders quickly, raising her eyebrows at Manners. "Wow, you did good."

After a five-minute walk from the bus stop, they arrived at the lieutenant's car, which was covered. Bolders helped her remove the cover and fold it, putting it in the trunk. He opened her door and then closed it after she got inside.

He walked around to the passenger side and got in, looking at her. "A Mercedes, I'm impressed," he said, looking around the interior. "Very impressive, Lieutenant."

They rode for fifteen minutes and arrived at a gated community. Manners pulled out her card and scanned it; the gate opened, and they drove through. He looked on both sides, amazed at the beautiful, large homes.

"How can you afford this on a Navy lieutenant's salary, Manners?" he asked.

She laughed and shook her head. "I live in the downgraded section."

He looked out the window again and joked, "There's a downgraded section to this place?"

They came to a stop sign, took a right onto a road marked 'dead end,' and headed down a large hill. He could see the beach below. The car turned into a driveway and stopped short of the garage door. Manners turned off the car.

"Home sweet home, Captain," she said, looking at Bolders. Excited to be home, she hurried out of the car.

Bolders got out as quickly as he could. Manners grabbed her small bag and hurried inside. Bolders walked toward the front door, looking around in disbelief. He stopped to admire the beautiful beach below.

Manners ran back to the door and stepped outside. "Come on, Captain, we can see the beach later."

He went inside and was impressed by the cleanliness of the house. Everything was spotless, from the white leather sectional to the fireplace mantel. Manners came out of a room near the sliding glass doors.

"Let me show you to the spare bedroom so you can shower."

He followed her to his left, past the fireplace, through the dining room and kitchen, and into a hallway.

They walked past a door. "This is the washroom, sink, and toilet only," she pointed out.

A few more steps, and she opened a door to a room. He followed her, looking around at the large double bed and oak furniture.

"This is the bathroom," she told him as he stood in the middle of the bedroom. "I'll get you some towels and a bar of soap," she said, and left the room.

Bolders walked to the bathroom door as she exited and looked inside. "Holy cow!" he exclaimed, taking in the pink tub and counter with a double sink. She returned to find him standing there, still looking.

"Is everything okay, Captain?" she asked, walking up behind him.

"This bathroom is bigger than my ship's quarters, including the bathroom," he replied. "And everything is pink."

With her right hand, she placed her palm between his shoulder blades, leaning around him to look in. "It's mauve—a color between purple and pink. It's very relaxing, don't you think?" she said.

He pointed at the soap. "That's mauve too?"

"No." She laughed, picking up the soap. "That's pink, and yes, the towels are pink too." Turning to walk away, she looked at him. "Hurry, Captain, I am starving."

Bolders finished showering and shaving, got dressed, and went into the living room but didn't see Manners. Her bedroom door was still closed, so he assumed she was still showering. He walked out the double glass doors onto the patio and down a brick sidewalk that led to the backyard. The stars were just starting to come out as it got dark.

Manners emerged from her room, didn't see him, and started toward the guest bedroom. She happened to look to her right and saw Bolders standing at the far end of the backyard. She walked up behind him. "It is beautiful, isn't it?" she said, standing beside him.

"It really is, Lieutenant," he said, glancing at her before looking back at the beach.

She looked at him for a couple of seconds. "Captain," she said, still looking at him.

Bolders met her gaze before she turned back to the beach. "Do me a favor, Captain."

"Sure," he replied, also looking at the beach.

"Call me Tanya or T. We're not working now, and I don't want to think about work. I will still call you Captain, sir, if you prefer."

"I'd like that, Tanya," he said.

She turned toward him. "Okay then, Captain, let's go eat."

Tanya started walking away first, and Bolders followed. "Mat," he said.

She stopped and turned. "Pardon?"

"Mat. My name, short for Mathew," he told her.

She smiled, almost taking his breath away. "Okay, Mat, let's go eat."

They walked back into the house toward the front door. She took her purse off the couch, slung it over her shoulder, and pulled out her keys. She held the door open as Bolders walked outside.

She locked the door behind him and asked, "You have a license, right?"

"I have a license," he replied.

She handed him the keys. "Good, you're driving."

"I don't know where I'm going," he said as she walked by him.

Turning her head, she said, "It's a good thing I do."

68

He followed her around the car to the passenger side, trying his best not to stare at her. He opened her door and ensured her feet were clear before closing it. As he walked in front of the car, he couldn't help but glance at her, despite trying not to. He opened the driver's door, got in, and was captivated by her long dark wavy hair draped over her left shoulder. Look at the steering wheel, he told himself, but those gray eyes of hers were hypnotizing, and he couldn't turn away.

She saw him staring. "Is everything okay?" she asked, pulling the visor down and opening the mirror to check her makeup.

"There's nothing wrong," he replied, catching his breath. "I've just never seen anyone so beautiful."

She looked in the mirror, then turned to him, and he caught himself. You idiot, he thought, looking away and out the front window.

"I am so sorry; I can't believe I said that," he stammered, nervous and trying to catch his breath.

She lifted the visor with her right hand and placed her left hand on his forearm that was holding the steering wheel. "Please don't apologize," she said. "I don't think I've ever had anyone look at me like that before. We need to go if we're going to eat tonight," she added, smiling.

They left and headed toward the steakhouse. When they pulled into the parking lot, Bolders drove around to the front closest to the entrance. Manners turned her head to the left, tilted it to the right, and looked at Bolders. Her long hair fell over her shoulder, resting on her forearm.

Her eyes widened as she raised an eyebrow. "Really, Mat, just really?"

"What did I do?" He looked at her with a short smile, causing her to start laughing.

With her shoes off and her feet on the seat, she put her elbow on the door and propped her head on it. "If the back is full, Mat, doesn't it stand to reason the front would be?"

Even though Bolders was a commander in charge of the Navy's deadliest warship, she had made him feel dumb. Manners looked at him and could see his discomfort. She placed her hand on the back of his neck, and his eyes widened in surprise. She moved her fingers in a slow circle on the back of his neck before letting her hand slide down to his shoulder.

He turned onto the back row and found a parking space at the very back. He backed the car into the space and looked at her. "We are here," he said as she checked her watch.

"We are twenty-two minutes late. I hope we can get our seat," she said as Bolders opened his door.

He hurried around to open her door, but she had already stepped out. "You look so hurt," she said with a smile. "Should I get back in and let you open my door?"

He stared at her, thinking, Mathew, you're screwing this all up. She started to laugh, and he felt he should say something. He opened his mouth, but nothing came out. She stopped laughing and looked at him in a way no woman had ever looked at him before.

"Are you okay?" she asked with a small grin. "Is there something about me that makes you nervous? I'm really trying not to do or say anything that would make me look like an absolute buffoon to you." She laughed, slightly bending her knees and putting both hands over her mouth, laughing while looking at him.

He raised his eyebrows with an upside-down grin, and she could see he was uncomfortable. She walked closer, placing her hands on his mid-arm and squeezing softly. She then lifted her hands to his face, gently placing her fingertips on each side of his chin.

"I'm not laughing at you, sweetie," she said with a large smile as she gently held his face.

Bolders felt her fingertips on his face, his insides shaking as he

70

hoped his exterior remained steady. His knees threatened to tremble, and he repeated to himself, Don't shake, don't shake. She moved her fingertips from his chin to the back of his neck and head, gently pulling his face down to hers as they looked into each other's eyes. She rose up on her tiptoes so he wouldn't have to bend down as much. Just before their lips touched, he closed his eyes. She kissed him, then slowly pulled back, looking into his eyes with a wide, toothy smile. She placed her palms on his cheeks as she lowered herself back down.

"Are you just a little less nervous now?" she asked, still smiling.

Not knowing what to say, he just nodded, trying to catch his breath. "You took my breath away," he admitted, his hands still on her waist.

While this was happening, Nelson was in the restaurant, walking back from the bathroom. He noticed a small crowd standing around a table, looking out the large window. Curious, he slowed down and took a look to see what the commotion was about. He looked out the window just in time to see them stop kissing.

In a slow and low voice, Nelson muttered, "You have got to be kidding me."

One of the women standing there turned her head and looked at him. "Honey, that is the type of kiss every woman I know wants to get," she told Nelson.

Another woman chimed in, "I just wish I could get my husband to look at me like that."

Nelson walked back to his seat and sat down at the table with everyone else. At the table were Taylor and his wife, Nancy, along with Riley and his wife, Sara, and Nelson's wife, Judy. Also present were Timothy Slate (base attorney) and his wife, Dorothy, and Melvin Benton (base attorney) and his wife, Maggie.

He looked at Taylor. "William, you ever seen Mathew go out on a date or kiss a woman?"

"Uh, I don't think I've ever seen him with any woman," William replied. "I've heard of him going out on a few dates with women when he went back home on leave."

Judy looked at her husband. "What about that really pretty girl that he had the picture taken with?"

William responded, "I saw that picture, and they were standing two feet apart from each other."

Everyone laughed a little, then the admiral asked why he was asking.

"Well, I just saw Mat kissing a woman in the parking lot along with all those women," he said, pointing.

They were still there looking out the window.

"Who was he kissing?" William asked as everyone listened intently.

"I'm not so sure, but it looked like Manners from a distance," Nelson told him.

"Lieutenant Manners," Admiral Riley said, surprised. "My Lieutenant Manners."

"Yes, sir, but as I said, it was from a distance," Nelson replied.

Tanya looked at her watch. "Oh my God, we are twenty-eight minutes late," she said, panicking. She put her left arm around his right arm, pulling him along. "Let's go."

As they walked past the last row of cars, they heard someone say, "Well, well, look who we have here."

Mathew and Tanya both turned to their right where the voice came from.

"Commander Mathew Bolders, isn't it?" asked a tall, muscular man. "We just need to talk to you for a minute," he said. "My name is Drake. I'm sure you remember me from the dock." He then nodded to two of the three large men with him, signaling them to approach Bolders.

The two men started walking toward Mathew, and Tanya dropped her hands to her sides.

One of the women watching turned and looked at Nelson's table. "Excuse me, sir," she yelled across the restaurant, getting everyone's attention. "Your friend that was kissing the girl needs help," she said urgently.

All five men and their wives rose from the table, along with others in the restaurant.

Outside, the two men reached Bolders, each grabbing an arm. They had so much power that he couldn't break free, despite his strength.

Manners, grabbing the left hand of the man closest to her, twisted his wrist and pulled him away from Mathew. She kicked him behind the left knee, causing it to buckle, then twisted his wrist more. The man fell to the ground, and Manners placed her knee on his jaw.

The other man holding Bolders jerked him forward. Bolders punched him in the jaw, making him stumble.

Manners raised her knee and slammed it down on the man's jaw, knocking him out. She jumped to her feet and started toward Bolders when they heard a loud voice.

"Hey, you and Bolders." The man looked to see Nelson.

Nelson ran toward the man, jumped, and kicked him in the chest.

The man fell, and Nelson was pushed backward. Another man charged at Bolders, but Manners jumped up and kicked him in the chest. She then spun around and heel-kicked him in the jaw, knocking him down.

The man Nelson had kicked was now charging at Manners. Bolders jumped in his path and punched him in the jaw. The man hit Bolders in the gut, taking his breath away, and Bolders fell. Manners and Nelson rushed to help as the man reached for Bolders.

Suddenly, another man appeared and struck him with a forearm to the jaw, knocking him back.

Tanya ran to Bolders, who was still on the ground. Drake took a few steps toward them when the stranger stepped between them.

"Are we done here?" the stranger asked Drake calmly.

"We just need to speak to the Commander, that's all," Drake replied.

The stranger looked back at Bolders and Manners, then back at Drake. "I think he's done talking. You need to leave now and take your goons with you."

Nelson, standing near the man Manners had kicked, helped him up.

The man jerked away from Nelson. "Next time we meet, sailor, you're dead."

Nelson, a former SEAL, didn't scare easily. He stepped forward and whispered, "Here's a secret: many men have tried, and many men have died." Nelson saluted the man, turned his back, and walked away.

Drake and his three men began to leave. The stranger walked over to Nelson, who was bent down by Manners and Bolders.

"He okay?" the stranger asked, referring to Bolders.

"We're okay," Tanya said. "Thank you very much."

"I liked the saying. Do you mind if I use it?" the stranger asked Nelson as he started walking away.

"You Navy?" Nelson asked, watching him stop.

"Nah, I'm more of an Army guy," he replied. "Green Beret." He walked away.

Taylor and the Admiral watched as the stranger walked away.

Taylor looked at the Admiral, shaking his head. "The Army is making them big nowadays, aren't they?"

The Admiral nodded. "You're not kidding, that boy's half a tree."

Slate walked up beside the Admiral. "That's one for us."

Taylor, standing on the other side of the Admiral, bent slightly forward and turned his head. "What do you mean one for us?"

Slate took a step forward and turned so he could see both men clearly. "Well, we know from the dock that he is somehow associated with Captain Pettus, if not working for him. The only thing that puzzles me is why he wants Commander Bolders so badly."

Taylor shook his head. "If that was a question, I don't know what Mat has ever done to anyone."

About five minutes later, the police showed up with fire rescue and paramedics. They started asking questions to customers who witnessed the fight. After interviewing a couple dozen people inside and outside the restaurant, they approached the three gentlemen. An officer looked at the Admiral, who was not wearing a uniform, and asked, "What is your name, sir, and where were you when it started?"

"My name is Nicholas Riley, and these gentlemen and those over there came out right after it started," he replied.

"So you didn't see how it started or who provoked it?" the officer asked.

"No, but it was obvious from the forcefulness of the other men."

Another officer came up behind the one questioning Riley. "Sergeant," the officer said, "we found out that the gentleman on the ground," pointing to Bolders, "was the one who was attacked."

"How did you find this out?" the sergeant asked.

"We interviewed those eight ladies over there," pointing at them, "and they saw everything before and after the assault."

The sergeant turned back to Riley. "Your friend over there, I didn't mean to imply it was his fault. We have to ask questions and treat everyone as a suspect until we find the truth."

Riley replied calmly, "We understand you have a job to do."

Taylor was the first to thank the sergeant for his service,

followed by the others. The sergeant walked away with several officers, getting in their cars and driving away. Riley, Taylor, and Slate went over to where Bolders was sitting on the ground.

"Is he going to live?" Riley asked the paramedic, looking at Bolders.

"Yes, sir," the paramedic replied. "He took a hard hit to the stomach that probably bruised the inside."

Taylor looked at Bolders. "At least we know you can take a hit, Mat," he said, shaking his head.

The medics got up and looked at Manners, who was on her knees beside Bolders, with her hand on his back.

"You ready to try and get up, Mat?" Nelson asked, bending down.

"Yeah," he said, nodding at Tanya.

She rose to her feet, and Nelson stood up, bending his knees to help Bolders off the ground.

Bolders couldn't use his right hand because it was bandaged from hitting the man. Most of the restaurant patrons, who were outside, clapped for him as he got up and walked to the door. Bolders stopped at the entrance, still a little weak, with Tanya and Nelson by his side.

"I'll be okay," Bolders told them and asked them to go inside.

"Are you sure?" Kevin asked him. "I don't mind staying here with you."

"I'm sure," Bolders replied. "You both go on inside, and I'll be along in a few minutes."

"You go ahead, Nelson," Tanya said.

Bolders looked at her and kindly said, "You too."

Nelson stood there for a second after Tanya told him to leave, and she reassured him it was okay to go. He left and started walking back to the table where everyone else was.

"You need to sit down over here," Tanya said, pointing to an empty chair in the waiting area.

Mat shook his head and, slightly dropping it, said, "You can go on inside, Tanya."

She lifted his chin with four fingers from her right hand and placed her left hand on the right side of his head, lightly rubbing it. "Babe, I'm not going in without you. And another thing," she paused, "if this is some kind of male macho thing, get over it," she said, smiling.

He smiled, then smirked. "Really cute, but I could get used to it."

"What?" she asked. "Me telling you that you have too much male pride?"

"No, the part where you called me 'babe'," he told her. "I could get used to it."

She looked at him, raised up on tiptoes, and lightly kissed him. "I think I could too. Do you think you can make it inside, and we'll see if there's a table left?"

The two walked through the entrance door to the hostess's desk. The hostess looked through her book and said, "If you would wait about twenty minutes, I'll get you a table."

Tanya looked at Mathew. "Do you feel like waiting for a while?"

"Yeah, I'll wait," he told her, and they turned to go into the waiting area.

As they turned, Taylor was standing there and said to the hostess, "They will be joining us." He then looked at Bolders and asked, "That is, if you both want to?"

Tanya immediately answered before Bolders could. "We would love to. I am starving."

Bolders laughed and looked at Taylor. "That would be great, Will."

CHAPTER 9

THE HOSTESS HAD a waiter bring a couple more chairs to the large table, and Mat and Tanya sat down. After they sat, the waiter came to take their order. Tanya and Mathew both ordered a steak, potato, and bean dinner.

As the waiter was about to leave, a man wearing boots, a large belt buckle, and a cowboy hat walked up to their table. He put his hand on the waiter's shoulder. "The bill for this table is taken care of," he said. He then walked over to Bolders and put his hand on his shoulder. "I take it from all the tight haircuts that you are all in the service."

Riley, looking at the man, said, "We're all Navy."

"Well, thank you all for your service, and I've got the tip too. Don't y'all worry about a thing."

The Admiral started to say, "You really don't have—"

Manners cut him off. "Sir, thank you very much for the meal. It is our pleasure to serve."

The man looked at Manners, smiled, and said, "You know, I never liked kung fu movies. I always thought they were too fake until I saw you out there, young lady. You've got quite the girlfriend there," he told Bolders, squeezing his shoulder before walking away.

Tanya, looking at Riley, said, "Admiral, sir, sorry for cutting you off." She continued, "He can afford it. Did you see that Rolex watch he was wearing?"

Nancy Taylor added, "Yeah, it wasn't a cheap one either."

Sara Riley, the Admiral's wife, kept looking at Tanya and finally spoke up. "Tanya, do I know you from somewhere?"

The Admiral pulled pictures from his wallet and placed them on the table in front of Sara. She looked at them closely, then at Tanya, and back at her husband. "She could pass for her twin," Sara said in shock.

Everyone looked at the pictures of Riley's first love.

"Is this why you had her at the base? Because she looks so much like her?" Sara asked Riley.

"I didn't know she existed until a couple of days ago," he said, watching tears form in her eyes. "I swear to you, Sara, I had no idea," he added, softly placing his hand on her upper arm.

Everyone at the table saw her push his hand away and look at her husband for a moment. She got up slowly and looked at the Admiral. "I'll see you at home," she said, a tear falling down her cheek.

He stood up with her and placed his right hand just above her left waist. Once again, everyone watched as she pushed it away.

Sara looked at her husband. "Nick, please don't touch me; we'll talk when you get home."

She looked down the table at Tanya. "Honey, I'm sorry you had to be part of this." Sara then turned back to Riley and started walking away from the table.

The Admiral started to go after her, but Tanya rose from her seat. "Admiral, let me, please," she asked as she stepped away from her chair.

Everyone at the table watched as he nodded, and she walked toward Sara. Sara was at the headwaiter's desk when Tanya walked up behind her. A busboy passed by with a stack of cloth napkins, and Tanya took the top one.

"Mrs. Riley," Tanya said softly, as Sara turned to face her. Tanya held out the cloth napkin for her to wipe her eyes. Sara took it and did so. "Mrs. Riley, I'm so sorry that this happened because of me, ma'am." The headwaiter returned to his desk. "Before you have him call you a taxi, could I please talk to you for just a moment?" Tanya asked.

Sara nodded, and Tanya turned to the headwaiter. "Is there a place we could sit in private and talk for a few minutes?" she asked.

The waiter, seeing Sara's need, led the two ladies up a short flight of stairs. They walked down a hallway to a door marked "crew break room." He opened the door and told them he would stand outside, but they only had ten minutes.

Mrs. Riley and Tanya entered, and the waiter closed the door behind them, saying, "You won't be disturbed."

The two women walked to a small table near the coffeepot. Tanya poured two cups of coffee, watching Sara take a seat.

"Mrs. Riley, how do you take your coffee?"

"Just plain," Sara replied.

Tanya brought the coffee to the table and sat down across from her. "Thank you for talking to me, Mrs. Riley," Tanya said with a small smile.

Tanya looked down into her coffee cup, then back up. Sara was still looking at her with sad eyes.

"May I call you Tanya?" Sara asked.

"I would really like that," Tanya replied.

Sara continued, "Nick doesn't know, but I have seen him and her together in church a few times. She was the most beautiful woman that anyone had ever seen before, just like you."

"Mrs. Riley, the Admiral showed us a picture of you at your wedding, and you were absolutely gorgeous," Tanya said.

"Thank you, but please call me Sara," she told Tanya, looking back down at the table. Sara looked up at Manners. "I remember Nick was so happy when they were together. I have never seen him without a smile." She smiled at Tanya. "Just like that man with you, he notices no one else in the room, only you."

Tanya continued listening to Sara.

"One day, he came to church, and he wasn't smiling. His light was gone. I stopped praying to have someone like him and just prayed for his happiness. Tanya, he was so broken. Later, we found out that the ship she was on had been hit by mines, and she was killed. I remember asking God one Sunday why he would take happiness like that away from someone who believed in him. I remember one Sunday when their usual place had been taken by a new couple. The church was full that night, and the only seat was by me, so he asked if he could sit. When we started to pray, he put his head on the pew in front of us. I heard him, and it broke my heart. Even my mom and dad were crying as we looked and listened."

Tanya watched as tears flowed down Sara's face. Tanya's own cheeks became wet as she couldn't control her emotions.

"I placed my hand on his back, and he started to cry more. So I held him, and the tighter I held him, the more he cried. It was such a sorrowful cry. I had never heard someone cry in such pain before until that night. The whole church stopped and came as close as they could to pray for him. There wasn't a dry eye in the church, and he held me just as tightly as I held him. One year later, we were married, and it took a couple of years for him not to call me her name. Now you show up, and I see that same look in his eyes as he did when he sat in church with her."

Tanya reached across the table, took Sara's hands, and looked at her.

"You do realize that God answered your prayer and his that night he sat down beside you. He gave you the love you always wanted and gave him a love that would hold onto him no matter what. I see a man when he looks at you that sees a woman he loves so much he couldn't live without her. When he showed us your wedding pictures on the ship, you should have heard the way he said your name. Sara, you believe in God. I can see that just from listening to you tell me how you prayed. God gives us things to prepare us for other things that are more meaningful in our lives."

Sara lightened as she listened to Tanya without interruption.

"God gave the Admiral a love that he thought completely filled his heart so he would know love. Then our gracious and loving God gave him a love that overfilled his heart and filled his life with great happiness. That's what I see when I look at you two. It is a love that I hope I will have in my life."

Sara walked around the table and hugged Manners as she stood up. "Thank you so much, Tanya. Thank you."

Tanya saw the door open, and there stood the headwaiter with all the guys. With her left hand, she motioned for them to go away as the two women held each other and cried. Tanya pulled away, holding Sara's upper arms, and smiled at her.

"Let's go see if the steak is on the table yet or not."

Sara and Tanya washed their faces in the break room sink and redid their makeup. As they were freshening up, Sara looked at Tanya through the mirror and smiled. "You know, I see that kind of love in Bolders's eyes when he looks at you, and I also see it in yours."

The two women went back downstairs after nearly twenty minutes. The headwaiter had returned with the other men. The women thanked him as they passed by and headed back to their table. As Sara and Tanya approached, everyone turned to look at them, smiling. Admiral Riley tried to smile, but his face showed more worry than anything. When they reached the table, Tanya sat back in her seat. Sara stood by the Admiral as he rose to his feet.

"Sara, honey, I love you more than anything, and I'm so sorry I hurt you, my love."

She looked and saw the pictures in the empty fry basket, ready to be carried away.

Before he could say anything else, she began to speak, "I have been a fool and didn't realize it until now." She reached out and took his hands in hers, with not only their table but others around them watching. "I thought I was living in a shadow and never realized that she was the shadow until now. You pick up those pictures, Nicholas, and put them back in your wallet. You pull them out whenever you feel you need to and look at them. I know that they remind you of a love you once had that led you to a bigger love you have now."

The Admiral, not saying anything, wrapped his arms around his wife and held her tightly as she did him. As this was happening, Bolders and everyone else at the table looked around the room. They saw most of the ladies at the other tables also drying their eyes.

At that time, the waiters brought out the twelve steak orders and their drinks. They all had a little wine and a couple of beers except for Bolders; he had one glass of wine and three piña coladas. Taylor and Nelson were the only ones who knew Bolders couldn't handle his liquor very well. Nelson's wife, Judy, started noticing Bolders not laughing or talking much anymore; he was just staring at Manners.

She looked over at her husband, Nelson, and said, "Mathew is drunk."

Nelson, looking at Bolders, said, "Mat, you okay, brother?" he asked, but Bolders didn't respond.

He kept looking at Tanya, so Nelson said it a little louder, "Mat, you okay?"

Everyone looked at him, including Tanya. "No, I'm not okay," Bolders said as he looked at Nelson.

He looked back at Tanya, and she asked, "Babe, are you okay, babe?"

Taylor, looking at Tanya, said, "Manners, he can't hold his liquor."

"You're right, and that's why it's her fault," Bolders told Taylor, then looked back at Tanya. "It's your fault."

"What did I do, babe?" Tanya asked gently, knowing he was drunk.

"You made my heart explode into a million different colors when you kissed me," he told her.

Everyone started to laugh, not being able to help themselves.

Bolders pointed at her. "You are so beautiful. It's your fault," he told her. "The first time I saw you, it happened."

"What happened, sweetie?" she asked, smiling at him and the way he was talking.

"Yes, I'm drunk, but all I do is think of you." He paused, looking at her.

She put her right hand on his left cheek. "It's alright, Mat."

"No, you don't get it," he said in a drunk voice. "None of you get it."

"Mat, maybe we need to go," Taylor told him.

He looked at Taylor. "No, I'm not going until I tell you what I need to say," he said, looking at Tanya, slurring his words. "Are you listening to me?" he asked Tanya, now swaying a little in his seat from side to side. Taylor and Nelson started to get up to help him.

Tanya held out her right hand for them to stay and placed her left hand on his arm to steady him.

Bolders looked at Taylor. "Brother, she doesn't understand." He turned to Tanya. "You don't understand." She started to say something, and he interrupted. "No, let me finish."

"What doesn't she understand, Mat?" Nelson asked as Bolders looked at him, then back at Tanya.

"It's all your fault," he said again, more softly. "You made me fall in love with you."

Everyone at the table heard him, and you could have heard a pin drop. Tanya started to cry, looking at him.

"You don't know what you're saying, Mat," she told him.

"I'm drunk," he said, looking at her, "but I'm in love with you; I know that."

Tanya caressed his left cheek with her right hand as she looked into his eyes.

CHAPTER 10

Nelson looked at Tanya. "Manners, let us get him back to the ship," he said.

Benton looked at him. "No, we can't do that because if the wrong person sees it, it might not be good."

"I'll take him to my house," Manners said. "I've got an extra bedroom, and I can keep an eye on him."

The men helped her get him to the taxi, and Nelson and his wife rode with them. They helped Manners get him into her house, sat him on the couch, and made sure she was okay before they left. Nelson and Judy, his wife, then went back to the waiting taxi and headed back to the base.

Bolders woke up in a very comfortable bed with a pounding headache. He opened his eyes in a mostly dark room, except for a small bit of light shining through the semi-thick curtains. It was just enough light to see the outline of the things in the room. He lay on his back, pulling the comforter up to his neck as he watched the outline of the ceiling fan spinning around.

All at once, a blinding light hit him in the face. He jerked the covers up over his head as he heard a soft, very sexy voice saying,

"Nine-thirty, time to rise and shine. You can't eat with the covers over your head."

"Tanya?" he said, more like a question than a statement.

"Yes," she said. "And you need to eat something. I also have some hot coffee here."

He slowly pulled the covers off his head, trying to let his eyes adjust to the light. "I've got a terrible headache," he told her, squinting as the light hurt his eyes.

His vision cleared, and he saw her standing there in blue jeans and a brown pullover T-shirt. Her hair was up in a bun with part of it hanging out. She was holding a breakfast tray. He looked around the room again, seeing more clearly now. "Yellow," he said in a low voice.

"Pardon?" she asked, not hearing him clearly.

"Yellow, the room is in yellow," he repeated.

He looked at her again, thinking to himself how beautiful her smile was. "Let me get up, and I'll sit up and eat," he told her, throwing the covers off. As the comforter flew up in the air, he yelled, "Oh shit!" He grabbed the covers midair and jerked them back down on him, looking at Tanya. Sounding a little confused, he pointed toward his feet. "I don't... I mean, I'm nude... where... how?"

Tanya started laughing really hard and then sat down beside him on the bed. She put the breakfast tray over his lap and kissed him on the cheek. "Let me tell you about last night." Tanya looked at him and asked, "What is the last thing you remember about last night?"

He smiled. "Well, I remember the highlight of the evening."

"You do?" she sounded shocked to hear him say that, given the shape he was in.

"Yeah, we kissed." He smiled. "And it was awesome. Then you had to save my butt in a fight."

"That's all you remember about the night?" she asked, thinking it was something else.

"I remember something about the Admiral and his wife. I think you went to talk to her, and that's it," he told her.

"You got falling-down drunk last night and said a few things that were a bit surprising," she told him.

He looked at her, raising his eyebrows and widening his eyes. "Look, I don't drink much, and if I said something I shouldn't have, I'm sorry."

"Yeah," Tanya said, smiling really big. "I really saw, along with everyone else, how you handled your liquor."

He looked at her as she took the breakfast tray and set it on the chair in the corner. She went back to the bed and sat down on the middle edge, facing Bolders with her left leg bent under her.

"Where are my clothes?" he asked Tanya, still lying under the covers.

She smiled at him. "After we talk, I'll get your clothes."

He shook his head and leaned back against the headboard. "Let me hear how bad I screwed up."

"You told me last night that you were in love with me and had been since first sight."

They looked into each other's eyes, sitting there silently.

"I know you were drunk," she said, starting to get up from the bed.

He gently grabbed her left arm, stopping her. "Just because I was drunk and don't remember doesn't mean I didn't mean what I said." He easily pulled her toward him, leaving room for her to pull away if she wanted.

She moved forward toward the head of the bed and lay down on top of the covers beside him. He rolled onto his left side and put his right arm around her.

"I'm not drunk now," he told her.

She looked at him, their noses almost touching. He kissed her softly, then looked into her eyes again. "I am truly 100 percent in love with you, Lieutenant Manners." He pulled her closer and kissed her again, this time longer.

She pushed away, stood up, and laughed. "You need to take a shower and get dressed so we can meet with the attorneys after lunch." She smiled. "I'll get your clothes. Take a shower; we need to go."

They took a taxi to the steakhouse, got her car, then drove to the base to meet the attorneys, Slate and Benton. They arrived at the JAG office, parked, and walked inside to the desk.

The secretary looked at Bolders and asked, "What can I help you with?"

Tanya, before he could speak, put her arm around his. "This is Commander Bolders, and I'm Lieutenant Manners. We are here to see Commanders Slate and Benton."

The secretary said, "Commander, please follow me. Commander Slate is waiting for you."

"We will be glad to follow you," Tanya said, looking at Bolders with a hint of anger. The secretary opened the door. "Commander, have a nice day."

They walked into the office where the Admiral, Taylor, and Nelson were seated.

"Come in, Commander," Slate said. "You and the Lieutenant have a seat."

"Oh, wow," Tanya said sarcastically to Bolders. "Look at that, Mat, Commander Slate noticed me."

They sat down. Benton leaned against Slate's desk, facing everyone.

"Firstly, we are not out of the woods, but we are in a much better position than we were, thanks to last night. We have five days before President Bachmann takes over, and they have a lot of pull."

He looked at Bolders and sighed. "I just wish we knew why they wanted you so badly."

"Look," Bolders said, "it is plain to see that I am being set up; we all can see that."

Slate, sitting behind his desk, nodded. "It's not that we don't see it. Of course, we do."

Benton added, "We have to prove that you didn't set out to start a war."

"That is totally insane," Bolders said. "How would I even know that?"

At that moment, the secretary buzzed in. Slate looked at everyone. "I'm sorry; excuse me for a moment," he said, answering the call.

CHAPTER 11

"THANK YOU, ENSIGN," Slate said to his secretary. "Tell them to hold just one moment." He put the phone on hold and looked at Bolders. "They searched your quarters this morning at Norfolk. Is there anything they might find, Commander?"

"No, nothing other than a closet full of clothes," Bolders replied.

"Okay, let's put them on speaker and see what they have to tell us." He pushed a button and took the phone off hold. "Okay, Ensign, put them on."

"Hello," said the voice on the other end.

"This is Commander Timothy Slate, Commander Bolders' attorney," Slate answered.

"I am Commander Larry Williamson, head security officer at Norfolk Naval Base, Commander Slate. We were ordered this morning at zero nine hundred by Captain Malcolm Pettus to search the quarters of Commander Mathew Bolders."

"What was the reason for this search, Commander Williamson, and why wasn't my client informed?" Slate asked.

"We received orders from Captain Pettus, signed by a judge, to do so under the suspected terrorism act. We are faxing over everything to you now," Williamson told him.

"Thank you," Slate said, then hung up. He quickly checked his computer for the faxed message. Benton walked out of the office to get the printed copy before anyone else could see it.

Slate looked at the Admiral. "Sir, I don't know what's going on, but we have to make sure it doesn't happen here."

"Tell me what you need, Tim," Admiral Riley replied.

"You still have a security team watching the ship, sir?" Slate asked.

Riley turned to Nelson. "How many of your team are still on the ship, Master Chief?"

"All but me, sir," Nelson answered. "They are on shifts."

Riley looked at Slate. "There you go. Tell the Master Chief what you need."

"Get your guys up and make sure no one comes on board without mine or the Admiral's permission, okay?"

Nelson got up and walked outside the attorney's office to make a phone call. As Nelson walked out, Benton returned with several pieces of paper in his right hand. Everyone watched as Benton handed the paperwork to Slate. Bolders noticed the look of worry on Benton's face. Tanya watched as Benton briefly glanced at Bolders, then looked back at Slate. Nelson returned and sat beside Bolders.

"Do any of you know a Lieutenant Commander Albert Monroe on the base security force at Norfolk?"

"I know him, sir, up close and personal, and in my opinion, he is a piece of shit and a kiss-ass," Nelson spoke up.

The Admiral looked at him. "Master Chief, that's some strong words about one of your superiors."

"Sir, begging your pardon, but I won't take that back. He is Pettus's right-hand flunky."

At that moment, Nelson's phone rang, and he stepped outside to answer it. He returned in a few seconds, holding his phone. "Admiral, sir, we have three base security officers and five more sailors trying to board the Tiger Shark."

Riley then looked at Slate, who asked Nelson, "Do they have a warrant?"

Nelson checked with his team member and replied, "They do not, only signed paperwork from Captain Pettus."

Slate looked at the Admiral, who said, "Commander Slate, your call; make it."

The Commander looked at Nelson. "Can you put it on speaker so I can speak with him?"

Nelson put the phone on speaker and told his team member, "This is Commander Slate; he's calling the shots."

The voice on the other end acknowledged, "Roger that, Master Chief."

"This is Commander Slate, JAG officer," he introduced himself. "Who do I have on that end?"

"Brock, sir. Petty Officer Nathan Brock, team member number two," the voice on the other end answered.

"Well, Petty Officer Brock, I need you to do whatever it takes short of killing someone to keep all visitors off that ship."

"Aye, sir, will do," Brock answered. "If that is all, sir, I need to start that right now."

Slate looked at Nelson. "Sounds like a good man you have there, Master Chief."

Slate rose from behind the desk and set his left hip on the desk with his right foot on the floor. "Commander Bolders, do you know an Iranian named Farad?" Slate asked. "Think very hard, Commander."

Bolders thought for a minute. "I can't remember ever hearing the name or meeting anyone with that name. It's Middle Eastern, isn't it?" Bolders asked.

"It is, and they found a short letter in your quarters at Norfolk giving the exact location of the Iranian destroyers that fired on you."

"What?" Bolders said, raising his voice. "That's impossible. I don't even know anyone with that name."

Tanya moved her left hand from her lap and took his right hand, holding it tight. She looked at Slate. "So where do we go from here, Commander?"

"Well, I know like the rest of you that Commander Bolders is not a terrorist. Now, we just have to prove it."

Bolders asked, "Just how do we do that? All the evidence points to me, it sounds like."

Benton handed a printed paper to Slate. "Don't that beat all, and they probably don't even realize it yet."

"It's being kept secret probably because of what's going on now," Slate said. "Melvin," he continued, calling Benton by his first name, "we need to verify this while letting as few people know as possible."

"I'm on it now," Benton said, then walked out of the office.

Slate looked at Bolders, staring for a moment. "Who did you piss off or kill?"

He picked up the paperwork he had on the case so far. "From what I'm seeing, everything has Captain Pettus's name on it, signed on this base."

Riley asked Slate, "What was that with Benton he is checking out?"

"Let me find out first, sir, and I'll let everyone here know," Slate replied. He pointed at Bolders. "You need to stay out of the public eye until Monday morning."

Tanya spoke up. "He's staying with me, Commander, if that's okay?"

"You're both officers, so they can't get you for that. I see no reason why he can't," Slate told her. He looked at the Admiral. "Do you have any security members on base that you can truly trust?"

"All my nine team members," Riley said, "with my life."

"Can we get a round-the-clock watch on Commander Bolders and everyone else here?" Slate asked.

The Admiral asked, "Do you think we all need security watch until the trial?"

Slate answered, "Whatever is going on with Commander Bolders, they could use any of you to get to him. Until it starts and until it ends, you all need security."

The Admiral got up from his seat and told Slate, "If I can use your phone, I'll make that happen right now. That's all I have. I really did enjoy last night," he added, laughing. "Especially how Commander Bolders handles his liquor." Everyone laughed. "We will all do it again when this is over." He looked straight at Bolders. "We got you, Commander."

At that moment, there was a knock on the door, and the secretary walked in.

"Sir," she said to Commander Slate, with a worried but excited look on her face.

"Are you okay, Ensign?" Slate asked as she closed the door behind her, leaning against it.

"There is a whole room full of Navy SEALs in the waiting area, sir, waiting to see you," she repeated, "a whole room full."

"Have them come in, Ensign," Slate told her, and she just stood there, looking at him. "Well, Ensign, tell them to come in," Slate said.

"They won't all fit in this room, sir."

Slate rose from his desk, and everyone else looked at the Ensign when she said that. Bolders watched as Slate walked to the door and opened it.

"Good God," he said, looking into the waiting room. "I just need the Commander of the team to join me inside, please."

A man walked into the office in his CUU (camouflage utility uniform) and walked up to the Admiral. "Lieutenant Commander McNeil, sir, SEAL Team Three reporting."

The Admiral looked at McNeil. "Lieutenant Commander, this is your boss until this is over," he said, pointing to Commander Slate. Commander McNeil, looking at Slate, said, "We're at your disposal, sir."

Slate walked up to McNeil and shook his hand. "I need you to put a team on everyone in this room for at least the next week."

McNeil looked at him and then at the Admiral. "Are you okay, Admiral?" he asked with concern.

"We all will be now that you guys are on the job," the Admiral replied.

Everyone rose from their seats and left with a security team not far behind each of them. After Bolders and Tanya got back to her home, he sat at the dining table, watching her as she picked up a pencil and notepad, checking the refrigerator and cabinets while writing things down.

"I know you like steak and potatoes, so what else do you eat, babe?" she asked.

He watched her make her list and then walked toward the bedroom. About ten minutes later, she came back out in short pants and a tank top. He was speechless as he looked at her standing there, moving her lips.

"Mat," she said loudly, almost screaming at him. "Did you hear anything I said?"

He looked at her and asked, "No, I'm sorry, what did you say?"

Tanya shook her head, walked over to him, and gave him a kiss. "Nothing, I'll be back shortly. I'm going to the store."

He watched as she went out the front door. Bolders sat around for a few minutes at the dining table, then got bored of sitting there drinking coffee. He went over to the sofa, turned on the television, and watched it for a few minutes. He had just started getting into a Western when he saw a shadow cross the living room out of the corner of his left eye. He turned his head quickly but saw nothing. He rubbed his eyes, then reached for the TV remote on the coffee table and turned off the television. Walking into the kitchen, he opened the refrigerator.

"Hmm," he said, seeing a few bottles of Budweiser light. Although he didn't drink much, he took one. He opened it by hand and closed the fridge door. Bolders felt a warm breeze on his back and turned to see the sliding glass door slightly open. He walked up to the glass door and stood there for a minute. I really thought it was closed, he thought to himself. He opened the door more and walked out onto the patio.

"Tanya has a very nice setup out here," he said aloud, admiring her patio furniture. She had beautiful black iron patio furniture, including a table, a loveseat, two chairs, and an end table. He walked over to one of the chairs with the end table between them. He set his beer on the end table, then jumped, looking up, thinking he saw something. He stood up from the chair, bending backward, and stretching his back. He then started walking toward the pool, set about thirty feet from the patio. He twisted his head to the left quickly along with his body, really believing he had seen something that time.

About forty feet to the left side of the house behind the patio furniture, he saw a heavy potted plant knocked over. He stopped, looked around, and walked toward the backyard fence, looking behind the shrubs. Must have been a cat or something, he thought to himself, starting to get really jumpy. He started walking back toward the patio chair where he left his beer. He heard something else and stopped for a second; he didn't look back and just shook his head. Mathew, you're losing it, he laughed at himself, then continued walking toward the patio chair. He reached down, picked up his beer from the end table, and turned to sit down. He leaned back in the chair, lifting the bottle to his lips and taking a sip. He leaned his head back over the chair, looking up at the late afternoon sky.

CHAPTER 12

THE SKY WAS a beautiful blue with a mixture of black and gray clouds, along with a hint of white and orange where the sun was going down. For some reason, it made him think of Tanya and the situation they were in right now. Is it even possible that this could really be love, or is it because she is so beautiful that I just can't stop thinking of her?

He then reached into his right front pocket and pulled out his phone, opening it up. He scrolled through his contacts to Taylor's number and, for about two minutes, just stared at it. He closed the contacts, lifted his left hand, took a sip of beer, and looked at the darkened phone in his right hand. He swiped the phone to light up the screen again and went back to the contacts. He didn't stop to think and pressed Taylor's number. It rang about seven times before he heard Nancy's voice.

"Hello."

Bolders hung up the phone before thinking, took a deep breath, and threw his head back over the chair again. His phone rang, and he looked down, seeing it was Taylor's number calling back. What if it's Nancy again? he thought. I can't talk to her about this. It stopped ringing, and he started to press redial, then changed his mind and began to put it back into his pocket. The phone rang again, and he touched the green call button to answer it. He pressed the speaker button so he wouldn't have to hold it to his ear.

"Hello," he answered, hearing Taylor's voice on the other end.

"Mat, you okay, brother?" Taylor asked.

"Yeah, just needed someone to talk to, I guess," Bolders replied.

Taylor, being his best friend, knew him better than anyone else in the Navy and could tell something was wrong.

"Mat, I'm your friend, so don't try to tell me everything is okay when it's not."

Bolders waited for about five seconds before responding.

"It's about Lieutenant Manners," Bolders said, pausing for a few more seconds. "I don't know if it's right."

Taylor heard the concern in his voice and put the phone on speaker. "Mat, I put the phone on speaker so you can talk to Nancy too, brother," Taylor told him.

"Mat," Nancy said softly on the other end, "is everything okay with you and Tanya?"

"I think so," he replied. "Then again, I'm not sure," sounding really confused.

"Tell us what's going on, brother," Taylor urged.

"The first time I saw her, I couldn't take my eyes off her. I dreamed of her, Nancy," Bolders said. "Her image is burned into my brain," he continued.

Nancy looked at her husband, smiling, and asked, "Bolders, where is Tanya now, Mat?"

"At the store getting groceries for the weekend, and I don't know if I'm moving too fast or not, Nancy."

"What makes you say that, Mat?" Nancy asked, giving her husband a worried look.

"Remember what happened before," he said, referring to another woman.

"You're talking about Debra. You were with her because you were lonely. You really liked her, I know, and it hurt when she found someone else," Nancy said.

Taylor spoke up, "What does all of this have to do with you two?"

"Will, I think of her all the time. She kissed me when we got back here, and I lost my breath. I know that sounds stupid or maybe too sensitive for a man to say, but God, Will, she just looks at me, and I get this feeling."

Nancy put her hand over her mouth and looked at Taylor, laughing.

"I want to always touch her. I want to take her home to meet Mama and Daddy. I have never felt like this before, and I don't know what I'm doing," Bolders continued.

Nancy started jumping up and down, throwing her hands in the air and screaming, "Yes, yes!"

Taylor put his finger over his lips and shushed Nancy.

Nancy slapped his hand away. "Don't shush me."

"Excuse me," Bolders said, not knowing if she was talking to him.

"Not you, sweetie," Nancy replied. "I was talking to your brother trying to shut me up. Listen to me, Mat," Nancy said excitedly. "You are in love, honey, oh my God. You two are perfect for each other because she is also in love with you."

"You don't think we're moving too fast, Nancy? And living in the same house and everything?" Bolders asked.

"If it feels right, then it is right, Mat. Does it feel right to you?"

"Well, the age thing, isn't it kinda wrong? I mean, there is a pretty big difference in age between us."

Nancy told Taylor, "Will, I'm going to slap the fire out of you in a minute if you don't be quiet. Mat, listen to me. Does it seem to affect her with you being older than she is?"

"It doesn't seem to," he told Nancy. He started to walk back inside.

"I can't believe it, Mathew Bolders is finally in love," Nancy said, excited.

He closed the door behind him as he walked inside. They heard the phone fall to the floor and then the sound of struggling.

"Mat, honey, what's going on?" Nancy said.

Then Taylor yelled, "Mat!" as they heard something break over the phone.

Everyone had a pager-like device that, when pressed, called their team running. Taylor and Nancy both pressed their pagers at the same time, now hearing silence over the phone. Their team came in and was told something was wrong with Bolders. They heard voices.

"Is he dead?" one voice asked.

"No, then take care of it," another voice said.

A team member got on the radio, calling Nelson, who was on watch over Bolders. "Team one, team one, Master Chief, your package is in danger. Repeat, bad guys in the house."

In less than ten seconds, Nelson and another team member were at the door. One shot the lock off the door with a shotgun. They entered from the front and back just as Manners was pulling into the driveway.

Nelson entered the house with his silenced M4 carbine. He held it up to his shoulder, turning and sweeping the room. The others came over the back wall onto the patio. Nelson saw Bolders lying on the floor by the patio doors, not moving.

He ran over and fell to his knees beside Bolders. "Mat," he said, putting his hand gently on his back.

Bolders's face was on the floor as Nelson checked for wounds. Manners ran into the house and straight to Bolders.

"Mathew!" she yelled, falling beside him. She knocked Nelson out of the way and lay down next to him. "Bolders, talk to me, baby," she cried, laying her cheek on his. Her tears fell onto his cheek as Nelson tried to lift her up.

The paramedics from the base arrived along with Taylor and three MPs.

A paramedic walked up to Manners, bending over. "Ma'am, we have to check him out."

At that moment, Bolders coughed and moved his eyelids. He batted his eyelids then opened his eyes, unable to see clearly.

He heard a man asking, "What hurts, Commander?"

He couldn't see who anyone was and only heard overlapping voices.

"Tanya, Tanya, are you here?" he said in a low voice.

She fell to her knees, then lay down beside him. "I'm here, babe. I am here," she said, putting her arms around him.

"Lieutenant," one of the paramedics said to Manners, "we really need to check him out."

"I have to get up now, Mat, and let them look at you," Manners told him. "I'm not going anywhere; I'll be right here, babe."

"Can you raise up for me?" one of the base medics asked Bolders as they helped him up.

Nelson walked over to the medic. "What did they do? Get him with chloroform?"

The medic replied, "He is showing all the signs of it."

As they helped him to his feet, he was still very unstable. One of the medics, after seating him on the sofa, walked over to Tanya.

"His back is bruised, and so are his ribs. He needs to get to the hospital tomorrow for X-rays," he told Manners.

Nancy walked over to Tanya. "We're going to stay here with you tonight, if that's all right with you?"

"That would be great," Tanya said, hugging Nancy.

Everyone started to leave as Nelson's reliefs arrived. "I'll make sure there is a roving patrol around the property tonight until morning."

After the last person left, Taylor sat down beside Bolders and they began talking.

Tanya raised her hands over her mouth. "Oh my God," she said. "I left the milk, meat, ice cream, and everything in the car," she told Nancy.

Manners and Nancy went outside, brought in the groceries, and put everything away before it went bad.

The next morning, Bolders woke up on his right side, looking at an empty pillow next to him. He raised up in bed, feeling every bone and muscle in his body. He sat for a moment, then sat up on the side of the bed. He looked at his side and legs, seeing all the bruises. His bruises were black and blue with red where blood had risen to the surface. Tanya came in and saw he was trying to get to the shower.

She had bought him new clothes last night so he didn't have to wear the same ones every day. After the shower, Tanya stood right outside with a towel in her hand.

"I can do this myself," Bolders told her, smiling as she raised her eyebrows.

"Well, Mr. Smarty," she said, smiling, "if you were alone, you would be doing it yourself," as she started to dry his hair.

She helped him into her walk-in closet where she had a built-in vanity table with a lighted mirror.

"Now sit," she told him, helping him into the vanity chair.

"Tanya, please," he said, "let me do something myself, okay?" She just smiled and ignored him.

He just shook his head as she dried him off completely and helped him get dressed.

"You are very pushy. Do you realize that?" he asked with a small laugh.

"Get used to it, it's called love," she said as she buttoned up his shirt.

They stood in the middle of the walk-in closet, and Bolders held both her hands.

"I know people think you and I are crazy, but I've never felt this way about any other woman." He sat back down, unable to bend well due to the bruising and soreness. He pulled Tanya closer. "I love you so very much," he said, looking into her eyes.

CHAPTER 13

He then put his arm around her waist and, with the tips of his fingers, pulled her very close. He kissed her softly on the lips, closing his eyes as he did.

After the kiss, he said, "If you ever get tired of me saying that, please tell me."

She put her hands on each side of his cheeks and kissed him. "I'll never get tired of that." She then touched her nose to his. "I promise that." She helped him up from the chair, and they walked out of the closet. "That suit really looks good on you, babe," she said as she straightened his jacket. She put her right arm under his left and placed her left hand on it as well.

"Where are we going all dressed up?" he asked, then remembered it was Sunday.

Before they opened the bedroom door, he stopped and looked at her.

"When we first met, I assumed you knew that I don't do church, Tanya," he said in a mild but stern voice.

She looked at him with a somewhat shy smile and those beautiful gray eyes. "Please, you won't have to talk to anyone or stand;

you won't have to do anything. All you need to do is just be there for me, babe, please," she added.

"Okay, this time," he told her, "but I won't make this a habit, understand?"

"I understand, and thank you, babe," she said as she opened the bedroom door.

They walked a few steps into the kitchen dining room, then slowly into the living room where everyone and their wives were.

Everyone was talking and not paying attention. Taylor saw Tanya and Bolders walk into the living room. "Holy shit!" he exclaimed.

Everyone turned to look. Nancy, Taylor's wife, looked at Bolders. "Mat, you need to wear a suit more often; you look very handsome."

"Okay, let's go," Tanya said as she and Bolders slowly walked to the front door.

Taylor and Nelson looked at each other in shock because not even Bolders's mother could get him into church. The church was about a ten-minute drive from Tanya's house, and everyone took their own cars. Bolders and Manners were in the first car, with Nelson behind them and everyone else following. Nelson noticed a cream-colored sedan that kept getting between him and Taylor. The vehicle kept getting very close to Nelson's car as if it wanted to pass. Manners stopped at a red light just before the turn into the church. Nelson pulled up close to Manners's car and looked in his driver-side mirror.

He saw two doors open in the car behind him, one on the front passenger side and the other from the rear on the same side. Nelson reached between the front seats and raised the center console. He pulled out a 9 mm Glock 19 and removed it from the holster, putting the empty holster back in the console and the pistol under his left leg. Nelson saw the two doors open fully and then feet hit the ground.

"Put your seat back, Nelson," his wife, Judy, said urgently.

Two preteen boys ran past the car and onto the sidewalk, heading up to the church on foot. Judy slapped Nelson hard on the back of the shoulder.

"They were kids, Kevin," she said, giving him a hard look and gritting her teeth.

She looked back at their little boy, then at Nelson, before looking back at him again.

"Kevin," she said softly to her husband. "I know you have to finish this. After this, you're done for a while, and we go home." Then she just looked at him, waiting for his response.

He replaced his pistol in the middle console and closed it. He took his right hand and put it on her left cheek. "I promise." He then kissed her.

At that moment, a horn blew; it was the car behind them signaling to go. They all parked as close as they could together in the parking lot, which was pretty packed. Manners had dropped Bolders off at the front of the church to save him from walking too far. After parking, Manners joined Bolders and waited for everyone else. Everyone with their kids met Manners and Bolders outside the entrance door. Bolders leaned against the wall, his back, ribs, and neck still hurting.

They all followed Manners into the church she attended when home. She usually sat near the front, but given Bolders' discomfort with church, she sat him closer to the back. The choir got up and started singing "What a Friend We Have in Jesus." Manners usually sang in the choir, but she stayed with Bolders today. Bolders was uncomfortable until they started singing and he heard Tanya. She had a voice like he had never heard before; she could really sing. It wasn't only Bolders who was mesmerized; everyone sitting with them was, too. The other members of the church, though they loved her voice, were used to it. As Bolders looked at her, he thought how lucky he was to have someone like her give him a second look. Bolders admired her dark hair pulled back tight, with little strands falling out the back and sides.

She wore little makeup, allowing her freckles to be clearly visible, and a touch of bluish eye shadow that set her eyes off. Her yellow blouse and white skirt with big yellow flowers, paired with yellow high heels, made her hard to look away from. As she sang, she turned her head to the left, seeing him looking at her with a look any woman would kill for.

She raised her left arm, placed her hand on his right cheek, and mouthed, "I love you, Mathew."

The singing ended, and the choir took their seats in the pews. Tanya and Mathew sat down, her crossing her legs and him sitting close together. Her left hand held his in her lap, their fingers interlaced. The preacher came up to the podium, opened the Bible, and laid his notes on it. He turned his head to the right, away from the microphone, and cleared his throat.

He laughed a little. "Everyone is looking up here at me, telling the person next to them, 'That's not Pastor Neil.' I promise I'm not an impostor," he said, smiling.

"My name is Noel. I'm sitting in for Pastor Neil today, as he is under the weather. I prayed about what to speak on today, and God spoke to me. I questioned Him, asking, 'Lord, is this what you really want me to preach to a new congregation?' But He told me again, and I submitted to Him," Noel laughed. "You know best, Lord, but I probably want to be asked back."

The congregation chuckled as Noel glanced at his notes. He preached a heartfelt sermon on faith, love, obedience, and patience.

At the end of the sermon, Pastor Neil addressed everyone with a gentle voice, "Always remember that God answers prayers and is faithful to His Word," he said, holding up the Bible. "When you ask your heavenly Father for something, listen and watch carefully, as He sends answers in various ways. It might come from a passing comment or a sign. And before we close, remember this: if you don't remember anything else from this service, remember that when you ask God a question, He will make the answer clear, but you have to listen and have faith. Ensure it's God answering and not the enemy, as he is always working against the Lord.

"Don't attempt anything on your own without God; it never ends well. Let us bow our heads," Pastor Neil requested.

Bolders and Manners, along with everyone else, bowed their heads. Pastor Neil began to pray as Tanya lightly squeezed Mathew's hand beside her.

"Lord Jesus, I ask that you grant everyone hearing my voice the faith to believe that everything is possible with You. I pray for the patience to wait and not act on their own, losing Your blessing. I ask for wisdom to discern right from wrong, to know when to walk away and when to stand firm. Father, give us the strength and courage to stand for what's right in Your sight. Please forgive us our sins and watch over us, turning our wrongs right. In the name of Your Son, our Lord and Savior, King Jesus Christ, we ask and pray, amen.

"For those I won't see tonight, stay blessed, and I hope the sermon was a blessing to you."

Tanya and Mat walked to the end of the pew and into the aisle, arm in arm. The pastor greeted everyone at the doorway, and Tanya and Mat waited for their turn. When they reached him, he shook Bolders's hand and lightly shook Tanya's as well.

"I hope you enjoyed the service," Pastor Neil said. "You two look like the perfect happy couple. You both embody what this sermon was about," he continued, as Bolders grew more nervous.

"It's clear God has a hand in your relationship. Remember to keep Him at the center, and it will bless you."

Tanya thanked the pastor, and Mathew nodded. They joined everyone else outside. Tanya had Bolders sit on a bench while she retrieved the car. They got in, and Tanya smiled at Mat.

As they started driving, Mat asked her, "What's wrong?"

"You really don't like church, do you?" she asked, holding his hand.

He looked at her sincerely. "It's not that I don't like church. I just don't like the lies."

She decided to wait until they reached her home to continue the conversation. They drove back in silence. Upon arrival, Tanya parked and turned off the car.

"Hang on, and I'll help you," she said. Grabbing her purse, she hurried around to Bolders.

He was already getting out of the car. "Wait, Mat, and I'll help you," she reached his door.

Bolders raised his left hand, signaling her to stop. He stood, wincing as the weight on his ribs caused pain. Tanya stepped forward to support him, but he moved his arm away, saying, "I've got it, Tanya," in a somewhat harsh tone.

He winced in pain as he moved, then looked at Manners. "I told you I got it."

She backed away, giving him space but staying close enough to help if needed. He started walking slowly from the car to the door, with Tanya closing the car door and walking beside him. She reached into her purse with her right hand, pulling out the house keys. There were three steps to climb to get onto the porch. He stepped up onto the first step with his left leg, grabbed his right side, and nearly fell.

Manners quickly grabbed him, holding his right arm with her right hand and gently wrapping her left arm around his waist.

In a kinder voice, he said, "I've got it; please don't help me."

Tanya pretended not to hear him and continued holding him. "Take another step, Mat," she instructed.

"I've got it," he repeated, this time with a hint of anger. "Now, please let go."

Manners had enough and snapped, "Stop complaining and get up the other two steps." She added, "You complain worse than most women I know."

While helping Mathew stand, she opened the door with her right hand, then guided him inside and onto the couch. She walked away, heading to the bedroom to change her clothes. Before reaching the bedroom door, she stopped, steaming with frustration. Bolders noticed and asked, "Are you all right?"

She spun around, stomped back to the couch, and bent over, placing her right hand on the back of the couch for support.

"No, Mathew, I'm not okay because you're acting like an ass," she said, looking him straight in the face. She waited for a response, and when he didn't reply, she continued, "How do you think it makes me feel for you to treat me like this and not knowing why?" She waited again for a response, but he remained silent. "Well," she added, "are you going to tell me if I did something?"

"Yes, you did," he finally spoke up. "I told you how I felt about church and God, but here you are trying to push it on me."

She straightened up and started to walk away but couldn't hold back. She spun back around, bent down into his face again, and asked angrily, "And how am I pushing God on you? Tell me!" She straightened up, then bent down again. "What did you mean when you said you don't like the lies; who lied to you?"

"Everything preachers say God will do, like the 'ask and you shall receive' bullcrap. I don't mind church; most of the people are very nice and kind."

She stood up and looked down at him. "Do you love me, Mathew? All I want is a yes or no."

Bolders looked up at her. "Yes, yes, I do," he replied sweetly.

Tanya looked at him for a couple more seconds, then turned and walked toward the bedroom.

"Do you really love me?" Bolders asked as she walked away.

"If I didn't, I wouldn't be putting up with your bullcrap right now; I promise you that." She disappeared into her bedroom for about thirty minutes and came back out in shorts with a towel wrapped around her head.

She took him into the master bedroom, where there was a separate tub, and ran him a warm bath. As she undressed him, his ribs were still badly bruised, and larger blood spots had appeared on his back and ribs.

"Babe," she said sarcastically, "Am I still allowed to call you babe?"

He gave her a look as he stepped into the tub, and she held him for balance.

"Well, I don't know," she responded, answering his look.

"You're acting like you're having second thoughts about us now, and you just don't know how to tell me," she said.

"Oh!" he exclaimed in pain as he sat down in the tub. "Get me out," he added, holding out his arms.

She bent down, and he wrapped his arms around her waist, pulling her into the tub with him.

"Mathew," she yelled, "I just took a shower!" Now she was sitting in soapy water up to her chest.

Despite his pain, with his right arm around her waist, he placed his left hand behind her head and kissed her.

After the kiss, he looked into her eyes. "I haven't changed my mind about us," he said, smiling.

She got out of the tub, removing her wet clothes and wrapping herself in a towel. After getting dressed, she helped him bathe, then helped him out of the tub and dressed him. As she moved to his left side to help him to the living room, he stopped her by putting his left arm around her.

"I will never change my mind about you, Tanya. I can't understand why it happened so fast, but I'm glad it did."

They gazed into each other's eyes for a few seconds before sharing a long, passionate kiss. They started to kiss again but stopped when they heard the doorbell. Tanya quietly thanked God, then gently pushed away from Mathew.

"One more thing," he said as the doorbell rang again. He touched her left cheek with his right hand. "If they find me guilty, I don't expect you to wait for me."

She began to speak, but he placed his right index finger over her lips. "I just want you to know you are the love of my life."

They started kissing again, but the doorbell rang for a third time. Tanya stopped, helped him to the sofa, and gave him a peck on the lips before walking to the door.

Manners reached the door and opened it, smiling at the sight of Slate, Benton, their wives, Taylor and his wife Nancy, Admiral Riley, Nelson, and their wives.

Nancy and Judy held up food cartons. "Look, we brought Thai so you don't have to cook," they said.

Sara Riley added as Tanya let them in, "A little birdie told us that Thai is your favorite food."

"Babe, look who it is! The whole gang, with the boss," Tanya said, referring to Admiral Riley. "Set the food here, and us ladies can sit at the dining table while the men sit in the living room."

Tanya turned her head as she heard Bolders moan and saw Taylor and Nelson helping him up.

"Babe, what are you doing?" she asked, rushing over to him.

"I'm going to get a plate," he replied.

She looked at him and the other two men. "Sit him back down," she instructed. Then, to Bolders, she said, "I'll fix you a plate, babe."

After everyone had their food and were seated, Slate addressed Bolders. "We need to go over what's going to happen tomorrow. Can someone get Lieutenant Manners over here? She's going to be in the middle of this too."

Admiral Riley fetched Manners from the table, and she walked back with him to the sofa. Nelson moved over to a footstool, allowing Manners to sit beside Bolders.

Slate began, "The prosecution is going to claim your relation-ship is fake." Pointing to Taylor and Nelson, he continued, "You two are his friends, so they'll say you're lying for him."

The attorneys talked for about two hours before everyone started to get up.

Slate addressed Bolders and Manners. "If he's in as much pain tomorrow morning as he is now, don't bring him in. Take him to the doctor; that would look good."

"I'm not running," Bolders declared. "I've done nothing wrong. I protected my crew and ship."

Slate, looking at Manners before walking out the door, said, "You talk to him. This is not a time to be proud."

After everyone had left, Manners went to the kitchen, reaching over her head to open a narrow cabinet door. Inside, on the left edge, were two bottles of pills. She took them down, retrieved a pill from each bottle, and replaced them in the cabinet. She then walked over to the fridge, poured a large glass of iced tea, and returned to the living room. She sat down beside Bolders on the sofa, her right leg curled under her left one.

"Here, babe," she said, holding her pinched fingers up to his mouth with the two pills in between them. She placed the pills into his mouth and handed him the glass of iced tea, which he used to swallow them.

"Well, I think we need to call it a night, Mat," Tanya said, rising to her feet from the sofa.

She helped Mat to his feet and began leading him to her bedroom.

Smiling, he looked at her. "You don't have to sleep in the spare bedroom tonight," he told her.

She glanced back at him as they reached the foot of the bed. "I have no intentions of it," she said, smiling.

After helping him into the pajamas she had bought on Friday and laying him down in bed, she went to the closet. She emerged in a long flannel gown that nearly dragged on the floor. She crawled into bed with him, turning his back to her and putting her arm around him. He began to yawn from the pain medication, and she pressed her face to the back of his head.

She whispered, "Do you really want to appear in court, babe, knowing what they're trying to do?"

Mathew nodded, then began to fall asleep.

She softly rubbed his back, her touch relaxing him and putting him to sleep even faster. She sang to him in a sweet whisper, "Oh How I Love Jesus," in a very beautiful voice. She then started to pray for him, her forehead resting on his back between his shoulders.

The next morning, Tanya had the covers over her head, sleeping soundly with the air turned down low. The radio was playing softly, but Mathew's voice was louder as he sang "Rock Me." She pulled her head out of the covers and looked over her right shoulder toward the bathroom, where Bolders was singing.

"Babe," she called loudly, but got no answer from Bolders. She yelled louder, but still no answer.

She threw the covers off and glanced at the alarm clock, which read four forty-eight. They didn't have to get up until seven thirty, so she jumped out of bed.

"What is wrong with that man? My God, please stop me from killing him and committing a sin." She walked to the open bathroom door and looked in at Mathew, who was facing the mirror with no clothes on.

"Mathew," she said.

He turned to her, saying, "Look at me, honey. It's great, right?"

In a grumpy voice, she replied, "Yeah, I've seen your body before. I need more rest."

She started walking away, then smiled when she knew he couldn't see her. She climbed back into bed, pulled the covers over her head, and closed her eyes with a smile on her face.

A moment later, she heard Bolders in the bedroom. "Hey, honey, where's my underwear?"

Tanya growled loudly, throwing the covers off her body again.

"Mathew, I love you, but right now, I could strangle you to death," she said loudly.

She went into the closet with him, grabbed a pair of underwear, and handed them to him, pressing them against his chest.

"Is there anything else I can do for you before I go back to bed?" she asked, looking at him.

"Look at me," he said, turning around in a circle. "What do you see?"

She looked at him and replied, "I see a dead man if he wakes me up again before the alarm goes off." She went back to bed, covered her head, and started to smile really big before closing her eyes.

When the alarm went off, she got up, sat on the side of the bed, and stretched her arms in the air. At that moment, the bedroom door opened, and Bolders walked in with a cup of coffee, handing it to her.

"Thank you, babe," she said, pulling his head down to give him a kiss.

He started to walk away as she took a sip of her coffee. She choked and coughed. "My God, babe, how many scoops of coffee did you put in the coffee maker?"

"Seven scoops, honey," he replied. "The scoop wasn't that big, and it was a pretty big coffee holder."

"Sweetheart, please don't fix coffee for us anymore, please." She put her feet on the floor. "I've got to go take a shower," she said, then kissed him; it was the thought that counted.

She took a shower, got dressed, and walked into the living room.

"What is that I smell?" she asked as she walked into the dining room and saw Bolders putting plates on the table.

He pulled her seat out to let her sit down, then went back into the kitchen to get breakfast. He came back with a large omelet and toast, placing it on the table.

"Wow, babe," Tanya said, "it really smells so good." She took a large fork and a nice-sized piece of the omelet.

She bowed her head and glanced at Bolders to see if he would do the same. After noticing her looking at him, he bowed his head too. She prayed, then took a bite of the omelet, holding it in her mouth for a second before spitting it out into her napkin.

Seeing him about to take a bite, she stopped him. "It looks like an omelet and smells like an omelet, but the taste is altogether something else."

She saw his feelings were hurt by the look on his face. She walked over and sat in his lap, putting her left arm around his neck and kissing him. "I'll fix you breakfast tomorrow, okay?"

She got up, and he said, "You didn't even notice I was feeling better. I noticed at four thirty this morning, babe, but it was too early for me. There's a great possibility that I may go to prison for the rest of my life," Bolders said, "and I can't believe I will go without knowing a woman," he added with a straight face.

Manners, taking a swallow of water, choked on it and started to laugh. "That's a good one, Mat, real good," she said, laughing, "and you said it with a straight face too." She went back to her seat, resting her elbows on the table and her hands under her chin. "You have two great attorneys and a lot of good people behind you, Mat."

She saw that her words didn't help, so she got up and walked over to him. "If I'm right, you have to go to church with me every Sunday and not complain once," Tanya told him.

He looked at her for a moment and then replied, "And that's my final." He smiled, holding out his hand to shake hers.

"Not so fast, Mister," she said. "I want to meet your family and be introduced as your girlfriend." She held out her hand. "Do we have a deal?"

He answered, "What the hell! I'm probably not coming out of this anyway," he said, shaking her hand.

She held her open hands out, saying, "Let's go to court."

CHAPTER 14

HE PUT his hands in hers, and they left the house. They drove for about thirty-five minutes and arrived in front of the base gate. They were checked in and went straight to the courthouse and parked.

Tanya turned off the car, opened her purse, and pulled out a small makeup case with a mirror. She started putting on blush and saw Bolders looking at her out of the corner of his eye. She put everything back in her purse and turned her head to the right, looking at Bolders.

"Babe, you okay?" she asked, seeing the look on his face that reminded her of losing a best friend.

"This is what I was talking about, Tanya. Every Christian I talk to says ask God and believe He will answer," Bolders said. "I don't know if God put us together like you said or if it was fate," he continued.

Tanya looked at him with eyes starting to sparkle like stars as the morning sunlight hit the water filling her eyes. Bolders went on, "If God did give me something as special as you, why would He take it away?"

He watched as a tear slowly glided down her left cheek, glistening in the sun. She lifted her hands, putting them on his cheeks, and pulled his face halfway to meet hers for a long kiss. She pulled back, her eyes shifting left and right, searching his. She brought her left hand from his right cheek and took his right hand with it.

She squeezed his hand, her voice firm and reassuring, "Mathew Bolders, just because God didn't answer you right away doesn't mean He isn't listening. You just wait, babe. You haven't seen anything yet. God wants everyone to see when He stomps his big foot," Tanya said, tears dropping onto the middle console. She turned and opened the door. "Let's not keep God waiting, love."

They walked up to the courthouse building, then up the stairs to the double door entrance. Bolders held it open for Tanya, and she caressed his right back and arm as she passed him. They saw Taylor first, then Slate and Benton, the two attorneys standing in the foyer of the courthouse waiting for them.

Slate looked at his watch, then back up at them. "Cutting it a little close, aren't we?" He looked closely at Bolders. "Commander, you are walking a lot better today," he said in a surprised tone.

"Very few bruises today," Bolders told the three men, who shook their heads in disbelief.

Benton, looking at him, said, "Didn't the doctor say it would be several days before the bruises would disappear?"

Slate then looked at Bolders. "I've never seen anything like it before," he said, shaking his head. "Well, let's go inside and start this circus and get it over with so you can get back to work, Commander."

Taylor held the door open as Benton and Slate walked in first. Tanya and Bolders followed, with Taylor right behind them. Everyone in the full courtroom turned to see who was walking in. Nelson and a few of the other crew members had saved Taylor and Manners a seat behind where Bolders and his attorneys would sit.

Bolders looked back at Manners, and she smiled at him as if she had no worries and told him she loved him.

At that time, a voice said loudly, "All rise for the Honorable Captain Juan Morales."

Everyone rose from their seats.

"You may be seated," the judge said as he himself sat down in his seat.

They all retook their seats, and the judge looked at the prosecution attorney. "Lieutenant Commander Carol, is it?" the judge asked.

"Yes, sir, Your Honor, that is correct, and thank you for having me, Your Honor," Carol replied.

The judge looked at something on his desk and then back at Carol. "Commander, I don't know how they do things in Norfolk, but here, we play by the rules. Are we clear on that?"

"Yes sir, Your Honor, very clear," Carol said as he rose from his seat to answer the judge.

The judge continued, "If I have to warn you more than three to four times on any one thing, you will leave my courtroom. Are we clear on that?"

Lieutenant Commander Carol rose from his seat again and answered, "You are completely clear, sir."

The judge then looked at the defense. "Commander Slate, good to see you and you too, Lieutenant Commander Benton. I will do away with formals with the defense and the prosecution for this trial. Mr. Slate, I know you realize how my courtroom works. As I have told Mr. Carol, I will not tolerate constant warnings."

Slate and Benton rose to their feet facing the judge. "We will keep things aboveboard, Your Honor, as best we can."

They then sat back down, and the judge turned to the jurors. "Men and women of the jury, this is a general court-martial, and as you have already been briefed, he is being tried as a traitor and a spy. If at any time you do not understand something or need it repeated, raise your hand, and I will recognize you." The judge then picked up his gavel and hit it on the base. "Court is now in session."

Mr. Carol for the prosecution rose from his seat and walked halfway between his table and the witness's seat. "Your Honor, the prosecution would like to call Ensign Marcus Bailey as its first witness."

Bolders seemed very surprised when Ensign Bailey was called as a witness for the prosecution. He watched as the young ensign walked past his table up to the witness stand and raised his right hand. The judge then told the ensign that he could be seated. Carol walked up to the witness stand, placing his left hand on the wooden rail that went around the stand. He turned his body slightly so the jury and Bailey could both see him clearly.

"Mr. Bailey, is it true that you served under Commander Bolders on the destroyer Tiger Shark?" Carol asked.

Bailey, looking at Carol, answered, "Yes, sir, that is correct, sir."

Carol then turned his head for a second, looking at him. "And Mr. Bailey, how long have you served on the Tiger Shark?"

"This was my first cruise on that destroyer, sir, and we were out for almost six months, sir."

"But the SAD destroyers usually stay out for a whole six months or more before heading back, is that not correct?" Carol asked the young ensign.

"Yes, sir, from my understanding, that is correct, but we had a lot of electrical and engine problems."

Carol then asked, "I guess that is why you all had to start heading back almost a month early?"

"Yes, sir, we lost all power twice while we were standing by for our relief ship to show up, sir."

"Mr. Bailey, what was your job on board the ship?" Carol asked the ensign.

"I worked in the engine room, sir; as a plumber, we keep all the pipes clean and free of clogs."

"Can you recall having been told about a rescue mission, Mr. Bailey, just a few days before you were going to reach port?" Carol asked.

"Yes, sir; it was three and a half days before we were supposed to reach port at Pearl Harbor, sir," the ensign answered.

Carol looked at the jurors as he asked the next question, "Mr. Bailey, can you explain to all of us and the members of the jury just what happened and what you heard?"

"Yes, sir, I had just come on duty and was going over the paperwork to see if there had been any problems on the previous shift. The head chief engineer, Chief Walters, had stayed up; it was very unusual for us to see him. He called us together and told us that we were about to go on a rescue mission, and everyone needed to be at their best. He also said that we might have to engage or be engaged, so we needed to keep everything going. I remember hearing him telling one of the other crew members that he had told the captain that he didn't think the ship could take it. The engines started to rev at a very high RPM and began to make a noise that was out of the ordinary."

Carol was still looking at the jury to see their reactions. "This would let him know if he needed to turn the heat up a bit or if he was doing well."

"Can you tell us what you mean by the engines sounding out of the ordinary?" Carol asked the witness.

"It was making a knocking noise, and it was starting to get really loud," the ensign told him.

"And when you were relieved by the next shift, you heard something on your way to your bunk, didn't you?" Carol asked.

The young ensign looked at the jury, then back at Carol. "Yes, sir, I did. Right before I reached my quarters, I saw Lieutenant Manners and Bolders talking, and then they kissed."

Carol looked shocked, then turned back to the jury. "You mean they were kissing right there in the passageway for everyone to see?" he asked.

"Yes, sir," the young ensign answered. "And I heard him tell her he was going to take those ships out."

"Wow," Carol said.

Benton rose from his seat. "Objection, Your Honor."

Carol turned to Benton and then to the judge. "I don't understand, Your Honor, on what grounds?"

The judge looked at Benton, as did Carol, and asked Benton to clarify.

"Your Honor, this is hearsay; there are no witnesses, just this ensign's word for it," Benton said.

Carol then addressed the judge. "Your Honor, of course, only he saw it because they were trying to hide it. They didn't want the whole ship to see it and probably thought it was so late that everyone was in bed."

The judge looked at Carol, then back at Benton, then at the witness, and finally back at Benton. "I'll allow it."

Carol turned to face Bolders's table with a small, sly smile, then looked back at the judge. "No further questions at this time," he said, then started walking to his table.

The judge asked, "Does the defense wish to cross-examine the witness?"

He waited for about thirty seconds and then asked again, "Mr. Benton, do you have any questions for the witness?"

Just as the judge was about to tell the young ensign to step down, Benton stood up. He walked up to the witness box where the ensign was sitting and placed both hands on the rail.

Benton looked him square in the eyes. "How long had you been off duty when you saw this?" Benton asked.

"About an hour, sir," Bailey answered calmly.

"Where were you coming from?" Benton continued.

"I had taken a shower and grabbed a quick bite to eat in the galley, sir."

"I see," Benton said, staring at the young ensign for a moment before turning to the judge. "Your Honor, I am done with the witness for now. However, I would like the right to recall the witness at a later date, if it pleases the court?"

"Very well," the judge said, about to release the witness from the stand as Benton walked away.

Slate rose from his seat, raising his right hand. "Your Honor, if I may, I have one or two more questions for the witness," Slate requested.

"Very well," the judge replied, instructing the witness to remain seated.

Slate walked up to the witness stand, glanced at the witness, then turned to look at Carol.

He then faced the ensign again. "Mr. Bailey, we have ourselves a real mess here, don't we?" Slate asked.

"I guess so, sir," the young ensign replied, unsure of what to say.

Slate walked over toward the jury, his hands held in front of him. "How old are you, Bailey?" Slate asked, turning back but not hearing the ensign's response. He stopped and looked at the jury for a moment before facing Bailey again. "I'm sorry, my back was turned. You didn't hear me, did you?"

"No, sir, I didn't; I'm sorry," the ensign answered calmly.

Slate approached him, saying, "I'm sorry, that was rude of me to talk to you with my back turned. Excuse me one moment." Slate then walked over to his table, picked up a vanilla envelope, and while still looking away from the witness, asked once more, "How old are you, Ensign?"

He waited for about a minute before turning around to face the ensign. "Did you hear what I asked you, Mr. Bailey?" Slate inquired as he walked back up to the witness.

Once again, the young ensign had the same answer, "Sorry, sir, but no."

"I had asked you how old you were," Slate said to the young ensign.

"I am twenty years old, sir," Ensign Bailey answered.

"How long have you been in the Navy, Ensign Bailey?" Slate asked.

Carol stood up. "Your Honor, just where is he going with this?"

The judge looked at Slate. "Commander, is there a reason behind these questions?" the judge asked.

"Yes, sir," Slate replied. "I'll be quick getting to it, Your Honor."

The judge gave Slate a serious look. "I hope you do, please," he said in an unfriendly voice.

Slate nodded and said, "Very well, Your Honor, I'll get right to it. How far were you, would you say, from Commander Bolders and Lieutenant Manners when you heard their conversation?" he asked the ensign.

The ensign looked at Slate, unsure how to answer, so he glanced at Carol.

Slate stood in front of him, blocking his view of Carol. "How far, Ensign?" Slate repeated.

"Fifteen, maybe twenty feet, I guess," the young man said nervously.

"Okay, let's see." Slate turned and paced off from the witness stand to his table.

He then walked back to the witness stand and told the ensign,

"That was twenty-one feet." He then started pacing off from the witness stand to the jury, then turned and walked back. He placed both hands on the wooden rails around the witness stand. "You know how far that was?" Slate asked the ensign, and the young man shook his head. Slate smiled. "It is exactly fifteen feet away from you, Ensign Bailey."

Carol rose. "Your Honor, I object to the questioning; the witness isn't sure."

The judge looked at Carol. "I'm going to allow this, so please take your seat," he instructed.

"Thank you, Your Honor," Slate said, walking back in front of the witness. "The Commander and Lieutenant must have been speaking really loud for you to hear them," Slate said. "I mean, they must have awakened everyone with their loud conversation, right?" he asked Bailey.

Carol stood up, starting to say something.

The judge pointed a finger at him. "Mr. Carol, if you even clear your throat, I will have you escorted out of here."

Carol sat back down.

Slate turned away from Carol and back to the witness. "Are you sure about the distance?"

"I don't know, sir," Bailey replied nervously. "I could be off by a couple of feet."

"Okay, we can get someone to measure the distance from the door to where you said they were standing."

"No, sir," the ensign replied. "It is pretty close to the distance."

Slate then looked toward his table, pointing with his left hand. "I asked your name from twenty-one feet away, and you didn't hear me, did you, Ensign?" Slate continued, "Then I walked to the jurors, which is even closer, and asked your name again." He looked at the ensign. "We all know that ships aren't the quietest places. Some areas are quieter than others, but where you were, it wasn't really loud, although it does get noisy."

The ensign started to say something, but Slate interrupted him. "Mr. Bailey, be sure you heard what you heard, son."

Bailey glanced at the judge and saw he was looking directly at him.

Slate took two steps back, put his hands in his pockets, and took a deep breath. "Ensign Bailey, do you know what the penalty for perjury in the Navy is, son? It's five years and a dishonorable discharge, which won't be good for a young man like you." He saw the young man growing nervous, then looked at the judge. "Your Honor, could I have a sidebar?" Slate walked up to the judge's bench. "Your Honor," he whispered softly, "I think he was told to lie, sir."

"What do you want to do, Mr. Slate?" the judge asked.

"If you're giving me a choice, sir, and if he comes clean, let him go and remain in the Navy."

The judge squeezed the bridge of his nose lightly. "See what you can do, Mr. Slate, and if he comes clean, he can walk out of here."

Slate walked back to the witness stand, placing his right hand on the wooden rail. He leaned on it, supporting some of his weight, and covered his mouth with his left hand. After a few seconds, he pulled his hand down from his mouth and over his chin, taking a deep breath.

"Ensign Bailey, I am going to ask you a couple of questions, and once you leave this witness stand, they will be your answers."

The young ensign looked at him nervously, his body slightly shaking. Slate could see him holding his hands tightly in his lap to keep them from shaking.

"Excuse me one moment," Slate said, holding up his right

pointer finger. He turned his back to the young sailor and walked over to his table.

He placed both palms on the table to support his weight as he leaned over it. Bolders listened as Slate whispered to Benton. With Benton sitting right beside him, Slate talked so low that Benton barely heard him.

"When I start walking back to the witness, I want you to pick up your phone and call someone. Make sure the person won't hang up on you, then walk out talking to them. I want to make him think whatever I say is about to happen."

Benton nodded in acknowledgment, not wanting to say anything that someone could read from his lips. Slate then looked at Bolders, nodded, and rose from leaning over the table. The attorney turned his back on Bolders and Benton and started walking back to the sailor in the witness box. Benton did as Slate had instructed, got his phone, dialed a number, and waited for an answer.

When someone answered the phone, Benton whispered loud enough for the ensign to hear, "I need you to check something out for me."

The attorney rose from his seat, walked around the table, and started down the hallway to the exit doors. As he passed by, Manners told Taylor that she would be right back and followed Benton. When Benton exited into the large open foyer, two large men were walking down an adjoining hallway in his direction. Benton didn't think much of it but turned to the right to keep anyone from hearing his conversation and started walking toward the exit door. Another large man was walking toward him, mirroring his movements. Benton told the person on the phone to hold on and put his phone to his side.

Lieutenant Manners stopped, observing the two men walking out of the hallway. She then started walking toward Benton, and the men changed their course away from him. The other large man turned around and walked back out the doors he had just come through. Benton realized they were coming for him and didn't try to hide it. He saw the look in their eyes just before they hurried out of the building. He had seen that look before in battle; it was as if they feared for their lives.

He looked up, expecting to see anything except what he saw—it was Lieutenant Manners standing there. He looked around the room again, and she was the only one besides him in the room. He stopped and looked around again, not knowing what had scared those men.

Manners stopped close to him before turning down the hallway on the left. "Are you okay, Lieutenant Commander?" she asked Benton as he stood there.

"Did you see those three men that were just here?" he asked.

"Yeah, the ones that just walked out of the building. Is there something wrong?" she replied.

"No, I guess not," he said, pausing. "Did you see anyone else in here?"

"No, just me, and I'm on my way to the little girls' room," she told him, seeming to be in a hurry as she went into the restroom.

Slate was still standing with Bailey at the witness chair and glanced toward the judge, who seemed to be growing anxious. "Your Honor, we could let the prosecution call their next witness while we wait and recall this one."

The judge looked at the attorney. "How much longer do you think it's going to be, Mr. Slate?"

Before Slate could answer, Benton walked through the door as everyone in the room watched.

He walked up to Slate and whispered in his ear, "Your wife said to bring bread and milk home."

Slate, looking at the judge, said, "I've got the information I need, Your Honor, if I may continue."

The judge looked at the attorney. "If we can, please yes, please continue."

Slate walked up to the witness, standing straight with his hands in his pockets. He stared at the young sailor for a moment, then looked at the floor, then back at Carol. He looked at the jury and then turned his head toward the judge.

He looked at the sailor and asked, "Mr. Bailey, I am just going to ask this one time only, then I'm going to walk back to my seat. Are you sure you've seen and heard what you just told the court you did?"

Slate then paused.

The sailor started to say something, and Carol stood up. "Your Honor, this can be called treating the witness."

Slate looked at Carol, then back at the judge. "Your Honor, I'm just asking for the truth. If he is telling the truth, we're done; if not, you'll get what my colleague found out."

The judge looked at Carol. "I'll allow it," he said, then pointed at Slate. "And you better not be wasting this court's time."

Slate turned his attention back to Bailey. "Well, Mr. Bailey, what is it, son?" Slate asked.

CHAPTER 15

THE NERVOUS ENSIGN shook a little and stuttered every other word, "I'm not sure, sir," he told Slate. The sailor looked down at the floor, his heels tapping on the ground.

Slate looked back at Carol, then at the sailor. In a kind voice, he said, "Ensign, look at me."

The sailor looked up at him, appearing on the verge of tears. "Ensign Bailey, listen to me, son. If there is something you need to say, I'll fight tooth and nail for you."

Slate walked right up to the sailor. "Ensign, will you tell the judge?"

Bailey nodded his head.

Slate looked at the judge, having asked the sailor that just loud enough for only him to hear.

"I'm calling a twenty-minute recess," the judge said. He then looked at Slate. "You join myself and the witness."

Judge Morales rose from his seat, and so did the witness. All three men walked into the judge's chambers, and Morales sat behind his desk. Slate and the young ensign sat in the chairs in front of the desk.

The judge looked at Bailey for a moment. "Ensign, you see that man next to you?"

The ensign looked at Slate, then back at the judge, nervously gripping the arms of the chair.

"You don't have to tell me anything at all, son. You can just turn and walk out of here." Morales watched as Bailey looked at the door, then at Slate, then straightened his head again to look at him.

"Do you want Commander Carol in here, Ensign?" the judge asked as he saw Bailey look at the door as if expecting someone.

"No, sir," Bailey replied. He then asked, "If I didn't tell the truth, what's going to happen to me, sir?"

Morales saw that he was even more nervous now, so he asked, "Do you want a bottle of water?"

"Yes, sir," Bailey replied. "A bottle of water would be good, sir."

The judge rose from his seat just as the marine was going to get it for him. "I got it, Sergeant," he told the MP. He walked over to the small fridge and got a cold bottle of water.

Morales walked over to the front of his desk and handed Ensign Bailey the bottle of water. He then leaned back, resting all his weight on the desk, folding his hands at his chest.

"Sergeant," the judge said, looking at the marine MP, "could you come over here for a minute, please?"

The marine MP walked around the table to where the judge was sitting and stood beside him.

"Sergeant, could you tell this young man what's going to happen to him if he was lying to me."

"I'm going to handcuff you and take you straight to the brig, no questions asked."

"Now, Ensign, I am not saying you're lying, and if you are not, I appreciate your honesty. But on the other hand," Judge Morales said, looking the ensign straight in the eyes, "I'm sending you away for a long time."

Bailey looked at the judge with wide eyes when he heard about being sent away for a long time.

"I know what you're thinking," the judge continued, his tone serious yet somewhat cheerful. Judge Morales looked at his watch, then back at Bailey. "You're thinking I can only give you five years, right? But you're about to contribute to putting a man away for terrorism against his own country. If Commander Bolders did what you said he did, he deserves it. However, if you're lying, I'm going to put you in his place."

"I will still get five years if I am lying to you, right, Your Honor?" Bailey asked the judge.

"You saw the other attorney, Mr. Benton, go outside and use his phone, son?"

"Yes, sir, I did."

"Now, he is telling me that he has evidence that you're lying." The judge shrugged his shoulders, looked at his watch, and then back at Bailey. "You see that man next to you, Ensign?"

"Yes, sir," Bailey replied after looking at Slate.

"He told me he had evidence you were lying but was willing to stand up for you and fight for you."

Bailey looked at Slate, and the attorney nodded at him.

"I did, Your Honor. I lied to you, sir, and I'm sorry," Bailey confessed.

Slate looked at him. "Did your attorney tell you to lie about Commander Bolders, son?"

"No, sir, it was a really large man. He killed my little sister's cat, Daisy. He then told me, looking at my sister, that he could snap a human's neck just as easily."

Slate looked at the judge, who returned his gaze.

"Why didn't you tell someone about this, Ensign?" the judge asked, sounding genuinely concerned.

"Your Honor, the man picked me up with one hand so he could look directly in my face."

"Have you seen this man here since then, Bailey?" Slate asked.

"We have to get back out there, so what do you think we need to do about this, Commander?" the judge inquired.

"Let's continue and keep this between us," Slate suggested. Then he looked at Bailey. "You understand that, Ensign?"

"Yes, sir, Commander," Bailey replied. "I won't tell anyone, not a soul."

The judge, Bailey, and Slate walked back out, and everyone stood, then were seated. Judge Morales noticed that Carol was watching the young ensign as he walked back to his seat.

Before Carol could call his next witness, and to prevent Bailey from testifying again, he spoke up. "The court will not hear anything else from Mr. Bailey until the end of the trial. I want the prosecution and defense to be clear on this." Morales then took his gavel and struck the base, saying, "This court is back in session."

He looked at Carol and said, "The prosecution may call its next witness."

"The prosecution calls Lieutenant Tanya Manners to the witness stand, Your Honor." Manners rose from her seat, walked up to the witness stand, and took the oath.

At the end of the oath, she looked at Carol. "So help me, God." She then walked into the witness booth, sat in the chair, and smiled at Carol.

The attorney walked up to the witness box and said to Manners, "You're really happy this morning, Lieutenant."

"I am almost always happy unless you make me upset, Mr. Carol," Manners replied.

People in the audience, along with the jurors, laughed at how

140

Manners answered. Carol gave a halfway smirk, then walked up to the jurors' box, looking at them.

He turned and asked Manners as he walked back toward her, "How long have you and Commander Bolders known each other?"

"Well, that's a two-part question," Manners said, smiling.

Carol turned to the judge, pointing at Manners with an open hand. "Your Honor, she is making a joke of all of this," Carol told the judge. "This is no place for jokes."

Judge Morales looked to his left at the lieutenant. "How is this a two-part question?"

"I've known him for six months, and he's known me for eight days, Your Honor," she answered.

Morales looked at the attorney. "Mr. Carol, it is a two-part question with a two-part answer."

Carol walked right up to the witness box, placing his hands on the rail and leaning into it.

"So in eight days, you and Commander Bolders became an item or romantically involved?" Carol asked.

The lieutenant turned her head to the judge. "May I reach inside my jacket pocket, Your Honor?"

He nodded and watched her as she did so. Manners reached into her pocket, pulled out a pack of gum, and took a stick from it. She unwrapped it, folded it, and put it in her mouth.

"Getting a little nervous, Lieutenant?" Carol asked, leaning closer.

"No, sir. I wanted to freshen my breath," she answered.

"Oh, it smelled just fine, Ms. Manners."

Manners held out the pack to him. Carol started to take a stick from the pack, and Manners said, "Oh no, please take it all."

The judge burst out laughing along with everyone else in the courtroom.

"Your Honor, she is trying to make a joke of the trial and this court," Carol said.

Morales looked over at the lieutenant. "He's right, Ms. Manners. Let's keep this aboveboard."

Manners turned her head to the right, looking at the judge, and tilted her head down slightly, lifting her eyes. "Your Honor, no disrespect to the court, but evidently, he hasn't been up in your face yet, sir, talking to you?"

Carol looked at the judge, and Morales tried to speak but couldn't due to laughing.

"Mr. Carol, there are doctors that can take care of that problem for you; they're called dentists," Manners told him.

"Your Honor, she needs to calm herself in this courtroom or be fined, sir," Carol insisted.

Morales started hitting his gavel on the base. "Quiet in the courtroom," he said, trying to keep from laughing himself.

Carol waited until all the laughing was over and the judge told him to continue.

"Ms. Manners, are you ready to answer my questions now?" Carol asked, standing in front of the witness box.

"Yes, and I'm sorry that my sincerity turned into a joke," she replied, looking at Carol and then the judge.

"Thank you, Ms. Manners," Carol said, accepting her apology. He walked up to the witness stand, stopping about two feet away. "Ms. Manners, did Commander Bolders spend the night with you on your first night out?"

Manners didn't hesitate. "We slept under the same roof that night, in separate bedrooms."

"So you haven't slept together yet? Is that what you are telling me, Ms. Manners?" Carol asked.

"No, sir, it is not," she answered. "Are you asking me if we have slept in the same bed yet?"

"I thought that is what I had asked you, Lieutenant," Carol said.

"It isn't what you asked, sir, but yes, the night after and last night as well, we did and will tonight, sir," Manners told him.

Carol started to say something, and Manners interrupted him, partially holding up her right hand and pointing finger. "Now, if you want to ask me if we made love or however you wanted to phrase it, no, we haven't," Manners said.

"When is the first time you two kissed, Ms. Manners?" Carol asked, folding his hands across his chest.

"Well, it's not like your last witness said, I assure you," she replied. "It was the first night in the restaurant."

Carol looked at her for a moment. Every question he had put to her, she answered without hesitation. "I thought I saw you tell him that you loved him earlier, is that correct, Ms. Manners?" Carol asked.

"Yes, I did. Is there something wrong with me doing that, Lieutenant Commander?" Manners asked.

Benton started to rise from his seat to object to the questioning. Slate reached across Bolders, stopping him.

Benton looked at Slate, who shook his head, then Slate whispered, "I think she's about to let him have it."

All three men at the table watched as Carol questioned Manners.

"No, there is nothing wrong with that at all. I just don't see how you can fall in love with someone in just one day," Carol said.

Manners looked at him for a couple of seconds. "How long did it take you to fall in love with your wife, Commander?"

"Your Honor, once again, she is mocking these proceedings. A stop needs to be put to this," Carol told the judge.

Slate stood up, addressing the judge. "Your Honor, I think the witness, like the rest of us, just wants to know where all these nonsense questions are leading."

Carol began to lose his cool slightly. "Your Honor, please do something," he said loudly.

The courtroom grew very quiet, and even Carol realized what he had done: yelling in the judge's direction.

Judge Morales just looked at him without saying anything, then began to squint his eyes. "Are you finished, Mr. Carol?" Judge Morales asked in a low but stern voice.

"Your Honor, I sincerely apologize for that outburst, sir," Carol said, adding, "I am so very sorry."

Judge Morales motioned for Carol to approach the bench with his right pointing finger. The attorney walked up to the bench where the judge sat and waited for him to speak. Morales leaned forward and motioned for him to come closer, and he did.

Carol was right up against the bench, looking the judge in the eyes. "Your Honor—" Carol started to speak but was cut off.

"Don't speak, Lieutenant Commander Carol; you just need to listen," Morales said in a very low voice.

Carol could tell by the judge's look and tone, even though it was a whisper.

"If you ever speak to me in my courtroom again like you did, I will have your ass behind bars." The judge then rose from his seat and leaned further over toward Carol. "Do you understand everything I said, Mr. Carol?"

Carol nodded his head and replied, "Yes, sir, I understand, and once again, I'm very sorry, Your Honor."

Carol walked back over to where Manners was sitting in the witness seat after Morales dismissed him.

"Mr. Carol, one moment please," the judge said, holding up his left pointing finger. "I want everyone in this courtroom to hear me because this is the only time I'm going to say it," Morales announced. "If there are any more outbursts in this courtroom, I will clear it," he added sternly.

"Mr. Slate, Mr. Benton, I know you haven't, but I'm giving you fair warning in advance," the judge continued. "If either of you raise your voice to me, I will have you removed and have counsel appointed to your client," the judge added. "Now I hope everyone in this courtroom understands what I have said because it won't be repeated. Mr. Carol, you may continue now," the judge said, looking at the attorney.

"I have no further questions for the witness, Your Honor," Carol said as he walked back to his seat.

Benton rose from his seat and walked to the witness box while straightening his jacket. "Ms. Manners, how are you today?" Benton asked as he stopped in front of the witness box.

"I'm fine; thank you, Commander," Manners replied with a smile.

"The prosecution found great interest in this, so I want to ask a quick series of questions, and I'll be done," Benton said.

Manners looked at Benton, nodded, and sat back in her seat.

"Did you kiss Commander Bolders on the ship at any time or in any place on the ship?"

She started to answer, and Benton cut her off before she could get started.

"If you don't mind, I'll ask all at once, then you can answer," he said, and she agreed. "And did you have sex with Commander Bolders at any time up until now?" he asked. "And the last question is, are you in love with Commander Bolders?"

Manners looked at him, nodding her head. "Yes to all but one, sir; no, we have not made love," she added.

Benton nodded at her, then turned to his right, looking at the jury. As he started walking back to his seat, he said, "I have no idea why they wanted that information, but now they have it." About halfway to his seat, he added, "Your Honor, I have no further questions for this witness."

The judge then looked at the lieutenant. "Ms. Manners, you may step down and return to your seat."

She exited the witness box and, as she walked past Bolders, gave him a slight smile before going to her seat.

The judge then looked at the prosecution. "Mr. Carol, call your next witness, please."

"Your Honor, the prosecution calls petty officer second class Anthony Douglas to the witness stand," Carol announced.

When Douglas was called, Slate and Benton exchanged a fist bump, and Slate rose from his seat.

"Your Honor, may my counsel and I have a sidebar with you?" Slate requested.

Judge Morales shook his head, took his right hand, and motioned them up to the bench.

The judge, looking at them one by one, said, "This better be really important, gentlemen."

"It is, Your Honor," Benton said as he placed three papers in front of him. "Your Honor, we didn't want to turn this in to you until we were certain, sir."

CHAPTER 16

THE JUDGE LOOKED at the paperwork and rose from his seat. "I want all counsel members from both sides in my chambers now," he said angrily.

He was so upset that he walked ahead of the marine MP, who had to run to catch up. The MP opened the chamber door, and the judge and others walked in. The judge sat behind his desk and looked at the attorneys, placing his palms on his desk. Before anyone could sit down, he jumped up from his seat.

He slammed his palms on the table. "I want to know what the hell is going on in my courtroom, gentlemen! This is starting to look like a damned conspiracy against the commander," the judge said loudly. He pushed his chair so hard that it went halfway across the room as he turned.

He walked away from everyone about twenty feet, putting his hands behind his head. He brought his hands down fast and turned to face everyone. He then started walking back to his desk and picked up the three papers.

"I've had it with you, Mr. Carol, and I'm in good mind to have you arrested for treason now."

"Sir, I don't understand," Carol said, looking at Judge Morales.

He slammed the paperwork down in front of him. "Sure you do. These men confronted you about this."

Carol read the report and then laid it back on the table. "Everything in there is true, Your Honor, but we were told he was a traitor."

Slate handed the judge another paper showing where a terrorist named Farad sent Bolders a message.

The judge took the paper and looked at it. "So the commander may be a terrorist," he said.

Slate then said, "Sir, look at the dates on that letter."

The judge, looking at it, asked, "Mr. Slate, what am I looking for?"

"Your Honor, the dates don't match," Slate explained. "This letter appeared in the commander's base housing three months after he was at sea."

Then Benton spoke up. "And the letter was dated six months after the death of Farad."

The judge looked at Carol and pointed at him with his left finger. He was holding the paper in his left hand and threw the wadded paper at Carol. "If I find out you knew firsthand about this setup, and that's just what this is," the judge said. He looked at Carol for a moment. "I don't care if it's one year or twenty years from now, I'll see you spend the rest of your life behind bars." Morales turned and reached for his chair, forgetting he had pushed it across the room in anger.

The marine sergeant retrieved the chair and rolled it to the judge.

He sat down and looked at the attorneys. "Get out of my sight, and I'll be out in a minute."

Morales sat in his chair for about ten minutes, elbows on the table, looking at the paperwork. Slate and Benton made it back to their seats and turned their chairs to face each other. Taylor, Nelson, and Manners leaned forward to hear.

"What happened in there?" Taylor asked Slate in a whisper.

"He saw all the evidence and wasn't happy," Slate told them.

Tanya looked at Bolders. "Babe, this is God putting his big foot down," she said. After telling Bolders that, she leaned back in her seat and folded her hands.

Nelson started to ask Manners something, and they heard, "All rise for the Honorable Judge Morales."

They all rose, then retook their seats as they watched the judge. Morales sat there for about a minute, looking at the defense, then the prosecution. He then looked at the jury and leaned back in his chair, letting out a deep breath.

"Ladies and gentlemen of the jury, thank you for your service," he began. "In light of new evidence, we have to dismiss all charges against Commander Mathew Bolders."

Tanya started to get up and run to him, but Benton stopped her.

The judge then spoke again, "Commander Bolders, you are free to leave with all charges dismissed." The judge took his gavel and hit it on the base before retiring to his quarters.

Manners then got up and ran around, grabbing Bolders around the neck. After all the handshaking and congratulations were over, everyone started leaving the courtroom.

Carol's co-counsel left, telling Carol he had a meeting he couldn't miss. Slate and Benton were starting to head out after getting all their paperwork together.

Carol, still gathering his paperwork, saw the defense attorneys leaving and said, "Commander Slate, Lieutenant Commander Benton, could I have a word, please?"

The two attorneys stopped and moved closer to Carol's table, noticing that Manners and Bolders were still behind them.

"I know you both probably think that I knew a lot about all of this, but I know just what I was told," Carol said.

Slate and Benton noticed he kept looking at the two double doors at the entrance of the courtroom.

"You two have no idea who these people are, and you are on their radar now, so be careful," Carol told them.

"Whose radar and why? Who are you talking about, Lieutenant Commander?" Benton asked.

"What did you mean by no idea of the people we're dealing with?" Slate asked.

"I don't have time to answer all these questions; just listen," Carol said. "These people are very dangerous and really, really powerful," he added, looking again at the doors. "Commander Bolders and Lieutenant Manners need to watch themselves."

This time when he looked back at them, he whispered, barely moving his lips, "Leave now."

Then all at once, he started yelling at them rudely. "Look, I have nothing to tell you, so just leave me alone."

Slate and Benton looked toward the door at the front of the courtroom. They saw Carol's co-counsel along with two large men, each about six-four to six-seven in height.

"What is going on, Carol?" Slate asked. "Let us help you," he added in the same breath.

Benton lightly slapped Slate on his left shoulder. When Slate turned to look, Benton pointed toward the door. Slate looked toward the door and saw the two large men walking toward them. Slate and Benton backed away from Carol a couple of feet. The two men walked up to where the three attorneys were standing and looked at Carol. Slate was six-one, and the shorter of the two men was about three inches taller than him. The other man was at least a whole head taller, about six-six or six-seven.

"Mr. Carol, are you alright, sir?" the smaller man asked the prosecutor.

"I was just telling these gentlemen I've got nothing further to say to them," Carol said.

The larger man looked at Slate and Benton. "Mr. Carol needs you to leave him alone," he said in a deep voice.

Bolders and Manners were still there, and Manners started walking toward Slate and Benton.

Bolders tried to hold her back, but she looked at him. "No, come on."

Manners, standing on Bolders' right side and holding his right hand, was between Bolders and Benton and had to look up at everyone due to her height.

"Is there a problem?" she asked the two large men as one of the marine courtroom MPs started walking up.

"We need to go," the larger man said, looking at Manners and Bolders.

The smaller man took Carol by his left arm, nudging him between himself and the larger man. They then walked toward the double doors and out of the courtroom.

CHAPTER 17

THE MARINE WALKED UP to them and said, "Unless you're here for the next trial, you have to leave." He was about to walk away but stopped and turned. "Congratulations, Commander Bolders. I'm glad you were found innocent, sir."

The marine then turned and walked away back toward the judge's chambers.

Slate looked at everyone and said, "Well, let's do like the man said and get out of here."

The two attorneys then picked up their briefcases and started to walk out of the courtroom.

Tanya turned and faced Bolders, reaching both of her hands toward his right one. She held his right hand with both of hers and started to walk backward, pulling him along. She gave him a small smile and placed her top teeth over her bottom lip. She dropped her left hand from his right and then turned as she lifted his right arm over her right shoulder. He followed her out into the corridor where everyone was waiting for them. As they walked into the corridor of the courthouse, he took his right arm from her shoulder and put it around her waist.

Taylor looked at Manners and Bolders, laughing along with Nelson and their wives.

Manners, looking at them, then looking at Mat, smiled and asked, "What is so funny?"

Taylor grinned. "You two, don't take this the wrong way, but talk about love at first sight."

Nancy chimed in. "Yeah, Nelson told us all how Mathew looked at you on the ship."

Tanya turned to Mathew, smiling broadly. "Oh, you looked at me like that, did you?"

Bolders, looking at them, said, "Don't listen to him. I look at everyone on the ship."

"Ahh, Mat," Taylor said, grinning. "If you looked at everyone like that, we all would think you had a problem."

With their hands still around each other, Tanya squeezed him a little closer, patting him on the belly.

Admiral Riley spoke up. "I think we need to celebrate the win in the courtroom today."

Manners responded, "Well, number one, this one here can't hold his liquor." She pointed at Bolders. "Number two, I'm going to cook at home tonight because we have a trip to plan."

Everyone looked at each other, then Nelson asked, "A trip? Where are you both going?"

"Well, your man here, Master Chief, just learned never to bet against God because you always lose."

Nelson replied, "Yeah, okay, but where are you going?"

"If I won, which I did, he has to introduce me to his mom and dad." She then looked up at Mathew. "Right, babe? We will see all of you later," Manners told everyone as she and Bolders walked toward the front door.

They walked out of the courthouse, taking their arms from around each other and now holding hands. Everyone else had shown up extra early for the trial, so they got to park in the garage. Bolders and Manners showed up almost last minute, so they had to park outside in the overflowing parking lot. While everyone else turned right out of the courthouse, Bolders and Manners turned left. They walked to the end of the building, then turned left to get to the parking lot. They had to walk about halfway down the side of the building to reach where the car was parked. They reached the parking lot and had to cross the narrow one-way road that ran alongside the building.

The security guard was at the entry-exit gate to the parking lot. "Commander, sir. Lieutenant, ma'am," the private security officer greeted them.

Bolders stopped, pulling out his wallet from his jacket pocket, searching for something. He then put his wallet back and started searching his pockets desperately. Tanya stood there with her arms crossed and a big smile on her face, her purse over her left shoulder. She then reached into it with her left hand and pulled out a parking ticket.

She started to laugh. "Are you looking for this, babe?" she asked him.

He looked at her, smiling and shaking his head, then reached for the ticket. She lifted her right hand with the ticket over her head and back. As Bolders reached for it with his left hand, he wrapped his right one around her waist. They smiled at each other as he pulled her closer and kissed her very softly.

The security officer cleared his throat loudly, and as they looked at him, he said, "Your friends are waiting."

Bolders looked at him. "What friends?" he asked.

The security officer, with his left arm extended, pointed to five men dressed in black trench coats inside the parking lot.

Bolders looked at them, then at Manners. "Tanya, you know them?" he asked.

"No, but they don't look like they are here to congratulate you, babe."

The security guard said, "I just assumed they were friends because they have been here for about forty minutes waiting."

Manners, with Bolders's hand still touching her waist, pushed him away and looked at the security guard. "No, they're not his friends," she said.

Bolders looked at her as the men started walking slowly toward them. "No, but look at their clothes; they're dressed like the ones that attacked you at home."

The security guard then stepped out beside Bolders. He took his ball cap off his head and placed it back on backward.

The five men walked up to Bolders, Manners, and the guard, leaving about three feet between them.

"Man, those guys are huge," the guard said aloud.

Bolders looked to his left at the security officer, then back straight again. Just as he looked back at the men, one of them charged at him. The security officer kicked him in the gut, causing him to stop. He then took his left knee and kicked the back of the man's right knee. The big man's knee buckled, and he went down. Another one kicked Bolders in the gut, lifting him off the ground. The other three charged at Manners as she ran to Bolders. They reached her before she reached Bolders. One was on her left, one on her right, and the other in the middle. Manners took three running steps and jumped into the air. She kicked the one on the right with her right foot in the chest. She spun around in the air with her back turned to the middle one. She took her left foot and kicked the one on the left in the throat. Still spinning, and just before her feet hit the ground, she struck the middle one in the left cheek with the back of her right fist.

The five men started to run away fast as Bolders and Manners looked toward the main road. They saw Nelson and Taylor along with a few sailors, army, and marines running across the parking lot. Nelson and Taylor reached the security guard and Manners as they were helping Bolders up.

Nelson looked at Bolders. "You okay there, Mat?" he asked.

"Yeah, I'm good. Thanks," Bolders replied, then looked at the security guard and held out his hand.

The security guard shook Bolders's hand.

"Thank you," Bolders said to him, then added, "Where did you learn to fight?"

"United States Army, sir, third battalion first special forces group, sir," the guard replied.

"Mathew Bolders, the commander." He introduced himself. He then turned to the lieutenant. "This is my girlfriend, Lieutenant Tanya Manners."

As the man shook hands with her, she cut her eyes left, smiling and looking at Bolders.

"Jeffery Willard, sir, and it was a pleasure," he said after shaking hands with Manners.

The navy FPs and marine and army MPs arrived on the scene and locked down the base.

One of the marine MPs came up to Bolders and Manners just as they finished talking to the guard. "Sorry, sir, but we can't let you leave the base until we find these men," he told the commander. "We can take you to get temporary billeting for the night if you would like," the MP added. "We would be more than happy, Commander, to take you and the lieutenant over there if you would like, sir. You could pick your car up when you get ready to leave."

The two of them followed the MPs to their car; just as they opened the back door, a message came over the radio. "All suspects have been apprehended." Then it said, "All base gates reopened."

"Well, babe," Tanya said, looking at Mat, "we can go home

now." She then thanked the officers, as did Bolders. The two of them got into the car and went back to Tanya's house.

After they arrived, Bolders checked the house while she waited right inside the front door.

"All clear, honey," he told her, coming out of the master bedroom.

"I'll take a shower first, babe, and I'll make dinner while you do," Tanya told Mathew.

Mathew took a shower, and while he was drying off, he caught a tantalizing aroma wafting through the air. Walking out of the bedroom, he tilted his head back slightly to savor the delicious scent. "Wow, honey, what is that?" he asked, his curiosity piqued. "It smells great," he added.

Tanya, busy in the kitchen, looked up and smiled. "Mathew, babe, would you mind setting the table for me?" she asked. He obliged with a nod.

After they ate, Mathew helped her clean the table and began loading the dishwasher. Tanya gently stopped him, saying, "No, don't use that. I only use it when we have a lot of company; otherwise, I prefer to wash them by hand."

So, they did just that—Tanya washed, and Mathew dried.

Mathew had already changed into his pajamas, while Tanya, still dressed for cooking, hadn't changed yet. After finishing the dishes, Mathew went over to the sofa, picked up the TV remote, and turned it on. He glanced over his left shoulder at Tanya and twisted his body slightly, patting the left side of the couch in invitation. She walked behind him, gently brushing her left hand against his cheek in passing.

"I'll be right back. I've got to put on my night clothes," she said, disappearing into the bedroom.

He sat on the couch for about ten minutes, watching the news about the base closure. When she emerged quietly, he caught sight of her out of the corner of his eye. Turning to face her, his breath was taken away by her beauty. Her dark hair, usually cascading past her shoulders, was now pulled back and tied up. Her almost cream-colored skin and gray eyes melted his heart.

A feeling of warmth and excitement surged through him, making his whole body tremble inside. She wore a pink negligee with a matching long, see-through gown that complemented her pink lips perfectly. She sat down beside him, resting her left arm on his right shoulder and caressing the back of his head with her fingers. She pulled his head closer to hers and kissed him gently. His breathing quickened as he started to shake a little. She pulled back slightly to let him catch his breath, smiling at him.

All at once, he said, "Can I ask you a question, Tanya?"

Her face was still very close to his, her eyes flickering between his lips and his eyes. "Do you have to ask right now?" she murmured, kissing him softly and quickly.

"How do you fight like you do?" he asked her in a low, gentle voice. "You fight and move like a vampire or something, honey. It's really unbelievable how strong and fast you are."

She stopped, her eyes widening as she pulled her face back from his, staring in amazement. "I'm sitting here in a see-through gown practically giving myself to you," she said, trying her best to stay calm but finding it very difficult. Her voice rose slightly as her anger started to show. "And you think that's unbelievable? This," she pointed to her body, "should be unbelievable to you." Her voice grew louder, and her anger more apparent. "And you like the way I jump, do you?" she asked, her tone sharp. "Then watch how fast I jump off this couch." She got up and stormed into the bedroom, slamming the door behind her.

He waited for a few seconds before getting up and walking to the bedroom door. He opened it and called softly, "Sweetheart, are you okay?"

Just as he finished speaking, something hit him in the chest and face. As he looked down, he saw a sheet, blanket, and pillow on the floor.

He then heard Tanya yelling, "You sleep on the sofa, and see how you like that." She pushed him out of the bedroom and slammed the door, and he could hear her crying.

He knocked lightly on the bedroom door, pressing the right side of his face against it. "I am so sorry, Tanya. I didn't mean to hurt you," he said softly. "Please open the door and talk to me," he added.

"Go away, Mathew," he heard her say, her voice filled with pain.

He went and sat on the sofa for a few minutes before heading to the laundry room. He grabbed a pair of jeans and a slip-on shirt that hadn't been ironed yet and put them on. He walked up to the front door and entered the alarm code he had seen Tanya use. Then he stepped outside and leaned his left shoulder against the left column.

He watched an old man and what seemed to be his wife pass down the street with their little dog. The woman glanced at Bolders and lifted her right hand in a friendly wave as they walked by. Bolders waved back with his right hand, nodding his head. They seemed very happy, he thought, noticing them holding hands.

He walked inside, grabbed a beer, and came back out to the porch, settling on the bench. Just as he was about to bring the bottle to his lips, he stopped. Turning his head to the right, he strained to listen to the faint sound of a feminine voice in distress.

"Help me, help me," the voice called out, growing fainter.

Bolders set his beer down on the flattened arm of the wooden bench and walked across the front yard to the fence. He tried to peer down the road, but the streetlights at the far end had gone out, casting the area in darkness.

"Help me, please; help me," the voice called again, now weaker.

He couldn't see anything in the unlit area, but the desperation in the woman's voice was unmistakable. He opened the front gate, stepping through and closing it behind him without hesitation. Thinking of his mother and how he would want someone to help her if she were in trouble, he started walking quickly toward the voice. When he heard a scream, he broke into a run until he came upon a body lying on the ground.

He stopped and quickly scanned the area to see if there was anyone else around. The still figure on the ground was wearing a dress the same color as the older woman he had seen earlier. Approaching cautiously, he knelt down on his right knee and reached out his left hand to touch her shoulder. She didn't move.

Positioning his hands on either side of her body to steady himself, he leaned over, trying not to disturb anything. As he looked at the woman's face, a smile slowly spread across it. Her eyes opened, and Bolders fell back in surprise, landing on the sidewalk.

She rose to her knees, revealing herself to be a very beautiful woman, quite different from the older lady who had passed by. Standing up, she looked at Bolders with dark, piercing eyes. She was about five foot seven. Glancing to her left toward a patch of wooded area, she spoke to no one in particular, "I want this one."

ALL AT ONCE, Bolders heard something behind him—it was a car. He quickly looked back, and the woman had vanished. The car stopped, and the passenger window rolled down.

The woman driving asked, "Are you okay, sir?"

Bolders smiled, glanced over his right shoulder, and then back at her. "I'm fine; thank you, ma'am."

The woman nodded and drove away. Bolders stood on the sidewalk for a couple of minutes before starting to head back toward Tanya's. When he got back to Tanya's, he noticed the garage door was open, and her car was gone. He walked inside the gate, up to the house, and up the steps to the door. He tried to open it but found it locked. His beer was still sitting on the arm of the bench, so he picked it up and sat down on the porch, placing his feet on the last step.

He sat there for about ten minutes, thinking about how foolish he had been. He considered himself the luckiest guy to have the most beautiful woman he had ever seen. His head was down, staring at the steps, when he heard tires squealing. He looked up quickly and saw Tanya getting out of her car, leaving it on the road, and running through the gate toward him. He got up and met her halfway across the yard, and she jumped into his arms.

She hugged his neck tightly, kissing him and telling him she loved him.

She put her feet back on the ground and looked up at him. "I thought you were gone." She wiped the tears from her eyes, saying, "I told you to leave my room, not the house."

Bolders looked at her and gently cupped her cheeks with his hands. "Tanya, listen to me. I will always be here; trust me. I'm an idiot sometimes, but I am not crazy."

She smiled at him, her eyes still glistening with tears.

Bolders then told her, "I do love you, Tanya, and I am madly in love with you."

At that moment, the old man and woman with the dog passed by again. The woman looked at Tanya and said, "You found him, I see."

Mathew looked at the old woman and then back at Tanya. "That's not an old woman," he said, pointing at her.

"Of course, it is, Mat. I passed by them while looking for you. I stopped and asked if they had seen you, and she said you were on the porch earlier."

"Tanya," Bolders said softly, taking her left hand with his right as they stood in the middle of the yard.

"Yes, love," she answered, looking up at him.

"I am so, so sorry for acting the way I did." He looked into her eyes. "Can you please forgive me?" Bolders asked.

She went up on tiptoes and kissed him softly on the lips, then said, "Of course and always."

Just then, it started to rain. Bolders noticed Tanya's car still parked in the road. "Get in the house, and I'll pull the car into the garage."

After pulling the car back into the garage, the rain poured down harder. Bolders walked back into the house through the garage door that entered the kitchen. Tanya was standing there, waiting for him.

Seeing her standing there, he said, "You are a beautiful sight for any eyes."

Tanya looked at him, smiling broadly. "You just saw me a minute ago."

He gazed into her eyes as he stepped closer and said, "And you were a beautiful sight then too."

Her smile faded, and she lifted herself up on tiptoes again to kiss him. She turned and started walking out of the kitchen. Looking over her left shoulder at him, she said, "I'm going to run a bath." She smiled at him and then looked away.

"Oh, you're going to take a bath," he said to her as he walked out of the kitchen.

She stopped before entering her bedroom, turned, and looked at him. "No," she said, motioning him toward her with a finger, "I am for you," she paused, "and me together, a bath," she added with a sexy look on her face.

"Oh," he said, starting to follow her into the bathroom.

He watched as she unzipped her house dress, and it fell to her feet. He gazed at her beautiful golden-like skin, and her beauty took his breath away. He stood there, thinking that he had something other men only dreamed about. Her skin, as far as he could see, was perfect and unblemished.

She walked over to him, pulling his shirt over his head and throwing it on the floor. She then took off the rest of his clothes as he stood there in shock. She stepped into the bathtub full of bubbles and sat down in the hot water. She watched as he nervously stepped into the tub. She could tell something was wrong but chose not to embarrass him by pointing it out.

They stayed in the water for about an hour, enjoying a glass of champagne as they soaked. Afterward, they showered off the bubbles, dried themselves, and went to bed. Bolders couldn't stop looking into her eyes as he leaned over to kiss her. Just then, the phone rang, and she turned onto her left side to answer it. She saw the clock beside the phone; it read nine-thirty.

"Who is calling me this late?" she said aloud as she picked up her phone. She looked at the caller ID. "Oh my God," she said, looking at Bolders. "Mathew, be perfectly quiet." She whispered, "It's my dad," then answered the call. "Hi, Dad, how are you doing?" she said, and Bolders watched as she listened. "I'm just laying here with my eyes closed, relaxing and enjoying the peace." She squeezed Bolders's hand tightly, reassuring him.

She talked to her dad for about an hour, during which Bolders listened, noting that nothing about him came up. When Tanya finally hung up the phone, she looked over and saw Bolders had fallen asleep.

CHAPTER 18

THE NEXT MORNING, Bolders woke up lying on his right side with Tanya's arm wrapped around him. He turned onto his back, causing her to moan and smile. She laid her head on his chest, and he placed his left arm under her head and around her shoulder, holding her tight.

She looked up at him, moved her body up, and started to kiss him. Bolders gently rolled her onto her back, his body partially on and partially off hers. Just then, his phone rang. They tried to ignore it, but when it stopped and immediately started ringing again, Bolders rolled onto his right side and propped himself up on his right elbow. He reached over with his left hand and picked up his cell phone from the end table. He glanced at the caller ID and turned his head to look at Tanya.

He saw her resting her chin on his shoulder. "It's my mother," he told her.

"Oh, Father," she sighed, falling back onto the bed. "I need a ring and a vow first, Father. I know, Father," she said in a low voice, staring up at the ceiling.

"Hello, Mama, is everything okay?" he asked, surprised by the early morning call.

He listened for a minute before replying, "No, it's just so early in the morning. I thought something was wrong."

"No, Mama, I'm in Hawaii right now, but we are coming to see you soon."

Tanya sat up in bed, covering her mouth with her left hand and smiling broadly.

Bolders glanced at her. "Yes, Mama, I've got a girlfriend, and she is great."

Tanya watched him intently as he continued the conversation.

"It will be in a few days, Mama. I will let you know then," he said. "I love you and Daddy too."

As he ended the call, Tanya got up and said, "I'm going to take a shower," and walked to the bathroom.

He jumped up and followed her, and they showered together. Afterward, she sat at her vanity in a towel, doing her makeup, while he dressed. As he walked out of the closet, pulling his shirt over his head, she started laughing and told him to stop. He paused and looked back at her.

"Come here," she told him. He walked over to her, and she pulled him down for a kiss. Tanya then straightened his collar and lightly pushed him away, saying, "Okay, all done."

He stood up straight and asked, "Honey, would you like a cup of coffee?"

"Yes, babe," she answered, then added, "put some Irish cream inside."

He nodded and walked out of the closet and the room. Heading into the nook off the kitchen, he walked to the front door. Upon opening it, he saw the paper at the bottom of the porch steps. He walked out, picked up the paper, and as he straightened up, he noticed someone standing on the sidewalk across the street. The person stood still, watching.

Bolders turned and started walking back up the steps onto the porch. He glanced back, and the person had disappeared.

He walked up to the glass door, opened it, and went inside the house. As he turned to close the front door, he exclaimed, "Oh shit!" and fell backward. The woman he had seen last night was standing right at the glass door, her nose pressed against the glass, smiling at him.

Tanya came running out of the bedroom. "Mat, are you okay?" she asked, her voice filled with concern.

He looked up at her from the floor. "I just slipped," he told her.

She looked around, seeing nothing he could have tripped on. She knelt beside him, placing her right hand on his head. "Are you sure you're okay, babe?" she asked, her concern evident.

"I'm fine, honey, really," he reassured her as he sat up on the floor.

He looked at the front door, and fear washed over his face. Tanya noticed his expression and turned to see the print of a nose tip on the glass door. They both rose to their feet, and she asked him, "What did you trip over, babe?"

"I guess it was my own feet," he replied, glancing at the door again.

She could tell by the look on his face that he wasn't being truthful. Bolders saw the worried look on her face and tried to smile, attempting to show her he was fine.

"I have to go and finish getting ready," Tanya said, standing there in her jeans and bra.

She took his left hand with both of hers, lifted it to her lips, and kissed it as she backed away. "I love you, Mat Bolders," she told him, noticing where his gaze was fixed.

She could see that he wasn't looking at her face. Stretching out her left arm, she gently lifted his chin with her finger. "My face is up here, babe," she said with a smile and a wink.

She started walking back to the bedroom, holding up her left pointing finger. "My coffee, babe."

He had made their coffee and was taking both cups to the bedroom where she was. "Here's your coffee," he said as he placed it on the vanity. Then he heard his phone ringing.

He had left it on his side of the bed on the nightstand and walked over to it. By the time he reached it, the ringing had stopped. He looked at the call history to see who it was but didn't recognize the number.

"I guess they will call back if it's important," he said aloud, placing the phone back on the nightstand.

At that moment, Tanya's phone rang, and she looked at the number, seeing it was a local call. She answered it, and Bolders, about to walk out of the room, heard her say, "Mat, honey, come here."

Bolders walked back to Tanya as she set the phone down on the vanity. "The admiral wants to meet us for lunch in two hours at Mickie's Lunch Box Cafe," she said, glancing at her watch.

He started walking into the closet. Tanya looked at him and asked, "What are you doing, babe?"

"Getting my uniform," he replied, taking it down from the rack.

"You're on leave, so you don't need that, honey," she told him. "Besides, we're not meeting on base."

"Wonder what's going on?" he said, standing behind her chair and looking at her in the mirror. "He probably just wants to make sure you're still alive and I haven't killed you yet," he joked.

She looked at him through the mirror, winked, and smiled before handing him her coffee cup. "Would you mind making me one more cup to go, babe? I'll be right there."

He fixed two to-go cups of coffee, one for him and one for her.

When she came out, she checked her watch again. "We have one hour and ten minutes to get there," she told Bolders as she walked up to him.

She looked at the coffee cups, both pink, and asked which one was hers. He held up his left hand, and she took it, taking a sip to test the taste. "Can you close the front door for me? We'll go out through the garage," Tanya asked him.

He walked to the front door and went to lock the glass door first. As he looked outside, he saw the woman from the previous night standing on the porch, smiling at him, and starting to walk toward him.

Tanya began walking to the nook, but she looked back and saw Bolders backing away from the door. She placed her cup on the kitchen counter as she hurried to him. She reached out her arms, wrapped them around his waist, and looked out the door herself.

"I'm losing it, Tanya," Bolders said, looking at her. "I'm starting to see things."

She walked with him over to the sofa, and they sat down. "What are you seeing, baby?" she asked, placing her right hand on his knee and caressing the right side of his head with her left.

"Remember the old lady and man we saw last night walking with their dog?" Bolders asked.

"I remember, babe. What about it?" she asked, watching him struggle.

"I heard a woman's voice in trouble down the road and ran to it. I saw a young woman, and there was something not right about her," he told Tanya.

"That's what you were doing when you said you went for a walk?" she said.

He nodded. "I saw her again this morning, and that's why I was on the floor. Now I just saw her again, but this time she was coming toward me."

She leaned toward him, raising herself up on her left knee on the sofa, and kissed his right temple. "What's wrong with me, Tanya? I feel like I'm going crazy," he said.

She then put both knees on the sofa, sitting on them, and used her right hand to turn his head toward her. "You're not going crazy, babe. I promise you," she said, looking into his eyes. "You've been through so much, baby." She continued, "People were trying to kill you, and others were trying to kidnap you." She kissed him gently on the lips. "I am here for you and with you, and I promise this will pass. Don't tell anyone else about this, babe. If you see that woman again, let me know." She smiled at him and kissed him again, then asked, "Do you think you can go meet the admiral?"

He said nothing and leaned in to kiss her for about two minutes. When the kiss ended, their foreheads still touching, he whispered, "What did I ever do to deserve someone like you?"

"I guess someone has said a lot of prayers for you, and mine was answered with you too, babe," Tanya added. She got up off the sofa and held out both hands for him to take. "Let's go get something to eat."

Bolders took her hands and stood up. This time, she went to the door while he headed to the car. Tanya looked around and said in a low voice, "If you want a fight, I'll give it to you."

She closed the door and walked out to the garage where Bolders was waiting for her. They got into the car, and Tanya drove them to meet the admiral at the restaurant. When they arrived, it was so busy they had to park down the street in a pay-to-park lot. Bolders and Tanya walked back to the restaurant, holding hands.

"A busy place, isn't it?" Bolders remarked as they walked inside.

"Yes, it is, but the food is fantastic," Tanya replied, leading him in.

Sara, the admiral's wife, saw them and stood up, waving her left hand in the air. Tanya saw her and pointed, "There they are," she told Bolders.

They made their way to the table where Nelson, Taylor, Slate, and Benton, along with all the wives, were seated.

Sara looked at Tanya and said, "You are so beautiful today."

The other wives agreed. Nancy added, "We were all talking last night, and you two look like you've been together forever."

The admiral cleared his throat and looked at his wife, Sara. "Let's order," he said as the waitress approached.

After everyone had ordered, the admiral leaned forward, resting his forearms on the table. "Mat, the current president and his vice president both stepped down today rather than facing impeachment. No one else wanted the position, so previous President Abraham Bachmann is stepping back in to finish this term. I left him a message, and he contacted me. He spoke with an acquaintance of mine and a friend of his. I think we may have just found you and your crew a new home. A new base has been set up to get all World War II warships up and running again."

Taylor then asked the admiral, "What are they going to be? Some kind of a floating museum or something?"

"That's what it sounds like to me, but the last I heard of it was the last time President Bachmann was in office. Anyway, Admiral Stanley Dean and his wife Loretta will be here in two days to meet you and discuss it. Evidently, he has a daughter here he'll be staying with."

Everyone watched as Tanya's face shifted from happy-go-lucky to something else.

"Are you okay, Manners?" the admiral asked her.

She looked at him. "Rear Admiral Stanley Dean is coming here to Hawaii?" she asked, her voice tinged with surprise.

"Is there a problem with you and Admiral Dean?" Riley asked, looking concerned.

Tanya looked at Bolders. "I didn't want you to find out this way, babe," she said softly.

"Find out what, Tanya?" he asked, his curiosity piqued as everyone else looked at her.

"He's my dad," she revealed, watching Mathew's eyes widen and the table fall into a stunned silence.

Admiral Riley spoke up, trying to lighten the mood. "Everyone, cheer up. This is going to be a good thing," he said enthusiastically.

Nelson, who was sitting across from the admiral, shook his head.

"What's wrong?" Riley asked. "Is there something I don't know about?"

Everyone looked at Nelson except for Tanya, who already knew what he was going to say.

"I heard Admiral Dean had her transferred after her training because the men kept asking her out," Nelson said. "He doesn't want her with anyone in the military, so I've heard," he added.

Riley looked at Bolders and Tanya, saying, "We need to get you out of that house before he gets here."

At that moment, Tanya's phone rang. She reached into her purse and glanced at the caller ID before answering. "Hello, Dad, how are you?" she asked, making it clear to everyone who she was speaking to. "Really?" Then she said, "When will you be here?"

Everyone watched Tanya, waiting to find out what was going on. They heard her say, "Yes, sir," followed by a surprised, "Where are you? Let me know, and I'll pick you up, Dad," she told the admiral. "I can't wait to see you and Mom too, Dad. I love you both too." Then she hung up.

Bolders looked at her, then at the admiral. "Sir, if I can be excused, sir?" he asked.

"Go ahead; I'll call you tomorrow and let you know where and when," Riley said.

Bolders got up and started walking away. Tanya looked at the admiral, who gestured for her to follow. "Go talk to him and we'll call you in the morning."

She got up and ran toward the door, not giving the doorman time to open it. She rushed past him, looking right and then left but not seeing Bolders.

The doorman looked at her and said, "If you're looking for the man that just walked out, he turned right around the building."

She took off running, hoping to catch him. As she turned left at the end of the building, she saw him. She stopped running for a moment and called out, "Mathew, Mat, please wait and talk to me!" she said loudly, catching the attention of everyone walking up and down the street.

Bolders never once stopped and continued to walk, so Tanya began to run again. When she caught up to him, she jumped right in front of him, blocking his path. "Please, let me talk to you, Mat," she said, tears in her eyes.

He looked at her, his own eyes welling up. "You knew this wouldn't last, didn't you?" he asked.

"Mat, I promise you it will work, even if I have to leave the navy for it to do so. I was going to tell you while we were visiting your family," she said, her tears flowing down her cheeks.

He turned and leaned his back against the brick wall, sliding down it until he was sitting on the ground. She squatted down in front of him, wiping his tears with her thumbs. "I love you so much and will do anything to keep us together," she told him.

He looked at her, wiping her tears with his fingers. "I've always been told that your first love hurts the worst. I believe it."

She stared at him for a moment. "I'm your first love?" she asked softly.

He nodded, and as he started to bow his head again, she held it up with both her hands. "I promise you, Mathew Bolders, I will also be your last love," Tanya told him.

They started kissing, unaware that a crowd of at least fifty people had gathered around them, and there wasn't a dry eye in sight. Many phones were streaming the event live, already gaining thousands of views. The kiss lasted for about five minutes, and their tears flowed so heavily that it was like a cup of water hitting the ground.

"Let's go home, babe," Tanya said, looking at him with her beautiful smile.

Bolders didn't notice all the people around them as he looked into her eyes. They started getting up, and everyone, including a few police officers who had arrived, began to clap. Back at the restaurant, their friends saw the scene and came to where Tanya and Bolders were, joining in the applause.

Taylor, looking at them, said, "Well, there is no hiding it now, so let's go find a place to eat all this food."

"We can go to our house," Tanya suggested, "and maybe go to the beach and eat." She knew that Bolders had been wanting to go to the beach.

CHAPTER 19

THEY ALL LEFT, receiving pats on the back and applause from the crowd. Riley looked at Bolders and said, "I can't keep your whole crew, but if it comes to it, I'll keep a couple of you."

They reached Tanya's car, and Bolders walked to the driver's door to open it for her. He then took her left arm with his left hand, turning her to him. Gently pushing her against the car, he put his arm around her waist and started kissing her again. Taylor called his phone, and Tanya took it from his front pocket.

"Hello," she said, breathing hard into the phone. She heard Taylor ask, "Where are you guys?"

"We're not hungry," she said, stopping from kissing Bolders for just a second as he kissed her neck. "You guys find somewhere else to eat tonight."

They got in the car, drove back to Tanya's house, pulled into the garage, and went inside.

The next morning, Mathew woke up to find Tanya up on her right elbow, resting her head in her right hand.

"I never thought it would be like that," he told her as she looked at him.

"I thought you were just nervous," she said, caressing his face with her right hand. "I was your first," she said softly, looking into his eyes as she pulled the cover back over them.

About an hour later, she raised up in bed. "Oh my God, I'm going to fix us some coffee." She got out of bed and saw clothes scattered all over the bedroom.

She put on her house coat and looked at Bolders. "Let's go out to eat," she suggested.

"Well, let's take a shower, and then we'll go," she said.

After finishing their shower and getting dressed, Bolders began to shave. "I'm going to get us some coffee, babe," she said as she opened the bedroom door.

She stopped and froze, not moving. Bolders walked up behind her, placing his right hand on her right shoulder and kissing her neck. "I love you, Tanya Manners," he told her, kissing up her neck.

She slapped him on the cheek and pushed him away. "This is not a good time, babe," she said in a low voice.

Bolders put his arms around her waist, standing behind her. He squeezed her and repeated, "I love you so much."

He looked up and saw a man in an admiral's uniform sitting in the living room chair. An Asian woman sat on the far end of the sofa.

"Oh, I think this is the perfect time, honey," the man said to Tanya. "There is coffee made for you both; get a cup and sit down," he instructed them.

They sat down, and Tanya started to say something, but the man interrupted, "Not you, I want to hear from him," never taking his eyes off Bolders.

Tanya's phone rang, and the man waited silently until it stopped. It started ringing again.

"Answer it on speaker," the man told her.

"Hello," Tanya said.

"It's Nancy, Tanya. Your dad is here; he got here early this morning," Nancy informed her.

"You're a little too late with the phone call," Tanya replied, then hung up.

"Turn that phone off. I want no more interruptions," Tanya's dad ordered.

Admiral Dean never took his eyes off Bolders. "How long has this been going on?" he asked.

Bolders looked at him. "I love your daughter, Admiral Dean," he said.

"Are you in the military?" the admiral asked, continuing to stare.

"Yes, sir, navy," Bolders replied.

Dean handed his cup to Tanya. "Go get me another cup of coffee, T," he called her by her pet name.

She got up and started to the kitchen to get her dad coffee. "Do you know how old my daughter is?" Dean asked Bolders.

"Yes, sir, I do. She's twenty-two, sir," Bolders answered.

"How old are you?" the admiral asked.

"I'm thirty-eight, sir," Bolders replied.

Dean finally took his eyes off Bolders and looked at Tanya. "T, I'm very disappointed in you," he said.

He looked back at Bolders. "Did you two at least use protection?" the admiral asked.

They exchanged a glance, and Bolders saw the look in the admiral's eyes.

"My God, you're thirty-eight years old; you should know better," the admiral said angrily.

"What is wrong with you?" Dean shouted. "You act like a virgin or something. Do you do this with every woman you sleep with?"

He then looked at Tanya. "You see what kind of man you're with?" he yelled.

"Dad," Tanya spoke up loudly, "I was his first," she told him.

"Oh my God, now he's going to be following you around like a little puppy dog."

"Dad," she said in a high-pitched voice, then looked to her left, "Mom, please say something."

"Stan, that's enough," Loretta, his wife, said.

"How do you know he was a virgin?" Dean asked, looking at her.

Her eyes filled with water, knowing her dad was going to be disappointed in her. "No," she paused.

"T," he said, looking at her.

She got up and ran to the bedroom, slamming the door. Bolders started to get up, but Dean commanded, "And where are you going?"

"I'm going to check on Tanya," he replied.

"You are going to sit back down now, or your career is over!" Dean shouted.

Bolders turned and looked at the admiral. "Do whatever you think you need to," he said.

Dean started walking toward Bolders, and Loretta stood up, stopping him with a glance. Dean placed his right hand on Bolders's right shoulder. "Let me go in first," he said.

Dean opened the bedroom door and went inside, closing it behind him.

Bolders walked over to Loretta. "Mrs. Dean, could I get you more coffee, ma'am?" he asked.

He got her coffee and brought it to her before sitting down at the other end of the sofa.

Loretta looked at Bolders. "I'm on your side because my daughter loves you," she said.

He started to say something, but she cut him off. "I'm not done. If you ever break my daughter's heart and hurt her, there's no place on earth you can hide from me," she warned.

She looked at him for a moment. "All I want to hear from you is that you understand what I just said."

"Yes, ma'am, I understand. Thank you," Bolders replied.

Dean walked over to Tanya, who was lying facedown on the bed, crying. He sat down, rolled her over, and sat her up, hugging her tightly.

"I'm so sorry I disappointed you, Dad. I never wanted you to find out," she said through her tears.

He hugged her even tighter. "Disappointed a little, but you are still my little heart. I just hope this one's it," he said gently.

She looked up at him, his white suit soaked, and her face a solid red from crying. "Why don't you go get cleaned up, and let's go meet a real hero. I think his name is Mathew Bolders," he suggested.

She looked up at her dad, and her crying turned into loud laughter. "Are you okay?" he asked as she got up from the bed.

"Wait right there, Dad," she told him, opening the bedroom door. "Babe, could you come in here for a minute?" she called out to Bolders.

He walked into the room and saw her father sitting on the bed, observing them. "Dad, meet the man I love, Commander Mathew Bolders. Babe, my dad," she said, laughing even harder at the expression on her dad's face.

She walked up to Bolders. "Mat, honey, you and my dad talk away," she said, walking out of the bedroom.

Bolders watched Tanya walk back to the living room and followed her, with her dad trailing behind.

"What's so funny?" her mother asked as Tanya came out laughing.

"The commander that Dad calls his hero, the one he came here to meet," Tanya said, pointing to Bolders.

"Oh my God," her mom exclaimed in shock. "You have got to be kidding me." Loretta started laughing along with Tanya, adding, "You wouldn't believe what your dad said about him."

Stanley walked out of the room, shaking his head. "Go ahead and laugh, Etta," he said, using his pet name for her.

Loretta leaned back on the sofa, mimicking her husband's deep voice. "Now, that's the kind of man our daughter needs, Etta, but no, she has to end up with someone like that," she teased.

The admiral walked out of the kitchen with two beers and handed one to Bolders. Tanya and her mother exchanged amused glances, then looked back at Stanley.

"Dad," Tanya said in a playful voice, "are you okay?"

"I'm fine," he said, holding up the beer and looking at it. "I'm not driving, you are, honey," he told Tanya.

Dean then looked at Loretta and Tanya. "Are we ready to go?" he asked them.

They all walked out of the house with Bolders being the last one out. He made it to the car before Tanya and her mother did and walked around to open Tanya's door for her. Once she got in, he closed it. Tanya was driving, so Bolders sat behind her in the back seat with the admiral. They drove through the security gate at the subdivision and out onto the main road.

Bolders saw a police car pass by and looked up at Tanya through the rearview mirror, holding up the beer bottle chest-high. "If you keep holding it up like an advertisement for Budweiser...," the admiral said, looking to his left at him. He then shook his head at Bolders and took a drink of his own beer. "That's how you do it, it's very easy," he said.

At that exact moment, Tanya noticed blue lights come on behind her in the rearview mirror. "Oh, way to show him, Dad," Tanya told him as she pulled to the right side of the road.

She turned on her flashers and put the car in park, leaving both hands visible on the wheel. "I can't believe you just turned it up right in front of him, Stan," Loretta told her husband.

"He's in an undercover vehicle. How was I to know?" Stanley replied.

CHAPTER 20

THE OFFICER WALKED UP to the left side of the car to Tanya's door. She rolled down the window and greeted him. "Good morning, Officer."

"License and registration, please," he asked, and she handed them over.

He took the paperwork from her, checking to make sure everything was in order. As he started to walk back to his car, two more police cars pulled up—one behind the other officer's car and one in front of them. The officer who parked in front of them got out and stood looking at Tanya. The other one walked up to the car on the right side, opening the admiral's door and looking at him. Noticing his uniform, they knew his rank. Tanya and her mother heard them ask her dad to step to the back of the car. She noticed the officer standing in front of her car starting to walk toward her.

The officer passed by Tanya and walked up to Bolders's door, opening it. "Can you please step out, sir?" the officer asked.

Bolders complied, and the officer politely asked him to turn around and put his hands behind his back. The officer handcuffed him, closed the back door, and walked him to the back of the car.

Admiral Dean hadn't been handcuffed but was placed in the back of the first patrol car. The first officer went back, opened the patrol car door, and had the admiral step out.

"Sir, could you step to the front of the car?" the officer asked Dean.

One officer stayed with Bolders while the other two started talking to Admiral Dean.

"How many of these have you had, Admiral?" the officer asked, picking up the beer from the hood.

"That is my first one," Dean replied. "I was just having one with my daughter's boyfriend."

"You still shouldn't have an open container in any vehicle, Admiral. You should know better," the officer told him.

"I do know better, Officer," Dean responded, pointing at Bolders. "I wasn't thinking. He just took out three Iranian destroyers that had killed most of a Coast Guard cutter crew."

The two officers motioned for the one standing with Bolders to come over, and they briefed him on the situation.

The first officer then asked where they were going, and Dean replied that they were heading to the base for a meeting. Bolders couldn't hear the conversation clearly, but he watched one of the officers get in the car and pick up the radio. Dean had mentioned they needed to be there by 1300H. The officer looked at his watch and told Dean that he wasn't going to make it. Tanya kept glancing at her watch and exchanged a concerned look with her mom in the passenger seat.

"We're not going to make it."

At that moment, Tanya and her mom saw several patrol cars pull up with their lights flashing. Tanya exclaimed, "Oh my God, Mom, what has Dad told them?" as she saw the officers walking over to Bolders.

They removed the cuffs from Bolders, and the officers saluted him and shook his hand.

One officer shook Bolders's hand. "I wish I could have been there to see it. You make me proud to have served in the Corps and to be an American. We're going to get you where you need to go. Just hold on, sailor."

Bolders and Dean got back in the car. The officer handed the paperwork back to Tanya and said, "Ma'am, we're going to make sure your boyfriend gets to his appointment on time."

Tanya followed them as they escorted her through intersections all the way to the base. Once they arrived, Tanya looked at her watch as they pulled up to the gate.

"Wow," she said, smiling, "we are ten minutes early."

Their credentials were checked, and they continued onto the base. They arrived at the restaurant, which was very famous on base and always crowded.

It was almost impossible to find parking spaces, and most people just rode the base bus there.

"I know I'm not going to find a parking place," she said as she pulled into the restaurant. She stopped in front of the building and looked in her rearview mirror at Bolders.

"Babe, can you go in and let them know that we're here but may have to park somewhere else?"

Loretta then looked to the left at her daughter, pointing with her right finger. "I don't think that will be necessary, T."

Tanya looked at where her mom was pointing. There were two soldiers standing at the edge of the building between four red cones. A small sign in a metal stand read, "Rear Admiral Dean," with "Reserved" underneath. Tanya noticed one of the marines walking up to the car, bending down to look inside as she approached. Tanya leaned partially around her seat, looking at Bolders in the back as he started to get out.

"Wait, babe," she told him, then let down her window.

The young female marine bent over and looked in the back seat around Tanya. "Is that Admiral Dean in the back seat?" she asked.

"Yes, it is," Tanya replied. The marine motioned for the other marine to come over. "Who else do you have with you?" she asked.

"I'm Lieutenant Manners, and this is Loretta Dean," Tanya said, pointing to her mother. Using her left thumb, she then pointed to the back seat. "Behind me is Commander Mathew Bolders."

The marine looked at him. "Pleasure, Commander, sir," she said, opening Bolders's door with her left hand and pointing to the restaurant with her right. "If you will, Commander Bolders," she said as he got out. "Once again, Commander," she added, smiling, "it is a real pleasure."

Tanya looked at her mother and whispered, "Seriously, and he's eating this up."

The other marine opened the door for the admiral and Mrs. Dean. Bolders started to open the door for Manners, seeing no one had yet, but the female marine stepped in front of him and did so. After opening Tanya's door, the marine turned back toward Bolders.

"Excuse me, please, ma'am," he said as he walked around her. He then approached Tanya as she got out of the car and held out his right hand to help her.

Tanya smiled, looking up at him and placing her left hand into his extended right one. He lifted his arm upward, holding her hand as she exited the car. He then walked with Tanya to the door, holding it open for her, her mother, and her father. The headwaiter followed them as he led them to their table.

The admiral, walking behind his daughter, looked at his wife. "Etta, an Italian restaurant called Pretzels," he said, shaking his head.

Tanya, hearing what he said, turned her head right, looking over her shoulder. "Dad, it's the best Italian restaurant food you've ever had."

They reached the table, which was hidden in a glass room at the back of the restaurant for special guests. A large table was set up in the back, and everyone stood up as they entered the room. Admiral Riley and his wife, Sara, walked around the table to meet Admiral Dean and his wife, Loretta. The two admirals shook hands, and the wives also greeted each other by shaking hands and shaking the other husband's hand.

"So I hear that this is a great Italian restaurant," Dean said. "Can't wait to try it," he added.

As Riley sat down, he said, "I thought it was a joke the first time Sara told me about it."

Sara then spoke up, slightly bending over the table with her palms touching the edge. "That's not the words my husband used," she said, speaking just loud enough for only the people at the table to hear. "He said, how could an Italian restaurant be any good named after a Pretzel."

Admiral Dean started laughing, looking at Riley. "That is almost the same thing I said."

"So I see you and the commander here have already met," Riley said, speaking to Dean.

"Yes, we did, quite personally, this morning," Dean replied, looking at Bolders and his daughter as he said that. He then looked back at Riley and added, "President Bachmann called me first thing when he was sworn back in three days ago. He somewhat filled me in on what was going on, and it got my curiosity up, so I agreed to come."

Riley, looking at Dean, said, "We've got ourselves a situation here."

Dean didn't let him finish. "You have a situation, Admiral, it's not mine yet," he replied, glancing at Bolders and his daughter.

"Much as I respect what Commander Bolders did, I don't know if it will ever be my problem after what I witnessed this morning."

The room fell silent, and Tanya looked at her mother, hoping she would say something.

Loretta knew her husband had his own way of handling things, and he did them very well.

Dean then looked at Riley and asked, "Is this part of the crew that is part of this deal?"

"Yes, they are some really fine people and great sailors," Riley answered.

"With all due respect, Admiral Riley, I don't need you to sell them," Dean said respectfully. "I would rather they did that themselves," he added, looking around the table at each person.

"You," he said, pointing at Nelson, "what is your function on the ship, sailor?"

"Master Chief Kevin Nelson, sir, head of security on the Tiger Shark."

"I heard from the president just a small amount of details about the recent rescue mission," Dean said. "I would like to sit down with you and discuss it in more detail before I leave," he added.

"It would be my honor, sir," Nelson replied. Just then, the waitress arrived to take their orders.

Everyone gave their orders, and Riley told the waitress to give him the check.

After the waitress left, Admiral Dean turned his head slightly to the right. "And you, what is your function, sailor?" he asked in a demanding voice, pointing at Taylor.

"Lieutenant William Taylor, sir. I'm the executive officer and have served under the commander for seven years."

"What did you do before that, Lieutenant Commander?" Dean asked Taylor, trying to make him nervous.

"I served under the previous captain of the Tiger Shark for four years, sir," Taylor replied.

The waitress returned with two other staff members to help with the large order. After they had finished, the waitress and her helpers cleaned the table.

Dean looked at Riley and said, "Bachmann said this wasn't an order. It's my decision to make." He then looked at Bolders and added, "Nothing against you," before turning back to Riley. "If I take the ship and the rest of the crew, will that work?"

"Yeah, we can make that work," Riley replied, taking a deep breath and glancing at Bolders.

Dean looked back at Bolders and then at his daughter before turning his attention back to Riley. "I want my daughter in the deal," he said, looking directly at Riley.

"I thought everything was good," Tanya said to her dad, watching his gaze shift to Bolders.

"You and I might have gotten along, and it's not that I don't think you care for my daughter," Dean said. "You can call me old-fashioned or not understanding enough," he continued, looking at his daughter. "He took everything from me," he said, looking at Tanya before turning his gaze to Bolders. "You took mine and my wife's whole world. I wanted her to meet someone, fall in love with the man, and come to me to ask for her hand," Dean said.

Bolders stood up, looking the admiral in the eyes. "I do love her, sir," he said. "When she is ready for me to ask her, I will come to you and get your blessing."

Tanya got up and walked over to her dad, not caring about the others watching. She sat in his lap, and he hugged her tightly. "I just want what's best for you, T," he said.

"Dad, look at him, please," she said. "He is what's best for me. Mathew is what's best for me."

With his voice starting to crack, Dean whispered, "I'm just not ready to lose my little girl just yet."

Tanya then told Dean, "I will always be your little girl, Dad, no matter where I go or what I do. And Dad," she whispered softly, leaning closer, "I'm ready whenever he asks you." She stood up, kissed her father on his left cheek and forehead, and said, "I love you, Dad." Tanya then returned to her seat beside Mathew.

"Commander Bolders, if you ever hurt my daughter—" Dean started, his voice stern.

At that moment, Loretta reached out her right hand and placed two fingers over her husband's lips, shaking her head gently. "I've already gone over that with him."

Dean smiled, glancing at Bolders. "Well, she'll be more dangerous than I am, so I hope you take heed in what she said." He then turned to the other end of the table where Riley sat. "I've got a few days. Let's continue this conversation later."

"That sounds very good to me," Riley replied. Then he asked, "Who would like a drink?"

"Yes, that sounds like a winner," Nelson said as he rose from his seat.

Bolders reluctantly stood up, not wanting to drink but also not wanting to look bad in front of Tanya's father. Tanya looked at Mathew as he got up.

"Babe, only two drinks and beer only, okay? Please," she asked Bolders.

"Oh, that's right; you can't handle your liquor, can you, Commander?" Dean teased, wrapping his arm around Bolders's left shoulder and neck. "You're going to be alright, I think," Dean assured Bolders as they walked toward the bar.

Riley stood up at the same time as Nelson and Taylor, and they followed Dean and Bolders to the bar.

"Well, that's a good sign," Riley said to Nelson, giving him a pat on the back.

Nelson looked to his right at the admiral, replying, "It sure is not a bad one."

The waitress returned to the table where all the ladies were still seated.

"Would you ladies like dessert or something to drink?" the waitress asked.

Loretta looked at everyone and then asked the waitress if she could arrange a ride for her and her party later. The waitress returned with coconut cream pie and two bottles of red wine. About an hour later, everyone at the bar was laughing and talking, having a great time.

Dean glanced at Bolders, placing his right hand on his back. "Are you okay, Son?" he asked with concern.

Bolders turned his head left and looked at the admiral. Dean could see that he wasn't okay; he quickly glanced around Bolders and called out, "Master Chief."

Nelson looked over. "You better go get my daughter. He doesn't look good," Dean instructed.

"I'm on it, Admiral," Nelson responded, getting up and walking back to the table to get Tanya.

"Oh," Sara exclaimed as she saw Nelson approaching.

Judy, Nelson's wife, asked him, "Is there something wrong, Kev?" using his pet name.

Nelson looked at Tanya. "Your dad sent me to get you. Mat had a touch too much."

Tanya got up and followed Nelson, asking, "How much did he have to drink?"

"I don't know, ma'am. I was sitting at the other end and couldn't see well."

Dean had his bar swivel seat turned to face Bolders, with his left hand on the edge of the bar counter, ready to catch him if he fell forward.

Tanya arrived with her mother right behind her. "How much did he have to drink, Dad?" she asked, seeing that Mathew was really messed up.

Loretta addressed Dean and Riley, who Bolders was sitting between, "Why did you guys let him drink so much?"

"It doesn't take much for Mat to get drunk, Mom," Tanya explained to her mother.

"When you told him 'a couple,' I didn't think you actually meant 'a couple,'" Dean remarked.

He looked at Loretta and explained, "He only had two draft beers and a piña colada, and that's all."

Tanya and Loretta helped Bolders up off the bar seat, and Tanya asked if they could get a ride to the gate.

Nelson got up and looked at Riley. "Admiral, with your permission, I can get someone to drive their car and have them picked up."

Admiral Riley agreed, and Nelson arranged it. He then assisted the two women with getting Bolders to the car. Tanya and Mathew sat in the back seat while a female marine drove Tanya's car. She got them home and helped the women get Bolders into the house.

Before she left, she asked Tanya if she needed help getting him to bed.

"No," Tanya replied with a forced smile. "I can handle that all on my own, thank you."

The next morning, Bolders woke up in bed and realized he was alone. He couldn't hear anything from outside the bedroom, but it was hard to hear from Tanya's room. He got up, took a shower, dressed, and walked to the door. Taking a couple of deep breaths, he opened the door and walked into the kitchen nook. From there, he could see the living room and noticed a few people gathered.

He walked into the living room and saw both admirals, Nelson, and Taylor, along with all their wives. He also noticed Chief Douglas Walters, the head engineer, and his wife, Stephanie, were there too.

Admiral Dean spoke up, addressing Bolders, "We all were taking bets on whether you'd wake up before noon."

Tanya got up from the love seat and walked over to Bolders. "Have a seat, babe, and I'll fix you some coffee," she said, kissing him on the cheek.

He went and sat down on the love seat. Tanya returned shortly with a cup of coffee. She sat down beside Mathew, folding her left leg under her.

Dean then spoke up again, "Son, you are not a good drinker at all."

Bolders responded, "I've never been big on drinking, just maybe a beer, and that's it."

"So please tell me why in the hell you went to the bar with us last night," Dean asked. "You could have stayed at the table with the girls and had one or two beers, son," he added.

Tanya jumped in before Bolders could say anything. "He was trying to impress you, Dad, that's why."

"Son, listen to me," Dean continued, "and any man sitting here can tell you the same thing because they're all married. You see, this woman sitting here," he pointed at his wife Loretta, sitting on his left side, "you get in good with her; it doesn't matter what I say—you're in. But you make an enemy of her, I take over."

All the men in the room nodded in agreement with what the admiral had said.

"Just remember, if you two ever get married, your job is to make her happy," Dean went on to say.

"Dad, enough please; let him wake up and enjoy his coffee," Tanya interjected.

"The ladies are going to the store, and we are going outside on the patio to talk."

Bolders watched as Admiral Dean got up off the sofa and waited for someone else to do so as well.

Dean looked at Bolders and said, "Did you think I meant everyone? I meant just you and I," he said, raising his left hand and pointing toward the patio door.

Bolders went first and sat down by the fire pit in an iron chair with a flowery cushion. It was a little chilly, so Admiral Dean lit the firepit. He then lit a cigar and sat down across from Bolders, propping his feet up.

"Admiral Riley and I were talking last night, and I didn't realize that Malcolm Pettus was your commanding officer."

"Yes, sir. I was out of Jacksonville, Florida until seven years ago, then the ship and crew were transferred to Norfolk."

"How do you like Norfolk Naval Base?" Dean asked Bolders.

"It's a decent base, I guess, but I don't spend much time there when I'm off," Bolders replied.

"So why is Pettus after you, Mathew?" Dean asked, taking a sip of coffee.

"I guess for disobeying his orders, or that's the only reason I can think of, sir," Bolders responded.

Dean looked at him, then took a drag off his cigar and blew the smoke out. "Norfolk was my base for thirteen years until Braylon Oswald got into office," Dean said.

"What happened between you and President Oswald, sir?" Bolders asked.

"Well, Pettus had pull somehow and kissed the right people's ass, and I didn't, so I got shoved out. When President Bachmann got into office, he opened up a base and wanted me to take old World War II ships and bring them back to life," Dean explained.

194

"Is it going to be like a floating museum or something like that, sir?" Bolders asked.

"Something like that, but with full fighting strength," Dean replied. "I was told there have been attempts on your life," he added. "There's no doubt in my mind that Pettus is behind it."

At that time, Tanya, Loretta, Sara, and Nancy returned from the store. Tanya set the two bags of groceries she was carrying down on the kitchen counter.

She walked into the living room and over to Nelson. "How long have they been out there?" she asked.

"Breakfast will be ready soon, so you guys get in here and wash up," Loretta called out as she stuck her head out the door.

Dean and Bolders got up, but Dean stopped Bolders and looked at him. "Pettus must think you have something on him or someone he's close to," Dean told him.

"Who do you mean he's close to, sir?" Bolders asked.

"Son, it could be one of the presidents or someone up on the hill in Washington. You have my daughter with you now, so I'll try to clean this up the best I can."

Loretta was walking back to the door when she stopped. "T," she called, "come here quick." Everyone turned to look when she said that.

Tanya arrived just in time to see her dad and boyfriend shaking hands.

"Okay, let's go eat breakfast before these women get upset with us," Dean said to Bolders.

They started to walk toward the kitchen, but Tanya stopped them. "You two haven't washed up yet," she said.

"We're going to wash up in the sink," Dean told her.

She just looked at her dad. "You do not wash your hands in my kitchen sink. Dad," she said, pointing to the bedroom. "Babe," she said to Bolders, pointing toward their bedroom.

They were at the table eating breakfast when Admiral Dean looked at his daughter and asked, "Let me ask you something."

She looked at him, tilting her head slightly to the left with a look of curiosity.

"When are you two going to see his parents? And I hope it is soon," he added.

"I was going to make the arrangements once I knew what was going on," she replied.

"Taylor," Dean said, looking at the lieutenant commander, "do you think you can get that destroyer to Los Angeles in one piece?"

Taylor almost choked on his food, then looked at Bolders, confused. "Does this mean that the commander isn't going with us, Admiral?" Taylor asked.

"If he was, I wouldn't be asking you to," Dean told him, then looked at Bolders. "Will, take the ship to Los Angeles," Bolders instructed, then he glanced at Dean, confirming his decision.

Everyone watched closely to see what Dean would say next, sensing that Bolders wasn't going to be transferred. Dean then turned to his daughter. "I need you to meet his parents and get him back as soon as possible."

Everyone took a deep breath, including Bolders, who hadn't been told anything either.

"I am only going to have one captain on base, and I'm going to need him back to take his fleet out," Dean said, walking over to Bolders and extending his hand. Bolders shook his hand, and Dean said, "Captain Bolders, welcome to Breakaway Base Los Angeles."

After the handshake, Bolders stood there for a moment, still processing the news. Dean said to Bolders, "Admiral Riley and I have some business to take care of." He then lightly slapped Bolders on the right shoulder. "I'll see you and my daughter at home for a family dinner tonight." He and Riley then walked away.

Bolders stood there for a few seconds until the admirals were well on their way. He then sat back down, looking up to see Tanya staring at him. After a moment, he looked back at Tanya again. "Did he just," he paused, "call me captain?"

Tanya was all smiles, unable to contain her excitement. She nodded quickly. "Yes, he did," she said, jumping into his lap.

Tanya and Mathew walked out back, and she stopped in front of him, wrapping her arms around his waist. She then looked up at him, slightly wetting her lips. "Kiss me, Captain Bolders," she told him.

He bent over slightly and kissed her, closing his eyes and feeling that familiar spine-tingling sensation. As the kiss ended, Tanya took his phone from his left side. When it was over, she stood there holding his cell phone in her right hand in front of him. He looked down at his left hip, realizing his phone was missing.

He looked back at Tanya, and she said, "Call your parents so I can get us a ticket."

"I will call them," he told her as he reached for his phone.

She held her right arm far behind her, keeping the phone out of his reach. He pulled her closer, but she bent her arm behind herself to keep him from getting the phone. He looked at her, and his smile faded. "That phone is the last thing on my mind," he said, kissing her again.

She lightly pushed on him, smiling up at him. "I have created a monster."

He tried to kiss her again, but she pulled her head back, still held tightly around the waist. She took the phone from behind her back and placed it in the middle of his chest, laughing. "Call your mother now."

He took the phone from her hand, holding it at his left side. "We can call her anytime," Bolders said.

She moved away from him, pointing playfully into his chest. "Anytime is right now," Tanya told him.

She walked away, and before she went back into the house, Tanya looked back at him. She put her right thumb up to her ear and her right pinkie up to her mouth, giving him the sign to call. Tanya walked into the house and closed the door behind her, then walked over to where the ladies were talking.

"Did you two get everything figured out?" Nancy asked Tanya.

"It will be when he calls his mother, and I can get our tickets," Tanya replied.

Judy, Nelson's wife, looked at her. "Tanya, if someone didn't know you two, they would swear you've been together for years."

Nancy chimed in, "We all were talking about that earlier this morning."

Judy said, "The way you both just fell for each other right away is something out of a storybook."

After about ten minutes, Bolders walked back in, just putting his cell phone back in its case.

Tanya looked at him and asked, "Well, what did your mother say?"

"She said that today wouldn't be soon enough," Mathew replied, "then she started talking about God," he added.

All the women looked at him after he said that, then walked into the bedroom. Loretta, with a shocked expression, looked at her daughter. "I thought he was a Christian, Tanya."

"No, Mother, he's not," Tanya answered. "He was raised in church but drifted away."

She saw the way her mother looked at her from across the table after she said that.

"Mother, please don't look at me like that. I am working on him and will get him back in church."

"T," Loretta said, her right elbow on the table and pointing at Tanya with her right index finger, "you know it takes more than just going to church to be a Christian, young lady," Loretta told her.

"Yes, Mother," Tanya said, letting out a deep breath. "I'm working on him."

"How long has he been this way, not believing in God?" Loretta asked, looking at everyone at the table.

Taylor spoke up, "All I know is something happened after he grew up, and he turned away from church. From my understanding, when he got away from church, he eventually got away from God."

"We have tried several times," Taylor continued, speaking of her and her husband, "to get him to visit church with us," she told Loretta.

Bolders walked out of the bedroom at that time, unaware of the conversation. He passed by everyone at the dining room and walked into the living room, looking on and under everything.

"What are you looking for, babe?" Tanya asked him.

"My wallet," he replied as he overturned every pillow and cushion in the room.

"If you will come sit down and have a cup of coffee, babe, I'll find it for you," Tanya told him.

He started walking toward the dining room, and Tanya looked at her mother. "Please don't say anything."

She got up and let Mathew have her seat, then fixed him a cup of coffee. She placed the coffee on the table in front of him, leaned over, and kissed him. As she rose, she looked at her mother, squinting her eyebrows, then walked into the bedroom. Tanya's mother, Loretta, is a straight shooter and usually says what's on her mind, especially when it concerns her family. Today was no different as she was trying her best to keep her mouth shut.

Bolders turned his head to the left, watching Tanya as she disappeared into the kitchen, heading to the bedroom. He sat at the table with everyone drinking their coffee, or juice in Judy's case. He noticed that Loretta kept looking at him differently than she had been before. He wanted to ask her if everything was okay but didn't want to sound paranoid.

After a few minutes, he couldn't help himself and spoke up. "Is there something wrong, Mrs. Dean?"

Loretta shook her head no, but then immediately said, "As a matter of fact, there is, Mathew. There is something very wrong."

"Is it something that I've done, Mrs. Dean?" Bolders asked in a mild, concerned voice.

"Yes, Mathew, it is something that you are doing to my daughter," Loretta replied, her voice upset.

"What do you think I've done to Tanya, Mrs. Dean?" Bolders asked, genuinely worried that he might have unknowingly done something wrong.

"We are a Christian family, Mathew, and from my understanding, so is your family, and at one time, you were too," Loretta said. "Most of the people we've met who work with and around you are Christians as well," she continued.

"Mrs. Dean, I don't know where this is coming from, but I love your daughter very much, and I can't imagine my life without her now."

"I can't imagine my little girl without God, Mathew," Loretta said, looking directly into his eyes. "That child was a miracle and has been to her father and myself ever since," she told Bolders, tears welling up. "The Bible says iron sharpens iron, Mathew. Do you know what that means?" she asked. "Do you really think that both of you will be happy going in different directions?"

"Yes, I do, Mrs. Dean," Bolders replied respectfully. "The reason I believe that is because of the love we have for each other."

"I just don't understand you, Mathew," she said. "You say she is the most important thing in your life—"

Before Loretta could say anything else, Tanya walked into the dining room, having overheard their conversation.

"Mother," Tanya said furiously, "what are you doing?"

Bolders turned his head slightly to the right, seeing Tanya standing almost in front of him. He started getting up, saying, "Your mother was just explaining to me why I am not good for you."

Loretta spoke up again, "You need to sit here like a man and discuss this problem instead of running away."

Bolders walked to the coffeepot, finding it empty. He set his cup down and started walking outside.

"Mother, how could you?" Tanya said to Loretta. "You claim you want what's best for me."

"I do, I really do, and a man that believes in God is what's best for you, baby," Loretta insisted.

"Mother, just how do you know that God didn't put us together for me to lead him back to Him?"

At that moment, the front door opened, and Admiral Dean, Admiral Riley, and Sara walked in. Dean looked at his daughter and wife, both with tears in their eyes and clearly upset.

"What in the Doc Holliday's Tombstone is going on in here?" the admiral asked, looking at the two women.

"Dad, Mother seems to think it's best to tell my boyfriend that I'm better off without him in not so many words. She thinks because he doesn't believe like we do that he is no good for me," Tanya explained.

"You need to sit," Tanya's dad told her, and she did, crossing her legs.

Loretta started to say something, but Dean looked at her. "Etta, I think you've said enough for now, don't you? He loves our daughter, and for whatever reason under God's brightly lit sun, she loves him," Dean told Loretta. "So, Etta, just let her be happy. It may just turn out like you want in the long run," he added. He then looked at Tanya. "T, go out and check on the boy," he told her.

Tanya saw that her dad had Dunkin' Donuts coffee and took it, pouring it into Bolders's cup. She handed the remainder back to her dad. She glared at her mother as she walked to the back door. She walked outside and sat in Bolders's lap, giving him the cup of hot black coffee.

"You made some more. That was quick," he said, referring to the coffee.

"I stole some of my dad's," she replied, smiling.

She still had tears in her eyes, and Bolders set his cup on the table, wiping them away with his right thumb.

"Please don't pay any attention to my mother, Mat. She just doesn't want to see me hurt."

"Tanya," Bolders said softly, looking at her, "I love you so much. Do you think she could be right? Because I don't want you to change one bit."

Tanya's expression changed, and she glared at him. "Mat Bolders, I never ever want to hear you say something like that again as long as you live." She then put her face close to his, lightly biting her bottom lip. "However, it is very nice to know that you love me that much," she said, then kissed him, wrapping her arms around his neck.

Everyone inside the house was watching them.

Stanley looked at his wife, Loretta. "Look at them, Etta, when have you ever seen our daughter so happy?" He then looked back at his wife again. "Can you tell me when you've seen her happy like that?"

Loretta shook her head, taking her left hand and caressing Stanley's arm as she watched.

"Her being this way is all I've ever wanted," the admiral told his wife. "And I know you do too. I would have preferred him to be a Christian, and I have faith that will happen in God's time," he continued. "I would have liked him to be a little bit younger and have just a bit more hair, but I'm not in love with him, she is. I think if the time ever comes, he will make our daughter a wonderful husband. I've already given him my blessings. So whenever he gets ambitious and decides to marry her, he doesn't have to come ask first."

They were still kissing, so the admiral got up out of his seat. "I better break this up before they both suffocate," he said, and everyone laughed.

He walked to the back door and opened it. "Mathew, son, could I speak to you for a moment?"

Tanya rose out of his lap and started to go inside as well.

"You just wait here, T; I won't be but a minute with him," her dad told her.

She sat back down, and everyone watched as Admiral Dean and Bolders walked back into the spare bedroom. After about a minute, Bolders and the admiral came back out of the room. Bolders started walking toward the back door, and the admiral sat back down at the table. Bolders opened the back door.

The admiral said, "Everyone, watch this," as he started to film it.

At that moment, the doorbell rang, and Nelson answered it.

"Oh my God," he said, "what are you all doing here?" he exclaimed as they rushed past him.

They also stood and looked at what was going on outside. Bolders held out both his hands for Tanya to take, and she did. He pulled her to her feet and looked at her for a moment. Then he reached into his back pocket and pulled out a velvet red ring box, kneeling down on one knee and looking up at her.

CHAPTER 21

TANYA'S left hand went up over her mouth as she said, "Oh my God," and her right hand went over her heart.

Mathew opened the box, revealing a half-carat gold diamond ring. "Tanya, I know we haven't known each other that long, but for me, it seems like a lifetime," he told her. "I lose my breath when you kiss me. You make me feel like I've never felt before. Will you make me the happiest man in the world and let me spend the rest of my life with you? Will you marry me, Tanya Dean Manners?"

She held out her left hand, with her right still over her heart, and Mathew placed the ring on her finger. He then got up off his knee, and tears rolled down her face. She wrapped her arms around his neck, and he put his arms around her waist. As everyone looked on, it was the most romantic kiss any of them had ever seen. Everyone inside began to clap, and Tanya and Mathew turned, smiling broadly. Bolders then looked closely at her, then walked with Tanya, holding her hand, to the back door. Everyone hugged their necks and congratulated them, even Loretta.

After she hugged Bolders's neck, she looked at him, holding

each side of his arms. "Forgive me, Mathew. I was wrong," she said, then smiled at him.

Loretta then told him, "There is someone else you need to see," as she stepped to the side.

"Mama, Daddy," Bolders said, and then he hugged his mama's neck first, then his daddy's. "Mama, this is Tanya."

She hugged their necks, and then Doris, his mama, put her hands on Tanya's cheeks. "Daddy," she said to Albert, her husband. "She is just a living doll, isn't she?"

"Yes, she is, Mama," Albert said. "Honey, you are as beautiful as an angel. Wait until everyone else in the family sees her."

Tanya was enjoying herself and was so happy, looking over at Bolders. Everyone watched the four of them talking and loved hearing Doris talk with her heavy southern accent.

Doris combed Tanya's long dark hair with her fingers. "Daddy, look at those eyes. Mathew was right, wasn't he, Daddy?"

Albert answered, "He absolutely was, Mama."

Tanya was smiling from ear to ear.

"What did Mat say about my eyes, Mrs. Bolders?" she asked Mathew's mother.

"He told us that you had the most beautiful gray eyes and that he melted every time you looked at him from the first time he saw you." She stopped smiling and looked at Mathew, turning to kiss him again.

When the kiss was over, he went and hugged his mama again, asking how she got there so fast.

"Your father-in-law and this other gentleman," pointing to Riley, "arranged to have one of those big jets come get us."

Bolders turned, looking at Admiral Dean, feeling emotional having his parents there to witness it.

He walked over to the admiral. "Thank you, sir," and then he looked at Riley, "you too, sir."

Riley told Bolders, "It was all that man," talking about Dean, "I was just there for the ride."

Dean then said to Bolders, "If you really want to thank me, keep loving my daughter and take care of her."

"Admiral—" Bolders began.

Dean stopped him, saying, "It is either Stan or Dean today, not Admiral."

Bolders nodded and spoke again, "Mr. Dean, I promise I will love and take care of her 'til the day I die."

The admiral looked at him and said, "I'm not the one you need to convince," he said, looking back at his wife.

"Mrs. Dean, I swear I will make her very happy," Bolders told Tanya's mother.

"Mathew, you have our little baby girl now, so don't tell me—show us," Loretta told him.

"Okay, everyone," Dean said in a slightly loud voice to get everyone's attention. "I was just told something by my new commander." He glanced at Taylor and the head of fleet security without calling anyone's names. Everyone laughed, and then Dean continued, "Anyway, I was told that she could cook some mean home biscuits. With the help of my newly found friend and fellow conspirator, Mr. Riley, we are going to grill some huge steaks. So, if it wouldn't be too much trouble, we would love for the lovely Mrs. Bolders to whip up some of those biscuits," Dean said.

There was a knock on the door, and both Tanya and Bolders heard it. Tanya started to answer, but Bolders stopped her. She was talking to all the women, so he went to the front door. When he opened it, there was no one there. He stepped out onto the porch, opening the glass door.

He looked to the left and then the right, seeing no one. Assuming it was a prank, he started back inside. As he was turning, he looked up toward the sidewalk across the street. There stood a beautiful woman just standing and looking at him from across the street. This time, she had two large, creepy-looking men with her, one on each side. Why am I so mesmerized by her? he asked himself. The only woman I've ever loved is right inside the house, he thought. All at once, she was right at the front gate, staring at him. The two men remained on the sidewalk across the street, watching the lady. He could hear her calling his name, but her lips weren't moving.

Tanya looked around the room for Mathew but didn't see him anywhere. She knew he had gone to answer the front door, but that had been several minutes ago. She then told everyone she was talking to that she would excuse herself for a moment.

Tanya walked to the front door, which was standing open. She could see Mathew standing in the middle of the yard, seemingly talking to someone. She looked around, ensuring no one else was watching her, then briskly walked to the front door. She stepped out onto the porch and stared for a moment.

Bolders saw the woman look up quickly toward the house, then he turned and saw Tanya. He turned back, and the woman and two men were gone.

"Babe," he heard Tanya call to him softly as he turned.

She wrapped her left hand around his waist, holding him tightly against her body. "Are you okay, babe?" she asked, looking out toward the sidewalk.

"I'm fine," he said, smiling at her. "Why wouldn't I be? I have you."

"Let's go back inside," she suggested. They walked in with their arms around each other.

A couple of days had passed since Admiral Dean and his wife Loretta had gone back to California. The Tiger Shark was out of dry dock and ready to go, and Bolders' parents had gone back home. Tanya and Mathew had packed their things a couple of days ago, so they were ready. It was the morning before Bolders and Tanya were supposed to leave for Breakaway Base Los Angeles. The Tiger Shark was scheduled to pull out of port at 1000 hours that morning, and Bolders wanted to be there to see them off.

Tanya woke up, hugging Bolders who was still asleep. She rolled over on her left side very carefully so as not to wake Mathew. She propped herself up on her left elbow and looked at the clock, which read 0530. With her left hand, she pushed herself up, looking at Mathew, not wanting to wake him just yet. She then used her right hand to pull the covers to one side and slid out of bed.

She went into the kitchen to start the coffee and then went to take a shower before waking Mathew. As she was getting out of the shower, Mathew was sitting up on his side of the bed with his feet on the floor.

"Good morning, love," Tanya said as she entered the closet.

When she came out of the closet, he was just getting up and heading to the bathroom.

"Babe, do you see what time it is?" Tanya asked as he went to shower.

It was 07:15 when he finally came into the dining room.

"I've got your egg and bacon sandwich and coffee to go, babe," Tanya told him.

They headed out of the house and to the base so Bolders could see his crew off. They arrived at the base and made their way to the docks, arriving at 08:45. He and Tanya, both in their uniforms with their new ranks, boarded the ship.

Taylor, now a commander, would be taking the ship to California on its five-day cruise. Everyone on the ship congratulated Bolders and Tanya on their engagement. It was finally time for all non-personnel to leave the ship before flooding the dry dock so it could pull away. Bolders stood on the land, watching the Tiger Shark back away from the dry dock; he almost wanted to tell them to stop. It was the first time in seven years since he first took command that he had watched her sail away without him. Tanya, holding his hand, could see it really bothered him and released his hand. While still standing beside him, she wrapped both hands around him and squeezed tightly. He put his right arm around her and did the same, watching the ship start to move forward, leaving the harbor.

A voice spoke to them from behind, and they turned, recognizing it.

"It doesn't get any easier, Mat," Admiral Riley said, standing with his wife, Sara.

Sara stood by Tanya as Riley stood by Bolders, placing his right hand on Bolders's left shoulder. "I can tell you, though, when you get home after a few months, you're not going to believe it."

Bolders looked at him curiously. "They really miss you," he said to the admiral.

"Well, let me put it to you this way," Riley said to Bolders, laughing. "The first couple of weeks, you don't want to leave the house, and the next couple of weeks, you're not able to."

All four of them laughed and joked about that for a minute or two. Bolders then looked back to sea, and the Tiger Shark was gone. Riley saw the look on his face, as did Tanya. Riley threw his right arm around Bolders, grabbing his right shoulder and squeezing it tightly.

"Lunch is on me and Sara today; let's go."

They ate, laughed, and joked for a while, and before long, it was time for them to say goodbye.

Sara hugged Bolders's neck and then Tanya's, saying, "I know we didn't get off to the best start, but I'm really going to miss you."

Riley shook Bolders's hand and then gave Tanya a hug. "It was a pleasure getting to know both of you."

They separated, with Tanya and Mathew going back to her

home and the admiral and Sara returning to base. After they arrived at Tanya's house and walked in the door, she went straight to the bedroom. He started to follow her, and she turned, laughing.

She pointed to the sofa. "Go, sit down."

About ten minutes later, she came out of the bedroom, and he turned to look at her. She wore a yellow bikini and wrapped a light blue towel around her waist. They went to the beach, and the whole time he couldn't take his eyes off her. When it was time to go in, she picked up the towels they were laying on. As Tanya bent down, he looked and saw that woman again, coming out of the water in a bright pink bikini.

Tanya stood up and saw him looking at the water behind her, so she turned and looked.

"Babe, what is it?" Tanya asked, seeing a frightened look on his face.

"Let's go to the house," he told her, hurrying to get away from the beach.

They went up the trail, which took about ten minutes to get to the house. When they arrived, she unlocked the back door, and Mathew followed her in, locking the door behind them.

"Babe, what is wrong?" Tanya asked, watching him. He looked at her and shook his head. She pointed at him. "Don't you tell me nothing, Mat Bolders. I see it in your face," Tanya said, her voice filled with worry.

He went over to the sofa and sat down, putting his elbows on his knees and his face in the palms of his hands. Tanya went over and sat down on his left side, placing her left hand between his shoulder blades. She softly caressed his back while resting her chin on his left shoulder.

"Please tell me what's wrong, babe," she whispered in his ear, then kissed his cheek right in front of his earlobe.

He lifted his head, turning to look at Tanya. "I saw that lady again, babe."

Her head was still on his shoulder; she softly kissed him, then raised her head. "I feel like I'm going crazy, honey. It all started just a few days before that rescue mission."

"You have been through a lot, babe," Tanya reassured him. "It will go away."

They went to bed, and she held him until he went to sleep, then waited a while longer. She moved her hand from around him and lay there for just a couple of minutes, seeing if he would wake up.

After a couple of minutes, she got up, and he rolled over. "Where are you going, honey?" Bolders asked.

"Just going to get some water. Would you like some, love?" she asked.

He nodded as she got up and went to the kitchen. She got two bottles of water and carried them back to the bedroom.

"Babe, here's your water," she said as she heard him mumble something, then roll over.

She set his bottle of water on her side of the bed on the table and stood there for a minute. She then walked out of the bedroom and eased the door closed behind her. With her right hand on the door-knob, she placed her left hand on the door, making sure it closed quietly. She walked to the back glass door and looked out for a few seconds as she took a swallow of water. She twisted the plastic top back on the bottle of water in her right hand, then unlocked the back door with her left hand, turned the knob, and quietly opened it. She closed it and took three steps away from the door, then stopped, looking around.

"I know you're out here, so show yourself," Tanya said to nothing but the midnight air.

Her hair was shiny black and hung down to her waist; she

walked closer to Tanya. The woman stopped just a couple of feet from Tanya, just out of her reach.

Tanya stared into the woman's dark eyes. "What do you want?" she asked.

The woman smiled at Tanya. "Are you really in love with him?" she asked sarcastically.

"You touch him, and I promise you'll find out," Tanya told her, almost gritting her teeth.

Tanya heard something behind her and slightly turned her head to the right. She made sure she could see the woman and also saw two large men appearing out of the bushes behind her. With her head still in the same position, she cut her eyes back to the woman.

"Still, after all these years, you aren't fighting your own battles."

"A princess never fights for herself," the woman replied. "Or didn't you know that?"

Tanya squinted her eyebrows. "I'll tell you what I do know."

The woman laughed in her face. "Please tell me."

Tanya took two steps forward, and the woman took two steps back. She heard the two men move closer to her. Without looking at them, she held her right hand out behind her. "If you two come any closer, your so-called princess will leave here alone." She looked back at the woman with a violent look in her eyes. "I'll rip your heart from your chest and feed it to the wild beast," Tanya warned.

The woman looked at the two men behind Tanya and said to them, "Let's go."

Tanya turned to go back inside and saw Bolders walk up to the back door. He took his right hand and opened it as he yawned.

"Are you okay, sweetheart?" Bolders asked Tanya, seeing her outside just standing there.

"I'm fine, babe," she told him, smiling and walking up to him, removing her housecoat.

They went to bed and didn't get to sleep until late. It wasn't long until the alarm went off, and Tanya stretched, saying no. Bolders covered his head up, and Tanya threw the covers back, getting up.

She patted Mathew on the buttocks. "Okay, you get up, we've got a flight to catch in four hours."

Tanya went into the kitchen, started the coffee maker, and then came back into the bedroom. She saw Mathew was still in bed with the covers pulled over his head. She walked over to his side of the bed and grabbed the covers, throwing them off him.

"Babe,"

"Please, just a few more minutes' sleep," Bolders pleaded. "We didn't get but two hours of sleep."

"Whose fault is that?" she asked, grabbing his legs and pulling them off the bed.

"It is your fault," he told her as he sat up, rubbing his head with his right hand.

"How is it my fault?" she asked, taking his hands and pulling him up.

"You are the one that lost your clothes outside," he replied.

"Yeah, because of you," she retorted.

They showered, sat at the table, and drank coffee, looking around the room.

"I'm going to miss this place," she said as she got up and went to the bedroom.

Tanya made the bed, cleaned the coffeepot, and straightened up the house. Before they knew it, there was a knock on the door. It was two sailors from the base, there to take them to catch their 09:30 flight. They arrived at Hickman Air Force Base and noticed they were the only ones there. Bolders walked up to an airman and asked if they were in the right place. The airman explained they were going to Los Angeles Air Force Base in El Segundo to pick up supplies.

"You and your wife," he assumed, seeing the ring on her finger, "are the only ones besides the crew on this flight."

The C-17 loadmaster came out to meet Bolders and Tanya, saluting them.

"We're putting your bags on the plane now, sir, and we can leave now if you're ready, sir."

Tanya spoke up, not giving Bolders a chance to respond, "Yes, let's get going."

"I was going to get something to eat, honey," Bolders told Tanya. "We still have almost fifty minutes."

Tanya, not letting Bolders stop, asked the airman, "Do you have food onboard?"

The airman turned and smiled. "Yes, ma'am, there are sandwiches and a microwave on board, ma'am," he answered.

They boarded the plane and took off. Five and a half hours later, at thirteen forty-five, they landed in Los Angeles, California. When they got off the plane, sailors were there to get their luggage and carry it to a van. The first thing they saw as they started to walk on the tarmac was Admiral Dean and his wife, Loretta, waiting for them.

Tanya hugged her dad and mom, and Loretta hugged Bolders. Mathew saluted the admiral, and they started walking to the car.

Loretta told Tanya, "We have a couple of homes for you and me to look at tomorrow."

She looked back at Bolders, then at her mother. "What about Mathew? He needs to see it too."

Dean spoke up, "He has a full day tomorrow ahead of him with the fleet."

Bolders then told Tanya, "Sweetheart, if you're happy with it, I will be too."

Tanya then asked her mother as they got in the car, "Where's the closest hotel to the base?"

"You two are staying with us," Dean replied, looking in the rearview mirror at his daughter in the back seat.

Tanya started to say something, but her dad cut her off.

The next morning, Tanya and Mat got up, showered, dressed, and went downstairs where the admiral and Loretta were sitting at the table waiting for them.

"You two have a seat, and I'll get you some coffee and home-made biscuits and bacon," Loretta told them.

"Mother, you made homemade biscuits?" Tanya asked in shock, then looked at her father.

Dean smiled. "They're actually not bad at all," he told them.

Loretta brought two plates to the table.

"I had your mother show me while we were in Hawaii," Bolders said.

He tasted it, and his fiancée gave him a look that said, Oh no, don't do it.

He looked at Loretta, nodding his head. "Wow! Mrs. Dean, these aren't bad at all." Then he took another bite.

Loretta beamed with a huge smile and sat down, looking at Bolders. "I'm glad you like them." She took her left hand and rubbed his right arm a couple of times.

After everyone had eaten, the admiral looked at Bolders, saying, "You and I have to get to work."

Loretta told Tanya, "We have some houses to look at."

The admiral was already living on base in one of the completed homes. Bolders and Dean didn't have far to go to get to work. They went down to the shipyard, which had another security gate to pass through. Bolders and the admiral sat in the back seat of the car, Dean on the right side and Bolders on the left.

Bolders looked over to the admiral, saying, "A lot of security for a dry dock, Admiral."

Dean looked at him, smiling. "Just a little more than a regular dry dock, Captain."

The car pulled to the left side, right behind the guard post, and Bolders watched as the driver got out. He opened Bolders's door, being closer, then walked around to open the admiral's, but he was already getting out. Bolders saw the admiral start walking toward the front of the car, so he did as well. They stood on a large hill with a small pathway too narrow for a car to travel.

A golf cart appeared, coming over the hill, heading their way.

Dean looked at Bolders. "There is our ride, Mathew."

The golf cart pulled up, and a lieutenant stepped out of the second seat. He saluted the admiral and said, "Admiral, sir, it's good to have you back, sir."

"Lieutenant, this is my future son-in-law, Captain Mathew Bolders," Dean introduced Mathew.

"Sir, it's a pleasure to meet you," the lieutenant said, then the three men got into the golf cart.

CHAPTER 22

As THEY RODE, the admiral sat in the seat facing the lieutenant, with Bolders beside the lieutenant.

"How are we looking on our go date, Lieutenant?" Dean asked.

"We are looking really good, sir," Lieutenant Hung replied. "We are actually ahead of schedule by about a month now, sir."

Hung looked at Bolders. "So you're marrying Lieutenant Manners?"

"I am," Bolders replied.

Right then, they topped the hill, and Bolders couldn't believe his eyes; he saw carriers, battleships, cruisers, and destroyers. They started descending the large hill into the harbor. They reached the harbor dock, and Bolders was still in shock, not believing what he was seeing. He felt like a kid in a candy store all by himself.

He looked at Dean, saying, "We heard in 2019 that these ships were going to be scrapped or made safer for tourists."

"Well," Dean said, looking at him, "you can see they are not scrapped and are safer for tourists. These ships will be going from state to state and country to country, letting people board and look around. They will also be able to show live firings to demonstrate the might of the navy. In the next few days, I will let you pick your flagship, and we will go from there."

They toured a few of the destroyers and a cruiser, which had been restored to almost original condition. The admiral had Hung take them back to their car at the top of the hill as it was getting late.

They reached the car, and Dean looked at Bolders. "Hey, remember, once we pass that gate, no talking to anyone else."

Bolders shook his head and then said, "This base is big, but not that big. Doesn't everyone on base already know about it?"

"They do," Dean replied as both men leaned over the top, talking to each other. "But you'll never hear them talking about it because you never know if they're from this base or not."

"Gotcha," Bolders said, understanding a little better now, and the two men got in the car.

Dean told the driver to stop by his office so he could check on something before he went home.

When they stopped, Dean said to Bolders, "Son, there's a bar across the street that has great onion rings. If you have a beer, only have one because my daughter will kill me if I bring you back drunk. You can come up to the office with me if you want; I'll be about thirty minutes."

Bolders decided to go across the street to the bar he saw named St. Johns. He went in, sat down at the bar, and looked around at how empty it was.

The bartender came over. "Captain, can I get you something?" the civilian bartender asked.

"I heard y'all have really good onion rings," Bolders told him.

He heard a female voice on his left side say, "Hi there, can I sit here, or is it taken?"

"No, ma'am, you can sit here; it's not taken," he told the voice, not seeing who was behind it yet.

When the lady sat down beside him, he looked over to say hello. When he looked, he saw it was that same beautiful woman from Hawaii that he had seen several times.

He started to get up from his seat, and the young lady spoke up, holding both palms of her hands up. "Please, don't go," she pleaded, turning her barstool to face Bolders. "Just hear me out, and I promise, you'll never see me again"—then she paused—"I promise, never again."

Bolders sat back down and turned his barstool toward her. He then looked around as if looking for something or someone.

She spoke up, knowing what he was looking for. "My bodyguards are outside. I came in by myself," she said, smiling at him.

"Bodyguards," Bolders said sarcastically, "lady, I don't think you need bodyguards. You forgot I saw you on the sidewalk looking like a vampire or something."

The young lady started to say something, and Bolders cut her off. "Just who are you and what do you want with me?" he asked, placing his right elbow and forearm on the bar.

"I am just worried about you, Captain Bolders," she said. Then she added, "Oh, and by the way, congratulations on your promotion."

"Who are you, lady, and why are you worried about me?"

"My name is Sintra, and I am a princess of a place that I won't mention right now for my safety."

"Okay, there's the who and now why; you have one minute," he told her, looking at his watch.

"The family you're with is not the safest family to be around, and that woman you're dating—"

Bolders cut her off. "You leave my fiancée out of this, or I leave now."

"All I'm going to say, and then you can leave, is be careful and watch your back."

She then got up and placed her left hand softly on his right cheek.

Her fingertips glided across his cheek as she walked away, saying, "The wrong woman always gets the good guys."

He turned and watched her walk away, noticing the way her body moved. Bolders wasn't the only one watching; the bartender was watching her walk away as well.

"Captain," the bartender said, "my God, you either have a gorgeous woman waiting at home for you or you don't like women."

"I've got the most beautiful woman you have ever seen in your entire life," Bolders told the bartender.

At that moment, he heard a voice behind him saying, "What beautiful woman?"

He turned around and saw the admiral walking up and taking a seat. Bolders started to get up, thinking he was ready to go.

"Have a seat, son," the admiral told him. "Neither one of us is driving, so we can have a quick beer."

He then looked at the bartender asking, "Barkeep, my future son-in-law hasn't had a drink yet, has he?"

"You're the one marrying Ms. Tanya?" the bartender said, looking at Bolders. "I can see why you brushed that young lady off," the bartender told Bolders.

Admiral Dean then looked at Bolders, then back at the bartender, asking, "What woman?"

"Just some woman that sat down beside me talking nonsense," Bolders told Dean.

"Some woman," the bartender said, "Admiral, she was beautiful and was all over the captain. The captain here just brushed her off like she was nothing," the bartender told the admiral.

"Where is this beautiful woman at?" Admiral Dean asked Bolders and the bartender.

"You were just about to pass her on your way out," the bartender told Dean.

"I didn't see anyone as I was coming in," the admiral told the bartender.

"Let us have whatever you have on tap, barkeep. We're off the next few days."

The bartender brought them their draft beer, and Dean lifted his glass, toasting Bolders as he raised his.

"Well, I know you love my little girl," the admiral said as he took a drink. He put the glass back on the bar and looked at Bolders. "Strange, I didn't see her. Well, anyway," the admiral said, "bottoms up; we both have a dinner date tonight."

The admiral pulled out a twenty and put it on the bar, telling the bartender to keep the change.

The two men walked out of the bar and headed for the car. Five minutes later, someone entered the bar and sat down at a barstool in the middle of the bar.

"What can I get you, ma'am?" the bartender asked the woman.

"I'll take a whiskey straight and whatever is on tap," she told the bartender.

He brought her drinks and placed them on the bar in front of her.

"Why don't you join me?" the woman asked, raising her right eyebrow more than the left.

"I can't; I have to take care of the customers," he told her, looking into her bright blue eyes.

She turned her barstool to face the room, looking around, then back at the bartender. "No one is here," she told him, then the tip of her tongue peeped out from her lips and raked the bottom one on the way back into hiding.

The bartender looked into her blue eyes and at her slightly tanned skin and long blonde hair.

"Well, I guess one drink won't hurt," he said as he poured himself a whiskey.

Bolders and Dean made it home, and the car let them out in the driveway. They walked up to the house, and Dean opened the door, walking inside followed by Bolders. They went to the living room and saw the ladies watching the TV very seriously. Loretta was standing behind the admiral's recliner with her elbows on the back of it, her hands over her mouth and nose. Tanya leaned over the back of the sofa with her right hand over her mouth. Stanley could see they were watching the news and saw police cars on the TV but didn't pay attention to what it was.

Stanley said jokingly as he walked toward Loretta, "You ladies act like someone died."

She turned around and grabbed him, hugging him tightly. Tanya turned and fell into Bolders's arms, crying and holding him tightly as well.

"What in the world is going on?" Stanley asked, looking at Loretta and then at the TV.

Tanya, with her head resting on Bolders's right side, looked at her dad. "You know Joey at St. John's bar," she said, with her right hand now on Bolders's chest. She then looked at Mathew. "You wouldn't know him, babe, but we've known him for years."

Stanley looked at Loretta and then at Tanya. "What happened?" he asked, looking at both ladies.

Loretta told him, "All we've heard is that someone killed him inside the bar," she said, looking up at Stanley.

"Are you sure it was him?" Bolders asked. "The admiral and I just saw him no more than about twenty minutes ago."

"Yeah, it's got to be some kind of mistake."

Then the house phone rang. Stanley answered it, and everyone listened to him talking.

"And you have a positive identification on the body, and you're sure it's bartender Joey?"

They saw him listening to the other party over the phone.

"Me and my future son-in-law both saw him no more than a half hour ago."

He listened again, then answered, "We would be more than glad to answer any questions," he told them. "I'm at home." He listened again, then said, "We'll be here waiting; come on by." He then hung up the phone.

Loretta looked at Stanley and asked, "Do we have time to eat before they get here, honey?"

"I would say so," Stanley replied, and they sat down at the table.

Just as Tanya started to take the meatloaf out of the oven, the doorbell rang.

"Close the oven, T," Loretta said to her daughter as Stanley went to answer the door.

"Mat, son," Bolders heard the admiral call, "could you come into the living room?"

Bolders walked into the living room, where two FBI agents, one marine MP, and CID detectives stood.

The admiral looked at them and asked, "Do you need to ask us questions separately or together?"

"We can ask you together, sir; that's not a problem," the CID detective told the admiral.

One of the FBI agents spoke up. "I would rather we question them separately," he said.

The agent looked at Dean. "Nothing against you, Admiral, but it's better we do it right the first time."

"Don't explain, I completely understand, and my family wants the person who did this caught."

One FBI agent and one CID detective went with each of the

men. They let the admiral stay in the living room while they questioned him. The other two took Bolders outside on the patio, and Tanya followed them. They sat down on the soft pillowed patio furniture, with Bolders sitting on the love seat and Tanya beside him.

"Before we get started, may I ask what relation you are to Captain Bolders, ma'am?" the FBI agent asked Tanya.

"I am his fiancée," she quickly answered. Then she asked, "Is there a problem with me being here?"

"No, ma'am, not unless he has a problem with it," the agent said, looking at Bolders.

"I don't have any problem with it, sir," Bolders told the agent.

The first question came from the detective, "Captain, the admiral said that you and he had seen the bartender earlier?"

"Yes, twenty or thirty minutes before we walked in the house and were told by Tanya and her mom what happened."

The agent then asked, "How long had you known the bartender before today?"

"I just met him today for the first time," Bolders answered quickly.

"Did you notice anything out of the ordinary while you were in there?" the agent asked.

"Not really, or at least not with him," Bolders told them. "He actually seemed like a really good guy."

The detective then asked, "You said at least not with him; what did you mean by that?"

"This woman came in and sat down by me, trying to strike up a conversation."

The detective asked, "Captain, can you describe this woman to us?"

"Sure," Bolders replied, "dark eyes, long dark almost black hair, about five seven, slim, very pretty."

"Was it your first time seeing this woman, Captain?" the agent asked.

"No, sir, she looked like a woman that hit on me once in Hawaii before I left," Bolders answered.

"But you're not sure, is that what you're saying?" the detective asked.

"That is correct, sir," Bolders replied, and then neither one said anything for about twenty seconds.

The detective looked at Bolders and asked, "What were you doing in there, Captain?"

"My future father-in-law had to go to his office and gave me a choice of going with him or to the bar."

"You didn't want to go with the admiral, Captain?" the agent asked.

"He said that the bar had great onion rings, and I love onion rings, so I went."

The agent and the detective looked at Bolders for a few seconds. "Can you think of anything else, anything at all, no matter if it seems important or not?"

He looked at Tanya, then at the detective. "She didn't finish her drink," Bolders said.

"I don't understand, Captain," the agent said.

"She ordered a whiskey and a draft beer," Bolders explained. "She only took one drink of the beer then left."

"What was so strange about that, Captain?" the agent asked.

"When you order a beer, you usually drink more than a sip, right?" Bolders asked. "Then she gave him a fifty-dollar bill before she left."

"We don't have anything else, Captain, and we do appreciate your time. And congratulations on your engagement. We hope you both will be very happy."

Bolders then asked, "Do I need to stay around or something?"

The agent gave a small laugh. "You and the admiral are not suspects."

"Sir," Bolders said as they started to walk away. Both men turned, and the agent asked, "Did you think of something else?"

"No," Bolders answered. "I don't know if I'm allowed to ask or not, but how did he die?"

The detective replied, "We haven't seen the body yet."

"I don't mind telling you, but you may want to leave, ma'am; it's not very good," the detective told Tanya.

"I want to know also," she said.

The detective told them, "His neck was broken, and his heart removed from his body."

"Oh my God," Tanya said, turning her head and covering her face with both hands, burying her head into Mathew's chest.

Everyone left, and Tanya and Bolders were still sitting outside on the love seat.

Tanya dried her eyes and turned to Bolders, bending her left leg and placing it in the seat.

"Was that the same woman that you had seen before, Mathew?" she asked as she sniffled.

"Yeah, it was, and she was trying to warn me about you and your parents," Mathew told her.

"I love you, Mat, and thank you for telling me," she said, placing her right hand on his cheek and giving him a quick kiss. She wiped her eyes and got up, saying to Bolders, "Let's go eat, Mathew."

They went back in and saw Stanley and Loretta sitting on the sofa.

"Did you both hear what happened to him?" Tanya asked her parents.

"He told us," her father said.

Then her mother added, "How can a person do that to another?"

Tanya then said, "I hope they pay for what they have done," she said, her voice quivering with anger.

Loretta then said, "He was such a nice young man and never met a stranger, I think."

The admiral then stood up from the sofa. "Well, let's eat," he said as he started walking toward the table.

Bolders followed him to the table, and they sat down. Tanya got the meatloaf out of the oven, and Loretta set a dishcloth down for her to set the hot dish on. Loretta got the cream potatoes off the stove and set them on the table as well. Tanya and Loretta fixed the men's plates and then sat down without making themselves a plate.

"You aren't going to eat, honey?" Mathew asked Tanya.

She pushed the plate away. "I'm not hungry, just thinking about what they did to poor Joey," Tanya said.

Loretta, trying to brighten up the mood just a little, said, "On a better note, T found a couple of houses to look at tomorrow."

The men ate, and Tanya picked at Mathew's plate with a fork, eating very little. The women put all the leftovers away in containers and placed them in the refrigerator.

"Well, I'm going to bed," Tanya said, kissing her mother on her cheek and her father on his forehead.

Mathew followed her to bed, and they lay in bed staring at the ceiling for a while.

"I understand if you find other women more attractive than me, babe," Tanya told Mathew as she stared at the ceiling.

"What?" he said in a surprised voice. "Honey, there is no one as attractive as you." He turned his head toward Tanya.

She then turned on her left side, saying, "I love you so much, Mathew." She leaned over and kissed him, then partially put her body on his.

"Your parents are in the other room," he told her.

She pulled the cover over their heads.

The next morning, Bolders woke up, turning onto his right side with his eyes still closed.

He took a deep breath and smiled. "I love you." And he stretched out his left hand to put around her.

He opened his eyes and raised his head a little, seeing that she wasn't in bed. He got up and saw his clothes were laying on the dresser. He took a shower, got dressed, and went into the living room, seeing them outside with the little firepit going. Tanya saw him and walked in as he was getting a coffee cup off the rack.

She got him a BLT out of the microwave. "Mom made this for you, babe," and they walked outside.

Tanya curled up to Mathew by the firepit as he ate his sandwich, talking to the admiral. They all got up and met the real estate agent, looking at five homes.

As they were leaving the last home, Tanya asked, "Mat, babe, which one do you like?"

The second one they looked at was a three-bedroom, three-bath, and he knew Tanya loved that one.

"I like the second one," he told her, smiling.

She then told him, "You're saying that because that's the one I like."

"I am because it makes you happy, and when you're happy, I'm happy, sweetheart," Mathew told her.

Two months had passed, and Tanya and her mother were busy painting the house to the color she wanted. Bolders and her father would help when they had time because they were busy trying to get the fleet ready.

CHAPTER 23

MEANWHILE, at Norfolk Naval Base, Captain Malcolm Pettus was in his office going over paperwork.

The intercom on his desk beeped, and he pressed the answer button. "What is it?" he said in an unfriendly voice to his receptionist in the lobby of his office.

"There are three gentlemen here who want to see you, sir," she told him.

"Do I have an appointment with them?" he asked.

"No, sir," she replied. "They're nonmilitary, Captain Pettus."

"Tell them to make an appointment because I have no time to deal with civilian matters right now."

About two minutes later, the intercom buzzer went off again.

"What is it this time, Ensign Morris?" Pettus answered very rudely.

A male's voice came over the intercom this time. "The prince requests an audience with you, Captain."

Pettus sat there for a minute, staring at the intercom, then leaned forward, stretching out his left hand to press the talk button. Just before his finger touched the button, his office door opened, and there stood three large men.

A blonde-haired man with curly hair down to his shoulders spoke up as the other two came in and had a seat.

"You need to apologize for being so rude, Captain," he said as he stood by the door.

"Yeah, yeah, okay, just close the door; I will later," Pettus told the man.

The large blonde-haired man walked up to Pettus and grabbed him by the neck, lifting him out of the chair onto his feet.

"The prince wants you to apologize now," the man said, getting right up in Pettus's face. He then released his left hand from the captain's throat and pushed him back down in his chair.

Pettus took his right hand and rubbed his throat where the man had been squeezing it. The man walked to Pettus's office door, opened it, and turned to look at the captain. Pettus got up from his chair and walked just inside the doorway where he could see the receptionist.

He made sure that she could see him as well and said, "Ensign Morris, I am very sorry for acting rude to you."

The ensign nodded her head and said, "Thank you, Captain."

Pettus walked back into his office, where the two men were sitting and the third remained standing. The third man stood by the door, watching Pettus until he sat back down. Once Pettus sat down at his desk, the man walked out of the office into the waiting room and closed the door. Pettus looked at the one man sitting to his left that he had never seen before. The captain got up and walked around the table, and the man never looked at him. However, the second man watched every step Pettus took until he stopped at the first man.

The captain held out his right hand to shake the first man's hand. The man sitting beside him got up and placed his left hand on Pettus.

"The father will not touch you, or you will never touch him," he said. Pettus looked at the man as he turned his head to look at the captain.

He stood up, towering over Pettus. "Malcolm, I never have to come visit people in person. You asked me for a favor, and I did it for you, and you knew what the price was," the man told Pettus. "However, you have yet to get me what I want, Pettus."

Pettus started to say something, and the man called father put his left finger up to his lips, saying shh to him.

He leaned his head forward to within inches of Pettus's face. "Malcolm, if you can't get me what you promised, then I'll see you again." He then whispered in a low growling voice that sent chills down Pettus's spine. "If you do see me again, Malcolm, it will mean I don't need you anymore."

The man called father and the man with him walked to the door, and the captain ran ahead to open it. When Pettus opened the door, there was the blonde man sitting on the front of the desk, talking to the ensign, and they were laughing.

He got up and gave the ensign a card, telling her, "I would really like to take you out tonight."

The ensign smiled, taking the card from the man. "If I don't have to work late, I would love to."

The blonde man looked at her. "I don't think you'll have to. He might even give you tomorrow off."

Pettus started walking back into his office and looked at the ensign. "Go ahead and take the rest of the day off."

Back in California, Bolders was just walking off the USS Midway—the ship he had chosen for his flagship.

Taylor was walking beside Bolders as they walked down the

dock to the end. "Can you believe how the navy hid this? I mean, all of this," he said, swinging his right hand around.

"Yeah, it's pretty impressive how they have managed to keep the real reason a secret," Bolders replied.

They reached the end of the dock, and Bolders stopped and looked at Taylor. "You know, Will, I still lay in bed and wonder sometimes if this floating museum is the real reason for this."

"What do you mean?" Taylor asked in a puzzled voice.

Bolders looked out at the fleet. "All of this firepower, I just wonder if they know something we don't yet."

Their ride had arrived, and the driver told Bolders that the admiral needed to see him and his XO in his office. The driver took them straight to the admiral's office and dropped them off.

As they walked into the office of Admiral Dean, the receptionist immediately rose from her seat. "Captain Bolders, the admiral is expecting you," she said and went and opened his office door.

Bolders and Taylor looked at each other with Taylor shrugging his shoulders and lifting his eyebrows. The two men walked into the office and saw Admiral Dean sitting on the front of his desk. They also saw Admiral Riley and his wife Sara sitting there laughing, talking, and having coffee. The receptionist closed the door behind them as they walked in.

"Come on in, Captain, Commander, won't keep you long. Admiral Riley and Sara just wanted to say hello."

"What in the world are you all doing here?" Bolders asked Riley and his wife.

"I had to see this historical fleet for myself," Riley told Bolders. "So you picked the USS Midway Rock'n Roll carrier as your flag-ship?" Riley said, smiling at Bolders.

"Okay," Dean told his future son-in-law, "you need to go get my daughter and get back here for dinner."

"Yes, sir," Bolders said as he and Taylor both exited the office.

About thirty minutes later, Bolders pulled up in his driveway and saw a strange car and also Mrs. Dean's SUV in the driveway. He knew that the admiral said that Tanya and he were coming to his house for dinner. He didn't understand why Mrs. Dean was here and immediately thought something was wrong. He hurried into the house, knowing that Tanya had been sick the past couple of days. He rushed into the house and saw his mama and daddy also there, and then he really got worried.

He didn't see Tanya as he looked around and then asked his mama, "Where's Tanya?"

Mrs. Bolders turned sideways in her chair, took her left hand, and pulled out the chair next to her. "Mat, son, come sit by me and let us talk to you for a minute," Doris, his mother, told him.

He got really defensive at that time, thinking something was wrong with her. "Where is she, Mamma?" Bolders asked in a voice that was a little panicked.

He knew she had been sick for a couple of days, but they assumed it was a virus.

Loretta looked at Bolders and said, "Mathew, honey, just come and sit down for one minute, okay?"

He walked over and hesitantly sat down in the chair, looking at his mamma and then Loretta.

"It's nothing that bad, sweetie," his mamma told him. "She just has a condition right now."

He noticed that they were starting to smile a little bit.

"This is a joke, right?" Bolders said. He then added, "Where is she?"

"She is in the bathroom right now, Mat, but it's best you don't go in there yet," Loretta told him.

"Why?" he asked with a small smile on his face.

"She has a condition, and she loves you, just not right now, baby," his mamma told him.

"What kind of condition is it? What does she have?" Bolders asked.

His mamma put her left hand on his right shoulder and told him, "She is expecting, honey."

He looked at her, processing the information, and asked, "Expecting?"

"Mathew, sweetie, look at me for a minute," Loretta told him. She watched as he looked at her. "She's pregnant, baby," Loretta told him, and a smile spread from ear to ear on his face.

"Really?" he asked excitedly, watching both women smile and nod. As he was rising from the chair, he stopped. "How long have you known?" he asked with genuine curiosity.

"Honey,"—Loretta looked at him, laughing now—"we just found out today."

He was so excited; he was confused and ran to the bedroom. He saw her lying on the bed with no covers and barefoot with her legs curled up as she lay on her left side. He reached for the multicolored throw folded at the foot of the bed. He picked it up, holding it up so it would unfold. He walked in front of her softly and gently laid it over her.

She never opened her eyes but said, "Mat, lay down beside me, babe?" She was on the edge of the bed and moved a little more to the center.

He saw her scoot over enough to allow him room to lie down beside her.

Mathew lay down, smiling really big, putting his right arm around her as they faced each other. She snuggled her head into his chest then pulled back, looking at him laughing.

"What is it, sweetheart?" Mathew asked her as she was laughing really hard.

"You need to shower like now, babe. You smell really bad."

He got up, smelling his left underarm but trying to be unnoticeable.

Tanya laughed really hard as she sat up in bed saying, "Trust me, babe, you stink." She came out of the bedroom and walked to the dining room where her mother and her future mother-in-law were sitting.

"You weren't too hard on him, were you, honey?" Loretta asked her daughter.

"I can't do that to him," Tanya told her. "He is trying to be extra careful," she said, laughing.

Loretta looked at her daughter and said, "Doris and I were talking and wanted to run something by you."

Tanya turned around, looking at her mom and Doris. "I'm listening," she said.

"Well, now that you're expecting, what about moving up the wedding by a few months?" Loretta asked.

"I'll talk to Mat about it," she told her mother.

At that time, Bolders came into the room.

"Talk to me about what, sweetheart?" Mathew asked.

Loretta's phone rang, which she had lying in front of her on the table. She picked it up with her right hand and looked at the caller ID.

She looked at Tanya. "It's your father," Loretta said as she answered it. "Yes, Mr. Admiral, sir," she said, winking at Doris. "How can I help you?" She burst out laughing at whatever he said, then she added, "We're having dinner here tonight. Then go shower, get the steaks, and get over here." She listened for a moment then spoke up, "You tell Nicholas and Sara they had better come with you. Hey, honey," she said quickly to catch him before he hung up, "your daughter and Mat have big news for you."

Mathew walked over to Tanya, standing by the stove, boiling tea to help her stomach. He put his arms around her stomach, standing behind her, and rested his forehead on the back of her head. He then moved his left hand up, pulling the hair from the left side of her neck, and kissed it. She cut her eyes at him, moving her head to the left, causing his head to move away from hers.

"Mathew Bolders," she said, turning her head as far as possible to the left, "don't you think you've done enough so far, babe." She smiled at him.

He put his mouth up to her ear. "I don't think I've done quite enough yet."

She swayed her body to the left, slightly turning in the same direction. "I think you've done more than enough for now, babe," she said, then kissed him quickly, smiling.

CHAPTER 24

THEY ALL SAT down at the table. Bolders, Doris, and Loretta were drinking coffee, and Tanya was drinking her tea.

They were talking about the wedding, and then Tanya spoke up, "Where else would we have it? I got the only open date for the Gardens for the next two years."

About that time, Dean, Riley, and Sara came in with Stanley, saying, "Steaks in the house," while holding up a platter.

"Babe, you want to get those and take them out to the grill?" Tanya asked Mathew.

He took the platter from Dean and put it on the grill counter outside by the pool. Bolders started coming back in, and Tanya held out her left hand for Bolders to take. He walked up, taking her left hand with his left and stood behind her, putting his right hand on her shoulder.

"So what did everyone have to tell me that you had me come over and use your grill instead of mine?"

Doris and Loretta started to try to explain to Dean what was going on.

Tanya could see this was going nowhere and just cut in. "We are moving up the wedding, Dad."

Everyone looked at the admiral because he pulled so many strings to get her the wedding at the Garden. It was the dream wedding she had always wanted, and he made it happen.

He asked them, "Why the emergency all of a sudden to change the date? I thought you were going to wait till Mat got back from his first tour before you got married."

"Well, Dad, in a way, it would be best for me and the baby to do it quickly," she told her dad. She looked right at him after saying it, thinking he would get it.

"Look, I don't know where your two heads are, but I just can't snap my fingers." Then he stopped. He looked at Bolders then at Tanya. "Did you say baby?" he asked her as a smile got bigger and bigger.

"Yes, Dad, you're going to be a grandfather," she told him, smiling.

He bent over, crying and hugging her tightly. "I love you, baby girl," he said, his voice choked with emotion, and just held her for a few minutes. He then rose up, his eyes shimmering with tears of happiness, and shook Mathew's right hand, putting his left arm around his neck, hugging him tightly.

He then looked at Riley, his face beaming with pride. "I'm going to be a grandfather; how about that?" he said with a broad smile. "So now you have to find a new wedding venue?" Dean said, still grinning from ear to ear. He then added, "How long do we have?"

Tanya looked at Bolders for an answer, and she saw him shrug his shoulders. "Oh, you're a real big help," Tanya told him, looking back at her dad.

Dean looked at his wife, Loretta, then back at his daughter. "We'll start working on it in the morning," he said. "We only have two weeks before the fleet pulls out, so we need to do it before then."

"You have a test run on the Midway tomorrow, right?" Dean asked Bolders.

"Yes, sir, zero eight hundred out the gate (port) and back by fifteen hundred," Bolders explained.

Admiral Riley then spoke up, "I can take the Midway out in the morning if the captain is needed here," he told everyone.

Stanley replied, "No, but thank you, Nick [Riley]. Mathew needs to take it out."

Bolders, still standing on Tanya's left side, placed his right hand on her left shoulder.

Still sitting at the table, she looked up at her fiancé and saw his eyebrows raised and heard him say, "I've got an idea."

She looked up at him and raised her left pointing finger in the air. "No, Mathew Bolders."

He started to say something else, and everyone watched her tell him again, "No, Mat, and I mean it."

Her dad then spoke up and asked her, "What are you saying no to, sweetheart? You may know him well enough to know what he is about to say, but we don't," Dean added.

Tanya looked at her father. "He wants to have the wedding on that ship," she said as she looked back at Bolders.

Mathew started to say something else, and she said in a very angry voice, "No, and I mean it, Mathew."

Dean said to his daughter, "That really isn't a bad idea, baby, you got the room to do whatever you want to do."

Bolders spoke up, "Just go look at it, honey, that's all I ask."

"We will postpone the test for a couple of days to give you time to go on board and look," her father told her.

The ladies then went to the patio to start putting the steaks and potatoes on the grill.

Back in Virginia at Norfolk Naval Station, Ensign Morris was standing outside waiting on a base bus. She pulled out the card that the blonde man gave her and dialed the number on it. She told the man where she lived on base and that she would sign him in at the front gate. After she went to the front gate, she went back to her apartment. Morris had been in her apartment for about thirty minutes and had just gotten out of the shower when her doorbell rang. With her towel wrapped around her, she went to answer it.

She cracked the door with the chain still attached to it. "Can I help you?" she asked the person at the door.

"Your Amanda Morris?" the voice said.

She replied, "Sorry, I don't know you."

As she closed the door and started walking back to the bathroom, she turned around all at once and screamed very, very loudly. Her scream was so loud that her neighbors on both sides and across the hall heard it. They called the base police and gathered outside her door. It didn't take long for the MPs to show up, and they got billeting to meet them at the room. The lady from billeting opened the door, and the chain was still attached. The MP broke it, and three officers went inside, finding her in the bathroom. Her body was laid out in the bathroom with her neck broken and a hole in her chest where her heart once was.

The next morning, Doris, Albert, and Tanya were sitting at the table drinking coffee, and Tanya was drinking her tea. Mathew walked out of the bedroom and saw everyone already dressed and looking ready to go. Bolders walked by Tanya, giving her a kiss on the forehead as he went to fix his coffee.

She turned and looked at him as he sat beside her. "That better not be my morning kiss, mister."

He laughed and leaned over to her, kissed her softly on the lips, and said, "No, that's the morning kiss. You all look like we're going somewhere," he said as he looked at everyone. "I thought we were taking today off since I don't have the test run for a few days."

"Dad wanted us to come in, so the ladies and your dad are going onboard the carrier to look around."

They all left for the base, and upon arriving, a car picked everyone up and took them to the Midway. A separate car took Bolders to the admiral's office, stopping outside. Bolders walked in.

He went into the admiral's office where he saw Marine MPs everywhere.

Dean held his hand up. "Captain Bolders," he said, "come in here, please. These officers want to ask you a couple of questions about Norfolk." Mathew went in and sat down with Riley and Dean, along with two other MPs.

"Congratulations, Captain, and we will let you get to your fiancé pretty quick. Do you remember a Ms. Amanda Morris at Norfolk Naval Base?" one of the officers asked him.

"That name doesn't ring a bell," he told the officers while shaking his head.

"Are you sure you don't remember the name, Captain Bolders?" the officer asked again.

"I really don't; I'm sorry; maybe if I could see or talk to her, I may remember her," he told the MPs.

The officer who had been the quietest asked Bolders, "Captain, did you go into Captain Pettus's office much?"

"A few times, not a lot," Bolders told him. "Why would you ask about Pettus?"

"Do you remember the young lady who worked in his office as the receptionist?"

"Yeah, I remember her, a very nice girl, but Pettus always treated her like crap. Why do you ask about her?" Bolders added.

"She was found dead in her apartment last night, with her neck broken and her heart ripped out of her chest."

Bolders, with a shocked look on his face, said, "That's the exact same thing that happened to the bartender, Joey."

"Did you see her around base with other people much?" the officer asked the captain.

"I really didn't see much of anyone when I was off," Bolders told them. "I was there three to four days after docking and the same before departing; the rest of my time was in Arkansas with my parents. I will tell you, though, that from the few times I met her, she seemed to be one of the nicest people on base," Bolders told them.

"You still have friends at the base, don't you?" one MP asked the captain.

"I still have a very few there, but not many," Bolders told the MP.

"If you hear of anything, direct or indirect, please call," the officer said and held out a card for him.

Bolders replied in a courteous way, "I still have one from before."

Bolders looked at Dean and Riley. "I thought they caught the guys that killed Joey."

Dean, looking at Riley and Bolders, said as he rose from his seat, "Let's go meet the ladies."

The three men went to the Midway where Tanya and the others were all over the ship, looking and getting ideas. Bolders and the two admirals were standing on the edge of the flight deck, talking and looking at the dock.

Bolders heard a voice come up behind them. "This ship is unbelievably huge."

Dean turned his head as far as he could to the right without turning his body, looking at Nelson.

"Master Chief, you haven't seen our wives, have you?" the admiral asked him.

"I just got an update from their security team saying they were on their way back up to the flight deck."

Riley laughed. "They have their own security team with them?" he asked.

"Yes, sir, Lieutenant Commander Manners is being called the first lady, and I couldn't keep a team away from her after what's been going on."

At that time, they saw the ladies and Albert with nine security officers.

"Good Lord," Dean said, looking at the team guarding them, "I don't think we have to worry about them."

"As I said, sir, no one gets close to the Lieutenant Commander or anyone in her party."

Bolders shook his head, smiling, as Tanya got closer to him.

Tanya, grinning from ear to ear, looked at Mathew. "What, Mr. Bolders?"

Mathew looked at her, smiling. "You are eating this up, aren't you?" he told her as she walked into his arms.

"Okay, guys, we've got it from here," Bolders told the security team.

Chief Styles stepped forward. "If it would be okay with the captain, sir, we would like to stay with the commander till she gets in her car, sir."

Nelson looked at Dean, saying, "Admiral, those guys are being called the first lady's mafia."

Tanya was very happy and excited about having the wedding after a few dozen women sailors helped with ideas for the wedding.

Dean and Riley stayed on base because it was getting late. Tanya and Bolders' parents had ridden with Tanya's mother to the base earlier. On the way home, it was just Tanya, Mathew, and his parents in the car.

Just as they were pulling in the driveway, Bolders' phone rang.

"Hello," he answered. "Okay, I'll be on my way; give me about thirty mikes [minutes], and I'll be there."

Tanya crossed her arms, looking at Mathew. "Was that my father?" she asked in a very unhappy tone.

"No, it was Nelson," he told her. "Something happened, and I've got to go back to base for a while."

Bolders made sure that they got in the house safely, and then he left again to go back to the base. Bolders arrived at the base and parked his car right inside the entry gate after he checked in. He got out of his car and walked to the back, leaning back on the trunk with his arms crossed over his chest. A pair of marine MPs that were driving through the small parking lot stopped where Bolders was.

The MP let down his window and put his bent arm on the door. "Everything alright, Captain?" he asked Bolders.

"Yeah, thank you, guys, just waiting on someone to come pick me up," he told the MPs.

The two marines drove off, and shortly after, a car pulled up with two sailors in the front seat. The one on the passenger side got out and opened the back door for Bolders.

As Bolders got into the car, the sailor said, "Sorry, we weren't here when you arrived, sir."

They pulled out of the parking lot, and Bolders told the driver, "I forgot something in my car." The driver turned the car around.

It had been about an hour, and Bolders's mom and Tanya were sitting on the sofa, watching a hospital show on TV.

"I want some ice cream," Tanya said. With her left leg curled under her, she leaned forward, picking her phone up from the coffee table.

She had it on speaker as she called Mathew, but the phone just rang and rang. She tried two more times with no answer.

"That man of mine," she said, "probably has the sound off."

THE FINAL BATTLE

Knowing he was meeting Nelson, she pressed another contact on her phone.

She looked at Doris. "I'll call Nelson. At least, he'll answer his phone."

"Hello," she heard Nelson say on the other end of the phone.

"I'm sorry to call you, Kevin, but can you tell Mat to turn his phone on?"

Kevin came back with a hesitant and somewhat confused voice. "Tanya, I haven't seen or spoken to Mat since we left you and him at the car leaving the base."

Tanya looked at her future mother-in-law and asked Nelson, "You didn't call Mathew?"

Nelson could tell she was getting panicked by her voice and said, "Just calm down, and tell me what was said."

Tanya then told him, "They must have sounded like you, Kevin." Her panic was growing. "Tanya, calm down."

"Where did he go, or did he say?" Nelson asked her.

"He was going to meet you at the base," she answered. "He said something happened on base."

"Tanya, just stay there, and I'll find him; just stay there." He hung up the phone with Tanya and got dressed quickly.

He dialed the front gate to the base and gave his security code. He then asked the marine, "Have you seen Captain Bolders come through the gate?"

"Yes, Master Chief, about an hour ago he came through, and an MP patrol saw him being picked up."

"Did they see who picked him up, Sergeant?" Nelson asked.

"It was a standard government-issued car, Master Chief," the marine told him.

"Can you get that MP unit to meet me in the parking lot of St. Johns bar, Sergeant?"

"Will do, Master Chief."

247

Nelson then drove straight to the bar.

Meanwhile, the car that picked Bolders up had turned down a side road. The road ran down past St. Johns bar for about three miles. It was a gravel road that ended at a deserted part of a beach, marked as "authorized personnel only."

Bolders tried to get out of the car, but the childproof locks had been switched on.

The man in the passenger front seat turned and said to Bolders, "Captain, trust me, no one will hurt you." He then held up a Taser. "However, if you don't calm down, I will use this."

They pulled up on the beach, and the men got out of the car and walked away.

"Where are you going?" Bolders yelled to the two sailors who were walking down the beach away from him.

He couldn't get into the front seat because of the bulletproof glass that separated the front from the back. He then laid down on his back on the seat and started to kick the door with his feet. The sailors had parked the car with the front tires halfway in the water. The tide would be rising soon, and there was a good chance that the car would be carried out with it. Bolders raised up and saw three figures in the distance walking toward him. They were too far away at the moment to make out, but they were getting closer. As they got closer, he could see it was the same black-haired woman from St. John's bar and Hawaii.

"Oh shit, this can't be good," he said aloud to himself as they got closer.

They stopped at the car and waited as he could see the water almost up to his door now. He saw the woman look at the man to her left and say something to him. The towering man started to walk toward the car. He reached the car door where water was starting to seep in through the door seals into the floorboard. He reached out his arm and opened the door after looking back at the woman for approval. The large man took Bolders' right hand, twisting it behind him. He then took his left arm, placing it around the captain's neck, holding it tightly. He started to walk Bolders up to where the woman was standing and stood in front of her. It was getting a little hard for Bolders to breathe as the man's grip on his neck tightened.

The dark-haired woman put her face right up to his and kissed him, then backed away. The man relaxed his grip a little so the captain could breathe better. She spoke in a foreign language that was like nothing he had ever heard. The man then released his grip from around Bolders' neck, forcing him to his knees. The man backed away but stayed behind him. The woman, standing about five feet from the captain, squatted down to eye level with Bolders.

"I tried to warn you about those people you're associating with and to stay away from them. You had your chance, and now that chance has passed," she said as she rose. She walked over to him, taking her right thumb and wiping away her lipstick from the left corner of his lips. "Shame, I didn't get to you before her. Should have, could have, would have," she said, smiling.

She then turned and looked at the larger man, telling him, "Do it."

He walked over to Bolders, lifting him to his feet with just one hand. They stopped, and all looked to their right behind them, as did Bolders. He hadn't heard anything, but he looked to see what they were looking at. He couldn't make it out, but he saw it was another large figure. He kicked the man in front of him hard between the legs.

The man fell to his knees with a deep groan as Bolders said, "No matter how big you are, that hurts." He looked up to see the woman swinging at him, and everything went dark.

"Mat, Mat, wake up" was the next thing he heard as he was coming to. He opened his eyes, trying to see who was there, but everything was blurry.

He felt a hand go under his neck and lift him into a sitting position. As his sight started to clear a little, he could see Nelson, Taylor, and Chief Walters (chief engineer). Bolders started to try to get up but was still out of it and fell back on his butt.

"Doc," Nelson called out, and Phillips came over, and Walters stood up to make way for the medic. The doc looked him over for a few minutes and then looked at Nelson, who was right across from him.

"He's going to be good after a day or two's rest," Phillips told Nelson.

They helped him up, and he saw the ship's security team along with Walters and some of his engine room people. He saw some of the cooks and galley personnel, all armed and securing a perimeter around the captain.

"Wow," Bolders said, "I've never seen those guys even hold a firearm," talking about the galley personnel. "They look downright scary," he added, making everyone laugh.

"You have a woman at home who is worried to death about you," Nelson told him. "What do you say we get you home to her?"

Nelson then looked at Walter. "Chief, you can get everyone back to the ship; me and the team will take it from here."

Taylor got on the other side of Bolders, telling Nelson, "I'm going with you."

They got in a black SUV, with one out in front and two more following behind. When they pulled up to the gate, the escort SUV sat there for about two minutes. They pulled up and over to the right side, waiting on the other vehicles to come through. When Bolders's SUV came through and pulled in behind, a team member was standing there. He walked up to the passenger side's back door where Taylor was sitting.

"Commander," the team member said, "we found the captain's phone, sir." He handed it to him.

As they were about two houses away, Bolders could see that Admiral Dean was also at his house.

They pulled up in the driveway, and the other three escorts parked on the side in front of the house. The team member driving got out of the car, and so did Taylor, sitting behind him. Nelson got out of the passenger side, and so did Bolders, and they started walking up to the house.

Tanya was standing up, pacing back and forth from the front window back to the table where everyone was.

"Honey, sit down. I'm sure everything is okay," her mother told her.

She stopped, turned, set her tea on the table, and took off running for the front door. She heard a car door slam and was on the front porch before anyone else could even get up.

She screamed, "Mat!" as she ran to him, wrapping her arms around him.

Tanya made him some iced tea and sat down beside him, rubbing her hands over the side of his head.

The next morning, there was a meeting that included the heads of departments on the base.

The meeting began with, "There have been things that have happened on our base. This is not only a place of work or a place where we gather to plan the defense of our country. This base is our home; it is where our family and our friends are. This is where some of us come to church and worship at the base church with our Christian family." The meeting ended with the admiral saying, "Let us look out for our military brothers and sisters. Let us look out for their families, let us keep them safe because keeping them safe helps us keep our country safe. I want to end this meeting with a prayer if I could. I know all of you don't believe, and if you want to leave now, I promise no one will ever say anything to you about it."

A few people got up and walked out, and no one gave them a

second look. Bolders got very squirmy in his chair, but he didn't get up and walk out.

The admiral then bowed his head and started to pray. "Dear Lord God, bless all those who remained sitting in this room who are believers in you, Christ. Bless those who got up and walked out of this room, and we pray for them. Bless our families, O Lord, bless our military brothers and sisters. Bless our contractor brothers and sisters who stand beside us in peace and in war and their families. Keep all of us safe, and, God, bless our country, our military, and those who serve it with us; in Jesus' name we pray, amen. Oh, one more thing, my daughter's wedding to this guy up here," he said as he pointed to Bolders sitting in the front row.

A lot of people had already seen the wedding gift list that was posted at certain places around the base.

"Having said that, I want all of you to give my future son-in-law a gift of prayer."

Everyone looked up, very curious about what else he was going to add.

"Please pray that God has mercy on him and doesn't let my daughter harm this young man. And please also pray that he gets this fleet out of the base port in one piece."

Bolders was mesmerized by her beauty and looked at his father, saying, "I can't believe I am so lucky."

There were all kinds of oohs and aahs from her beauty. She made it to the altar with her father, and he gave her to Bolders. Dean then walked over to Bolders's side, being the second best man. Bolders took Tanya's hands, looked into her eyes, and cleared his throat before saying his vows. He didn't have to read his vows from the paper because every word was in his heart.

"Tanya Dean Manners, I fell in love with you the first time I ever saw you. The first time we kissed, my heart exploded; that's the only way to describe the way I felt. Tanya, you are the woman I want to spend the rest of my life with and raise our kids with. I promise for as long as I live that I won't ever make you regret loving me."

Then Tanya started with hers. "I have never experienced a love like this other than for God. My heart aches for you when you're away; it's happy when you're near and falls to pieces when you're hurt. I promise I will love you, with God only being above you. I promise you that our love will be a love to outlast time. Mathew Bolders, I love you."

The pastor had them say the I dos, and then rings were exchanged. Then they kissed, and the pastor and parents finally had to step in, saying it was enough. They went to Paris, France, for their honeymoon and spent a glorious week.

When they got back to Breakaway Base in Los Angeles, Bolders only had two days to get ready. Doris and Albert said they were going to stay a few days with Tanya after he left. The day of departure came, and Tanya, along with their families, went to see him off. There were four carriers, four battleships, four light cruisers, and two heavy ones, along with seventeen old and new destroyers. It took only a couple of hours to get them out to sea and in formation. Onboard the Midway, on the bridge, Bolders and Taylor were standing, looking out the window.

Bolders turned his head right, looking at Taylor, who was standing about two feet away. "Will," he said to Taylor, "get me the heads of all departments including the CAG, the air boss, yourself, and Nelson. Make sure everyone is there"—then he looked at his watch—"in three hours, which will be fourteen thirty."

The time came, and Bolders entered a galley using it as a temporary briefing room. Everyone stood up as the captain walked to the head and leaned against the first table.

"Can everyone hear me clearly?" he asked, and everyone's heads nodded. "First, let me say, welcome aboard the first fully operational floating museum fleet in history. Next, let me say, I have heard it being said that I am not a pilot. Let me tell you that is correct." Some of the people in the room laughed. "Others are asking why I am the captain of this carrier and this fleet despite not being a pilot. I also hear that I got this position because I am the admiral's son-in-law. Let me start with that one," Bolders said, folding his arms over his chest and looking around the room. "I was given this position before he even really knew me and have recommendations from two admirals and the president. I know when to jump into the fray and when to go around it; that's why I was chosen. The CAG and air boss, along with others who have served on carriers before, I will, from time to time, seek your advice.

"Now, just because this is a museum show fleet doesn't mean that we may not have to defend ourselves if the occasion ever arises. If it does arise, I want us to be ready to defend this ship and every other ship in this fleet. We will be running regular carrier operations while we are at sea so we don't get slack. Now, does anyone have anything to say or add?" Bolders asked. "I am all ears," he added. "Commander David Mumford, CAG, where are you, sir?" Bolders asked, speaking out into the crowd.

The officer stood up. "Right here, sir," he answered.

"Where is my air boss, Commander Richard Winters?" Bolders asked.

Another naval officer stood up.

"And Master Chief Nelson and my XO, if you could all remain behind, and the rest, you are dismissed. I look forward to getting to know each of you more," the captain added.

Everyone left the room, and just the few he had asked to stay behind remained.

"Everyone here knows your jobs, and you know them better than I do," Bolders said. "That is something that we can all agree on, right?"

Everyone in the room agreed with him as he looked at each one. "I am always open to suggestions and have an open-door policy; however, I expect everyone to go through the chain of command. We have five days of sailing time to our first stop at Pearl Harbor, Hawaii. I want us to drill until we get there, and we are still an American fleet, so we need to maintain fleet security. Okay, I am done now," Bolders told them. "Does anyone have anything to add?"

No one said anything, so he dismissed everyone and asked Taylor to stay. Everyone left the room.

Taylor stayed and walked up to Bolders. "Well, Captain, how are you liking it so far?" he asked, smiling.

"Ask me that same question in about another week, and I'll give you an answer," Bolders told him.

CHAPTER 25

"I was on a carrier for a year, and it's just like a town, Mat," Taylor said. "Everyone has an opinion about the mayor," he added. "Come on, and I'll buy you a cup of coffee, Mr. Mayor," Taylor told Bolders, laughing.

One and a half weeks had passed, and the fleet was getting ready to leave Hawaii. Bolders went over the radio with the ship's crew from the entire fleet.

"Everyone did an exceptional job; we got not one complaint," Bolders told all the ships. "Okay, I need to meet with the CAG and the air boss in my office," Bolders told Taylor.

Bolders was in his office when there was a knock on the door.

"Come in," Bolders said, seeing it was Mumford and Winters.

They came in and had a seat.

"We have orders, gentlemen, to support an evacuation of Devil's Island."

"Did something happen on the island, Winters?" asked the captain.

"All I know is that the lease on the island is up, and they want all military and church personnel off the island by tomorrow noon," Winters replied.

Mumford then said, "We will need helos for that, and we're too far away, Captain."

"I know, so we're going to put a couple of A-6s in the air along with a couple of Tomcats for air cover. The Air Force will be landing aircraft and evacuating personnel. This will be an around-the-clock operation, gentlemen, so let's show them that the old girl still has it."

As Mumford got up, he looked at Bolders. "Very impressive, Captain."

Winters added, "Yeah, good call, sir."

Six hours into the mission, the captain heard the A-6s talking to the E-2 Hawkeye radar plane from the bridge.

"There are multiple unidentified moving in on the evacuation point, A-6 one."

"A-6 one to mother (carrier), permission to check out force moving in on our guys."

The CIC responded, "Cleared for one thousand, A-6 one, be careful."

In about one minute, the bomber reported, "A-6 one to Midway, there are about a thousand moving in on them."

Bolders picked up the mic from the bridge, asking, "How far away from our guys are they, A-6 one?"

"Seven to eight hours, best estimate, your one," the A-6 replied.

"Get me the CAG up here now," Bolders told Taylor.

Mumford showed up on the bridge about ten minutes later.

"CAG, what would you suggest we do to try and get them to stop advancing?" Bolders asked.

Mumford started to respond, "What I would do is—"

Bolders stopped him, handing him the mic. "Do it, CAG."

"A-6 one, do a flyby at treetop level; try to scare the crap out of them," Mumford instructed.

"Roger that, CAG; A-6 one going back down," then said, "passing over now."

The E-2 Hawkeye came over the radio. "They have halted, Midway."

Twenty-four hours had passed, and the mission was finally completed, and everyone was taken off the island.

The next morning, twenty-nine hours from passing by Devil's Island, one of the CIC personnel called Lieutenant Commander Wayne Dillard, who was in charge of CIC.

"What do you have, Ensign?" Dillard asked.

"You need to hear this, sir," the ensign told Dillard as he turned the speaker on.

"Anyone out there? Please help us, please," a woman's voice said.

"How long has this been going on?" Dillard asked the ensign.

"Been hearing something during the rescue mission, but it was too much static, sir. Contacted a couple other ships, and they got the same, sir; just figured it was the crew on the island."

The voice came over the radio again pleading.

"Find out where the captain is right now," he told another crew member.

"On the bridge, sir," the female crew member responded.

"Tell him to stay there; I'm on my way," Dillard said. Then he told the ensign, "Don't lose that lady."

Dillard arrived on the bridge out of breath.

"Lieutenant Commander, you okay?" Bolders asked him, seeing him breathing hard.

"There is a woman on that island, sir; turn your radio to eight, sir."

"Is anyone out there? Please, God, send someone," the female's voice asked, crying.

Bolders stood there listening to her and looked around at everyone. They were all looking at him as if to say, "Are you going to answer her?"

"Contact every ship in this fleet and tell them no one is to answer that," Bolders ordered.

Everyone looked at him, but he was the captain, and they did so.

"We have to make sure this isn't something to lure some of us over there."

The first thing that went through his mind was the lady with the black hair. Then he thought, That's crazy; how would she even know or be this far out?

"Please help us. I've got two small children, if there is anyone out there," the woman's voice pleaded again.

Bolders walked away from the radio and over to his chair and sat down.

Dillard looked at him. "Captain, aren't you at least going to find out what's happening?"

Bolders put his right elbow on the arm of his chair and his hand over his mouth and chin.

The young lady came back over the radio begging. "Please, if there is anyone, please, O God, let them hear."

It was killing Bolders not to answer, but he needed to think about his crew and the other ships. Bolders stayed on the bridge until early evening, and the lady never came back over the radio.

"I'm going to turn in," Bolders told the crew on the bridge as he got up and walked off.

He got to his quarters, and Taylor came up behind him.

"Mat, you have a minute to talk?" Taylor asked the captain.

"Sure, come in," Bolders told him, walking into his quarters.

Bolders sat in one of the dining room chairs and asked Taylor to sit.

Taylor sat down opposite the captain. "Mat, that wasn't you earlier today with that woman," Taylor told him.

"I know a lot has happened to you and now a wife and baby on the way; it's a lot," Taylor continued. "Well, I'm going to let you get some rest," he told Bolders and rose from his seat.

"Will, I'll see you in the morning, and thanks for everything, my friend," Bolders told him.

The next morning, there was a loud knock on the door, and it opened with Nelson stepping into the dining room. He ran over and knocked on the captain's bedroom door and opened it.

"Captain, it's Nelson, that lady is back on the radio," he told Bolders.

He looked at his clock, and it was 03:30. It didn't take the captain long to get ready and get back to the bridge. As Bolders was walking onto the bridge, he heard the lady pleading.

"Is there anyone out there, please answer for God's sake, please."

Everyone watched the captain as he walked over to the radio. The woman then came back on the radio. "They're coming back on board; I have to go."

Bolders turned and looked at everyone in the room, then outside into the darkness.

"Get me the CAG," Bolders said as he turned and looked at an ensign. He looked at the young ensign as he turned and started to walk toward the exit. "Hurry, son," Bolders said, "I need him here ten minutes ago."

The young ensign ran off the bridge, and within fifteen minutes, the CAG was running onto the bridge.

"Sorry, Captain," he apologized for his appearance. The ensign said, "It was an emergency."

He had his shirt hanging out, shoes on with no socks.

"I don't care how you look, Commander. I need a pilot," Bolders told him.

By this time, Taylor was also on the bridge, listening to everything.

"What kind of pilot do we need, sir?" Mumford asked the captain.

At that time, the lady came back on the radio. "Is anyone out there?" she asked again, crying and sobbing.

This time, Bolders could hear a little boy as she talked. "Mommy, I'm hungry."

Then they heard a little girl's voice, "We can't, Lee, the bad people will get us if we go to get food."

"Please, in the name of Jesus Christ, please answer me."

Bolders could hear that she was starting to give up by the tone of her voice. "Please, if not for me, for my children, it has been about a day with no food or water."

Before Bolders even thought about it again, he grabbed the mic. "This is the US warship Midway; we hear you, ma'am."

"Oh, thank God; please come and get us before they come back."

"Before who comes back, ma'am?" Bolders asked the lady.

"I don't know who they are, but they killed the crew and ate some of them."

Bolders turned and looked at the ensign again. "Get me Lieutenant Bingington now, and hurry, boy."

"Ma'am, what makes you think they're eating the people?" Bolders asked her.

"There is one that me and my ten-year-old daughter saw lying in this room."

"Where are you at in the room now, ma'am?"

"In the radio cabinet with the doors closed."

Mumford then told Bolders, "Have an E-2 on catapult one, and also two helos ready to go at your word, Captain."

"Where are you at, ma'am?" Bolders asked her.

"We are in a cove, is all I know, sir," the woman said. "I heard my husband say that."

"Where is your husband at now?" Bolders asked her. "Is he close by? Do you know?"

"I think he…" she started to cry and couldn't finish what she was saying.

"It's okay, ma'am; let me introduce myself," Captain Bolders said, his voice calm and reassuring. "My name is Captain Bolders, and I'm the captain of an aircraft carrier."

The woman on the other end replied, "My daughter has always wanted to be a pilot for as long as I can remember."

Taylor coordinated with Bingington, who quickly got his team ready, while CAG prepared the pilots.

"Tell your daughter we have a fantastic pilot who will give her a ride when you get onboard," Bolders assured her.

The Hawkeye took off, followed by the SEAL team five minutes later.

"What side of the island are you on, ma'am?" Bolders inquired, attempting to pinpoint her location.

"We're in a cove, Captain; that's all I know," she responded, her voice tinged with panic.

Then a voice crackled over the radio, "E-2 to Midway; we found what seems to be a 250-foot yacht in a cove on the far west side of the island."

"This is helo five-five-two; we're en route to retrieve the package, about five miles out," another voice chimed in.

"Ma'am, we have people on the way to get you and your kids now," Bolders informed her.

"This is helo one; we have the target in sight, one minute out," reported yet another voice.

"Ma'am, can you hear a helicopter yet?" Bolders asked.

"Captain, this is team lead; we have several people onboard armed with spears, it seems," the team lead reported.

Bolders turned to Taylor and Nelson, incredulous. "Spears!" he exclaimed. "Do not fire on anyone unless you are in danger, team lead," Bolders instructed Bingington.

"Roger that, fire only if engaged; we copy, sir," came the response.

Bolders turned back, shaking his head. "Spears, really?" he muttered. The next thing Bolders and the others on the bridge heard was, "Three bad guys down."

The woman's voice came through the radio, panic evident. "We heard gunfire," she said.

"That's our guys, ma'am; you're going to be okay," Bolders reassured her.

"They're here in the room," she cried out, then screamed. "Help me!" The children joined in, their screams heart-wrenching.

"They've got my kids," the woman said, her mic stuck on.

The crew heard everything.

"Hey, ass wipe," Bingington's voice came through, followed by several shots from silenced weapons.

"Captain, package is safe and multiple bad guys down," Bingington reported.

"Get out of there and get back here, Lieutenant," Bolders commanded.

On the main deck, they heard the team communicating with the helicopter.

Everyone was winched up into the helo, and the pilot announced, "We are RTB."

Bolders and the crew began to celebrate until they heard, "Helo one hit, repeat, helo one is going down."

A SEAL team took off from the Yorktown on Bolders' orders.

"XO," Bolders said to Taylor, "let's get those marines up on one of those amphibs."

The helo crash-landed on a small beach near a thick forest. Everyone inside was okay, just a few bumps and bruises. They exited the helicopter along with the woman and her two children.

Bolders listened to the radio as helo two reported, "Bingo fuel RTB, team lead."

Bolders turned to Taylor, "Get me Nelson and his security group up here now."

As he waited for Nelson and his team, the radio crackled again. "Team one, copy; this is team four from Yorktown."

After a moment of silence, the response came. "Team four, this is team one; we hear you five by five."

"We're going to try and winch you out now; copy, team one?"

Before he could respond, Nelson came onto the bridge along with his number two, Styles. The Yorktown's helo crackled over the radio, "Being fired upon, Yorktown, repeat, being fired upon. This is team four; we are bailing out into the water," and then the pilot added, "team four off."

CHAPTER 26

MEANWHILE, back at home, Doris and Albert woke up in their bed. They had been home for two days and were immensely proud of their son. Doris had bragged to everyone about what a beautiful daughter-in-law she had.

"I'm going to the Donut Palace," Albert announced.

It was Doris's favorite place for coffee and donuts, just a mile from their small farm.

"Mamma," Albert called, "I'm going to the Donut Palace. What do you want?"

Doris glanced toward the corner of the room, as if looking at someone. Albert followed her gaze but saw no one.

"Are you okay, Mamma?" he asked, concerned.

Doris looked at him and smiled. "I'm fine, Daddy, just thinking about our boy."

"I'll take two blueberry muffins and a large coffee, Daddy," she replied.

Albert kissed her, as he always did before leaving. "I love you, Mamma. Be back soon," he said.

"Daddy," she called, stopping him before he exited the bedroom doorway, "our boy is going to be okay, isn't he?" she asked, smiling.

"He's going to be fine, Mamma," he assured her. "Are you sure you're okay?"

"I'm fine, Albert," she answered, "I love you and Mathew and now Tanya so much, Daddy."

"We love you too, Mamma," Albert said, then added, "I'll be right back."

Doris heard the door close, and then the pickup pulled away.

Doris smiled, looking at the corner. "Is there any way to have just a little more time?" she asked, her eyes fixed on the empty space as if listening to someone.

After a moment, she spoke again to the empty corner, "I know you have, but I have grandkids on the way. If I just had a while longer," she pleaded. Then, with a resigned sigh, she said, "I understand."

Back onboard the Midway, they monitored the air traffic.

"Yorktown helo one hit, going down," came the urgent report over the radio.

"My team is ready to go, Captain," Nelson informed Bolders.

"Get those guys back here," Bolders commanded as Nelson rushed off the bridge. He turned to Taylor, "Have those marines ready if we need them."

A few minutes later, two helos lifted off the Midway's flight deck. Twenty minutes later, Nelson's helicopter was also hit.

"Helos four and five hit, helo five attempting to reach the carrier," the pilot reported.

Nelson's helicopter crash-landed on the beach. Over the radio, a crew member shouted, "We got bad guys out the ass, boss [Nelson]."

Suddenly, Bolders heard, "Man down, we got a man down."

Then Nelson's voice came through, "It's only a flesh wound, I'm okay."

Bolders picked up the ship's phone and called CIC. "Have you contacted Breakaway or Pearl yet?"

"Negative, sir, we can only communicate with the ships in the fleet and our teams on the island."

He hung up the phone and heard over the radio, "E-2 Hawkeye to mother [Midway], multiple bad guys moving in on our men."

Bolders turned to the ensign, "Get me the whole security group and those marines ready." He then looked at Taylor. "You've got the ship 'til I return, my friend," he said, patting Taylor on the shoulder with his left hand.

"Mat, you're the captain; you can't do this," Taylor urged him. "If they get too close, have those battleships light 'em up."

Bolders left the bridge and headed down to meet the departing security group. Taylor ordered two A-6s loaded with twenty-eight MK-82 five-hundred-pound bombs. Bolders watched from the back of the Chinook as the flight deck receded. The Chinook he was on dropped to treetop level, and the other three followed suit. The rear gunner in the back door spoke to someone, then turned to Bolders, pointing to his earpiece with his right finger. He indicated for Bolders to switch to channel two.

Bolders complied and said, "On two."

"Captain," the pilot said, "we're going to have to drop you off three miles from where the teams are, sir."

The helicopters landed, and eighty men dismounted from the three Chinooks. Bolders approached Nelson and Bingington as he got closer.

"Captain," Bingington reported, "you and your men stopped and turned back when you heard gunfire."

One of the marines looked at Bolders. "You're not going to turn back, are you, Captain?"

"Hell, no, son," Bolders responded. He then addressed everyone behind him, "Let's go get our guys."

Bolders and his men stopped at a large clearing about two hundred yards wide. They could hear rifle fire from across the clearing. Suddenly, rifle shots came from the rear of their group, accompanied by shouts. In the distance, they saw what appeared to be two men with swords.

"Keep your eyes open," Bolders instructed the two men in front with him as he moved to the back.

He saw two marines with the sides of their necks bitten out and another who was stabbed through the right shoulder downward. Turning to the rest of the group, he ordered, "Anyone comes near you that's not one of us, don't leave them standing."

Bolders sprinted back to the front as rifle fire erupted. He arrived to see five bodies lying before them.

"Sir," a marine said, "you said if they weren't with us, sir."

Bolders patted him on the shoulder. "You did good."

Suddenly, rifle fire broke out from every direction. Bolders was hit and swiftly dragged to the middle of the open field. A couple of Marines started to go after him, but he made them stop. The attacking soldiers ceased their assault, and the rifle fire stopped. Nelson and everyone else watched as what seemed to be a few thousand men appeared in the field. Two large men emerged from the middle of the crowd, standing about twenty feet apart.

A striking black-haired woman, dressed in black, walked out from the army. She stopped about forty feet from the soldiers she commanded and about a hundred yards from Bolders. When she spoke, it sounded as though she was right in front of him, her voice crystal clear.

"I don't see what my daughter sees in you," she said to Bolders.

"Who are you?" Bolders yelled, trying to be heard from a distance.

"You don't have to yell. I hear you just fine," the woman replied in a low voice.

He tried again, "Who are you?" speaking as if she were right in front of him.

"Better," she said, walking towards him. "My name is Lilith, the wife of the one true God."

"And who would that be?" Bolders asked, his right hand on his sidearm.

"Satan, you know him, don't you?" she said. "Remember in church?"

"Yeah, but in church, he wasn't a God. I remember that much," Bolders retorted.

The two men walked behind Lilith, close on either side, about ten feet back.

"Well, the closer I get, the better you look, but I still don't see what Sintra sees in you," she remarked.

Bolders saw two more women followed by four men emerging from the crowd. Lilith got within forty yards of Bolders and stopped, waiting for the others. Nelson and Bingington and their teams stepped out, rifles ready.

"Captain, walk to me," Nelson instructed as each man found a target.

The marines on the other side did the same, finding their targets.

Bolders recognized the black-haired woman he had seen in California and Hawaii.

"You," he said, "you killed those people on base," Bolders accused her.

"No," the blonde said to him, "that was me if you're referring to the bartender. I'm sorry; my name is Aradia," she introduced herself, smiling.

Lilith nodded, and two men started walking toward Bolders.

"Walk to me, my friend," Captain Nelson urged, moving closer to Bolders.

As the men reached for Bolders, Nelson and his team fired, killing both. Instantly, flashes of red and orange light pierced Nelson's side and hit three more of his men. Bolders saw this as he drew his sidearm. He aimed at Lilith, but her son struck Bolders through the stomach. Gunfire erupted as Bolders's men took cover and fired back at the demons.

"Kill him," Bolders heard Lilith command as two more approached him with large spears.

CHAPTER 27

ALL AT ONCE, everything stopped except for the men advancing to kill Bolders. Lilith and her daughters, along with her sons, stepped back. A whistling sound, like something slicing through the air, was heard. A small figure in gold armor slammed to the ground, sliding on gold kneepads. It cut the demon on the right, severing its legs above the knees. Then it jumped into the air, holding its sword behind it in the right hand. It spun around in midair, decapitating the other demon. It faced Lilith before landing on one knee, the tip of its sword touching the ground.

With its back to Bolders, Nelson could see the figure clearly. "Oh shit," he muttered.

The head of the small warrior in gold turned to look at Bolders. "Hi, babe, I'm here now; you hold on," she said to Bolders, who was now bleeding badly.

She rose and walked back to him, looking up to heaven. "Father, please."

Bolders started to choke on his blood as Tanya cried aloud.

"Jophiel," Lilith said, shrugging, "oops, but you can go with him."

Both of her sons and daughters charged at Jophiel, who raised her sword but wouldn't leave Bolders. The marines and others took aim as a marine yelled, "Light their ass up!"

Suddenly, seven more small figures hit the ground. Their white wings spread out from the gold armor. They held spears and swords as one went to Jophiel and the other stepped forward. Angelette stood by Jophiel as Nefta stepped forward.

"Lilith, you piece of shit, you and your daughters wanna fight? We'll give you one," Nefta declared.

Lilith and her family retreated quickly. At the same time, her horde charged toward the female angels.

"Your father won't be sending help because it's not time for Armageddon yet," Lilith yelled, laughing. "You are all going to die." She then shouted, "Kill them all!" As she did, their black wings emerged.

Nefta and the other female angels braced themselves. Suddenly, something hit the ground with such force that the dirt flew up like a cannonball impact. The demons, along with Lilith and her children, stopped in their tracks. A large angel, carrying a massive two-edged axe, had arrived.

"Joel [Jo-El]," Lilith said, her eyes wide as she backed up.

"Joel!" Jophiel screamed, turning towards him. "Please pray to the Father to help him," she cried, still praying herself.

Allocen, Lilith's son, started towards Joel, but she stopped him. "Are you crazy?" she scolded. "He will kill you."

Nozel, her other son, drew back a bow and shot Jophiel in the stomach, hitting the baby. She fell beside Bolders. "I love you, my love," she told him.

Joel let out a yell that hurt everyone's ears. He raised his large axe and threw it at Nozel, striking him in the chest. Lilith screamed loudly, "Kill all of them; bring me their heads."

Suddenly, nine more large angels landed, their white wings

spread wide. The demons halted, and a large figure emerged from the horde.

"Stop!" he yelled, walking over to his injured son, now joined by nine of his angels. He walked halfway and stopped, as one of the white-winged angels approached him.

"Micheal, I am surprised the old man let his best archangels come," the figure said.

"Maybe he wants me to go ahead and put an end to you, Satan," Michael retorted.

Bolders saw Tanya, now almost dead, and found the strength to look up. "I do believe you, God and your Son Jesus Christ. It is in His name I ask you to take me and save her and my child," he prayed.

Satan, hearing this, gritted his teeth and tried to get to Bolders. Michael stood in front of him, grabbed Satan, lifted him up, and slammed him hard to the ground. Satan rolled away from Michael, not rising but facing him. Dagon, one of Satan's generals, charged at Michael. Gabriel jumped in front of him and hit Dagon with his left fist, knocking him to the ground with such force that he needed help to get up.

Bolders continued begging God to heal Tanya.

Michael, along with Raphael and Gabriel, walked to him. "God has heard you," Michael said, looking down at Bolders with a smile.

The marines and other groups watched as Michael, Gabriel, Raphael, Joel, Uriel, Remiel, Saraqael, Raguel, Azrael, and Zerachiel gathered around. They put their hands on each other's shoulders as Michael knelt in the middle. The others held one hand toward heaven and the other on Michael as they spoke in a language no one understood. Suddenly, a cloud appeared in the shape of a face, made of solid white clouds with curly hair and a beard. Its eyes shone like two bright stars in the midday sky. A soft but deep voice came from it, causing the trees to sway like a hurricane wind and the dirt to jump around like heavy rain on a calm lake. A blinding light surrounded them, so bright no one could look at it. When the light faded and the archangels moved away, Bolders and Tanya rose from the ground. The angels, both male and female, walked back out, forming a battle line. Then thousands appeared in the air, swords drawn and shields raised.

Choppers landed, getting the soldiers out. Nelson, who had also been healed, ran to Bolders.

"You two, let's go," Nelson urged.

Tanya looked at Nelson and said, "He has his own ride." She grabbed Bolders and said, "Hold tight, babe."

CHAPTER 28

IN A FLASH OF LIGHT, they were on the carrier, waiting for the helos. They finally got ahold of Admiral Dean and were told to report back to base. Everyone looked at Tanya with her heavenly wings and golden armor. After she changed, she met Bolders on the bridge along with everyone else.

Taylor looked at her and then at Bolders. "Only Mathew would marry an angel," he remarked.

All at once, the thundering voice and the island disappeared in a white cloud. They heard a loud scream cursing God, knowing it was Satan.

Taylor looked at Bolders and asked, "Do you think it's over?"

"I hope so, I really hope so, friend," Bolders replied.

Tanya, now standing behind the two men, turned to look at the island. Her eyes widened, and her eyebrows raised as she took a deep breath. Bolders noticed her back was to him as she stared at the island. He called her name twice, trying to get her attention.

Finally, he reached out with his left hand and touched her upper arm. "Baby, you alright?" he asked.

She jumped slightly, then turned to face him. "I'm sorry, babe," she said. "I heard you." She placed her right hand on his left side.

She then looked back over her left shoulder with a worried expression before turning back to Mat. "Things are certainly never going to be the same again," she said, looking at Taylor and then at Mathew.

Rising on her tiptoes, she kissed her husband and walked off the bridge, saying, "I love you, babe."

To be continued.

AUTHOR'S NOTE

Purnell Myles's novel is a work of fiction and fantasy, where military language and operations are not intended to be accurate reflections of real procedures. Ship names are used fictitiously, and all characters are products of the author's imagination. The most realistic elements of the book are the references to God, Jesus Christ, and some of the heavenly angels, as well as the evil one, Satan.

ABOUT THE AUTHOR

Purnell Myles served overseas for seven years in convoy rescue and recovery in Afghanistan and Iraq. During his time abroad, he met his wife, and they have now been married for twelve years. He is retired and lives in Florida with his wife and dog, Ceasar.

www.ingramcontent.com/pod-product-compliance
Lightning Source LLC
Chambersburg PA
CBHW030633110726
47901CB00002B/427